A FATAL OBSESSION

A DCI DANNY FLINT BOOK

TREVOR NEGUS

INKUBATOR BOOKS

Published by Inkubator Books
www.inkubatorbooks.com

Copyright © 2023 by Trevor Negus

Trevor Negus has asserted his right to be identified as the author of this work.

ISBN (eBook): 978-1-83756-279-4
ISBN (Paperback): 978-1-83756-280-0

A FATAL OBSESSION is a work of fiction. People, places, events, and situations are the product of the author's imagination. Any resemblance to actual persons, living or dead is entirely coincidental.

No part of this book may be reproduced, stored in any retrieval system, or transmitted by any means without the prior written permission of the publisher.

PROLOGUE

1.00 a.m., 14 May 1989
Black Orchid Nightclub, Newcastle

Garry Poyser and Billy Gifford were standing outside the front entrance of the Newcastle nightclub, having a laugh at the expense of two women who had just left in a parlous state. Both women were extremely drunk and unsteady on their feet, tottering along on dangerously high stiletto heels.

Billy chuckled and said, 'By Christ, bonny lad, look at the state of them. What a plight.'

Garry laughed out loud and said, 'I know what ya mean, kidda. I diven't fancy yours much, like.'

As the two bouncers watched the drunken women stagger off towards the city centre, their relaxed attitude changed instantly when the manager of the nightclub burst through the main doors.

He was white as a ghost and lathered in sweat. The two bouncers immediately thought a brawl had started inside the club and began moving towards the main doors.

Seeing the doormen's reaction, the manager held up his hands and said, 'There's no fighting, lads; don't panic. Billy, go inside and use the phone in my office to call for an ambulance. No, scratch that. Call for three ambulances.'

As Billy ran inside the club, Garry said, 'Jesus, boss. What the fuck's going off in there? Has somebody been knifed?'

Sucking in air to try to calm himself down, the manager said, 'It's nothing like that, Garry lad. Three young girls have collapsed on the dance floor. One of them looks in a bad way. That new barmaid, Heather, was doing mouth-to-mouth on her as I came out here to get Billy. Some of the lads inside are starting to get a bit arsey; that's why I needed Billy inside.'

'You said three girls. Are the other two okay?'

'Not really, the bar staff are looking after them. I just hope those ambulances don't hang about. The shit's really going to hit the fan when the owners hear about this lot. I don't know what's happened to those girls, but I reckon it's got to be drugs.'

'Drugs? Nah. Not here, boss.'

'I'm telling you, that's what it looks like to me. I'm going back inside. Keep your ears open. If it kicks off in there, Billy will need you to back him up. In the meantime, stay here and keep an eye out for those ambulances. When they arrive, send the paramedics straight down to the main dance floor, got it?'

'Will do, boss.'

As the club manager ran back inside, Garry thrust his hands deep inside his black bomber jacket. He could feel the small bag that still contained the half-dozen ecstasy tablets he hadn't managed to sell. He knew these Es weren't the best he'd ever had, but he was desperate for cash. The round white pills with the dragon motif already had a bad name, but he had five hundred to shift and bills to pay. He hadn't expected any punter to have such a bad reaction, let alone three at the same time.

He knew as soon as the ambulances had been despatched, the police would also be informed. He needed to get rid of the pills in his pocket, sharpish.

Looking around, he saw an overflowing waste bin outside the nearby McDonald's. He could hear sirens approaching in the distance, so he sprinted down the road, and after a quick look around, he thrust the clear plastic bag containing the white pills deep inside the bin.

He raced back to the nightclub and was standing outside the main doors as the first ambulance pulled up. Two paramedics jumped out and grabbed the stretcher from the rear of the vehicle. Concern was written large on their faces.

Garry held the door open and shouted, 'In here, mate. Straight down the stairs to the main dance floor.'

As soon as the paramedics had entered the nightclub, Garry reached inside his jacket for his cigarettes and lighter. He had just taken the first drag when a second ambulance pulled up. He took another deep drag and directed the crew inside.

He was stubbing out the finished cigarette when Billy came back outside, shaking his head.

'Is it still quiet?' Garry said. 'Nobody's kicking off, are they?'

'Nah, it's all quiet. I can't quite believe what I've been seeing, mind. I reckon one of those girls is dead. They're working on her now, but I don't think they can get her heart going. She looks toast to me.'

'Nah, never.'

'I'm telling you, mate. I reckon she's fucking pegged it. The cops are going to be all over this place. If you've still got any of those pills on you, you'd better bin the fuckers.'

Garry had heard enough. 'I'm outta here, Billy. I've sold over twenty pills tonight; some fucker's bound to grass me up. If I get nicked again, the cops will throw the fucking key away!'

'You'd better get going, bonny lad. When the cops start asking questions, I'll stall them for as long as I can. You need to grab your stuff and get as far away from here as you can.'

Garry stared at his fellow bouncer and growled, 'You wouldn't grass me up, would you, Billy?'

Billy Gifford had worked alongside Garry Poyser for the best part of two years, and he knew the levels of violence his colleague was capable of. At just under six feet and of slim build, Garry wasn't the biggest. But what he lacked in size, he more than made up for in speed and boxing ability. Pair those skills with a liking for extreme violence, and Billy knew to be more than wary of his smaller colleague.

Billy was a big man and could handle himself, but there was something vicious about the way Poyser worked that worried him.

He half smiled at Garry and said, 'I wouldn't do that to you, Garry lad. Get going before it's too late.'

Garry gave a thumbs-up and sprinted off into the night.

The door to the nightclub opened, and a stretcher carrying one of the three young women who had succumbed to the effects of the ecstasy tablet was brought out. The girl's face was ashen, and an oxygen mask was providing her with much-needed oxygen.

As Billy stared at the stricken young woman, he asked, 'How are the other two?'

One of the paramedics said, 'One will be on her way to hospital shortly; the other one we couldn't help. Your boss has asked me to tell you to make sure nobody leaves the club until the cops get here.'

'Bloody hell, that's terrible. What the fuck's happened?'

The paramedic shrugged. 'Looks like a drugs overdose to me. That's what we've informed our control to tell the cops, anyway.'

As the ambulance sped off into the night, with its blue lights flashing and sirens blaring, Billy muttered under his breath, 'For fuck's sake, Garry. What the hell have you done?'

1

10.00 a.m., 30 September 1990
Hunters Croft, Rufford Road, Ollerton, Notts

As he limped down the long driveway towards the house, Stan Jennings drew deeply on his cigarette. The taxi driver had been ordered to stop at the gates so Stan could enjoy the walk and gather himself for what was bound to be yet another awkward conversation with his one and only client, Harvey Jarvis, the television personality known across the country as Guy Royal, formerly lauded as 'the King of Light Entertainment'.

The leaves on the trees, which lined both sides of the winding driveway, were already starting to change from the lush green of summer to the russets, golds and reds of autumn. This was, without doubt, Stan's favourite time of year, and this was also his favourite view of the house. The historical Elizabethan manor house dramatically came into view as he turned the driveway's final corner.

The beauty of the picture-perfect country house, set against the autumnal colours of the trees, took his mind off the constant aching pain in his right leg. He walked with a pronounced limp, and had done so since the age of nineteen, after his leg had been crushed in a near-fatal car accident. The sports car he was travelling in had been driven at speed into a wall after his lifelong friend Harvey Jarvis lost control. Stan often wondered if Jarvis only employed him now, as his agent and manager, out of a sense of guilt. It had been his poor driving, after a night of heavy drinking, that had caused the accident that had effectively ended Stan's own burgeoning show-business career.

Whatever the reason, it had turned out to be a match made in heaven. Stan had found he had a natural gift for management and had used all his show-business nous and connections in the industry to engineer his best friend's meteoric rise to the very top. The first thing he'd done was to insist on the name change. Overnight, Harvey Jarvis became Guy Royal, and it seemed his client's career had taken off from that pivotal moment. Royal instantly went from being a bit-part entertainer on the northern club circuit to the most sought-after act on all the country's television channels. There wasn't a light entertainment producer in the business who didn't want Guy Royal to host their new show.

With his affable northern bluntness and cheeky charm, he was adored by millions. Men liked his down-to-earth approach, and women admired his good looks, smart appearance and sparkling blue eyes. Everything had looked set for Guy to have a long and illustrious career.

Stan shook his head at the thought of his client's fall

from grace, which had been equally as swift and dramatic as his rise to fame.

Guy Royal was a flawed character, and once the truth of his abominable behaviour was in the public domain, there was nothing Stan could do to save his friend's career. The tabloid newspapers, aided by former wives and envious entertainers, had gleefully published details of Royal's drug-fuelled orgies with prostitutes, as well as giving lurid accounts of the abuse he had subjected his former wives to.

After the newspapers had published their stories, the television companies dropped Royal like a hot brick. Stan now struggled to secure him offers to play minor parts in Christmas pantomimes, such was his fall from grace. Most of that reluctance to employ Royal was the bad press coverage he had received over the last few years, but part of it was also the fact that he was now forty-eight years old, and his once handsome features had now been replaced by the bloated, blotchy face of an addict. His halcyon days at the pinnacle of the show-business world were well and truly over for Guy Royal.

But as he approached the beautiful house, Stan's mood lightened, and those troubling thoughts disappeared.

He was relieved to see his mustard-coloured MGB GT sports car still in good condition. Not so long ago, when he had made this same walk after yet another argument with Royal, he had found the car he'd previously owned burned out.

Guy had been so mortified about torching the car, following the booze- and drug-fuelled argument with his long-suffering friend and manager, that he had immediately gone out and bought the MGB GT.

Stan smiled as he recalled the event. That was Guy Royal

all over. When he was sober, you couldn't wish to meet a nicer person. When he was drunk or high on cocaine, he was Royal all right, a right Royal pain in the arse.

Stan had left the house the previous night in a taxi, with the prostitute he'd hired for the former TV personality. She was a regular visitor to the house, where she provided her services for Royal.

Royal had spent the day drinking and partying with the woman. Until she'd grown tired of his perverted demands and the threats of violence if she didn't comply with those outrageous demands.

She wanted to leave, but understandably also wanted the money she was owed before she left. A blazing row had ensued after Royal refused to pay the woman.

It had once again been left to Stan to sort out the mess created by his intoxicated client. When Royal had seen Stan paying the woman and heard him saying he would also use the taxi he'd called for her to go to Nottingham, he had kicked off big style and started hurling threats and abuse at Stan. Royal's ugly tirade had culminated in him telling Stan to 'fuck off out of the house!', along with the woman.

That was nothing new.

Stan had ignored the abuse, most of it, and just got in the taxi alongside the prostitute. After dropping her off first, he'd spent the remainder of the night at his small flat in the Mapperley Park area of the city.

What had been new were the former entertainer's vicious comments about what Stan could expect from his will.

The smile disappeared from his face as he thought about those comments. There had always been an unwritten verbal agreement between the two men that if anything happened to Royal, then Stan would inherit the house and all its contents. Guy Royal had recently amended his will to make that agreement into a legally binding one.

It was a regular occurrence for Stan to go unpaid for months at a time. The deal on the house was the sweetener that meant he never complained when he wasn't paid. Last night Royal had made it crystal clear that his manager would be getting nothing from him, including the house, and that he was going to amend his will again to that effect.

Stan had weighed up his options overnight and reached a decision during the early hours of the morning. He would demand an explanation from Royal when he was sober and seek assurances that he wasn't going to amend his will again. He couldn't risk ending up with nothing, not after all the years he had put in, guiding Royal to the top, making him a star. It had been his drive and ambition that had pushed Guy Royal to become one of the most recognised people in Britain.

It had been his vision and hard work that had created the King of Light Entertainment.

None of his client's subsequent calamitous fall from grace could be attributed to his management skills, and he deserved to be rewarded.

Stan took a last drag of the cigarette, flicked it down onto the gravel driveway, and limped up the stone steps to the front door.

He tried the door handle as he took out his key. He was shocked to find the door was unlocked. He knew he had locked it the night before, as he left with the prostitute in the taxi.

He expected to find Royal asleep somewhere in the house, having passed out where he'd dropped.

That was his usual form.

Stan closed the door behind him and was surprised to see keys in the lock on the inside.

He shouted, 'Harvey!'

The house remained deathly silent. Stan started to experience a growing sense of unease, and an all-too-familiar tightness began to form around his chest as he looked around the hallway before making his way towards the lounge.

He was overweight, grossly unfit and suffered with angina and asthma. The injured leg prevented any kind of meaningful exercise, or at least that was what he always told himself, and his poor diet, his smoking and drinking, all conspired to mean his health was in a precarious state. The longer the brooding silence filled the house, the more that tangible feeling of fear inside him grew.

Beads of sweat started to form on his forehead. Breathless, he stopped and leaned against the wall in the hallway, searching his jacket pockets for the blue inhaler he always carried with him. Taking two puffs, he steadied his breathing, trying to reassure himself that everything would be fine, and that his friend would just be passed out in a drunken stupor, somewhere in the house.

As he walked into the lounge, that much-needed reassurance was instantly banished. The first thing he saw was the ribbon of dried blood at his feet. Reluctantly, his eyes followed the trail of blood that stretched out across the wooden parquet flooring. He let out a gasp when he saw his lifelong friend lying face up on the floor, in front of the stone hearth. The blood that had trickled across the floor had come from a huge wound at the back of Guy Royal's head. His once blond, now greying, hair was matted with dark black, dried blood.

Stan avoided stepping in the congealed blood as he approached his friend. Kneeling at his side, he could see a single neat hole with a trickle of blood on Royal's forehead, just above his left eye. Gingerly, he felt for a pulse in Royal's neck. The flesh felt cold to the touch. There was no hint of a pulse.

Nothing.

Stan Jennings half fell, half staggered backwards at the realisation that the man he had worked alongside for the last thirty years had been shot and was now dead. Inadvertently, he stepped in the tacky blood and left a trail of sticky footprints across the lounge floor. As he heard the noise the sticky blood on his shoes made as he left the room, a wave of nausea swept over him. He staggered out through the front door and vomited his breakfast on the gravel driveway.

When he finally stopped dry heaving, he sat down heavily on the stone steps. That familiar feeling once again began to circle his chest, the tightness steadily increasing at an alarming rate. Trying not to panic, he fumbled for the silver pill box in his jacket pocket. He quickly placed one of the small black pills under his tongue and desperately tried to control his breathing, which had become little more than a series of rapid, shallow gasps.

After five tense minutes, his breathing began to return to normal, and he could feel the tightness around his chest starting to diminish.

Knowing the immediate danger of an angina attack had passed, he took the cigarette packet from his jacket pocket.

With his hands still shaking, he lit a cigarette and took a long drag.

He needed to calm his nerves before going back inside to call the police.

It was only as he exhaled the smoke that the tears started to flow.

2

11.45 a.m., 30 September 1990
Hunters Croft, Rufford Road, Ollerton, Notts

Detective Inspector Rob Buxton took the warrant card from his jacket pocket and presented it to the uniformed officer standing at the entrance to the long driveway that led to Hunters Croft.

The young officer returned the identification and said, 'You'll see where the other vehicles are parked, sir. DI Cartwright wants to keep the main turning area, outside the front of the property, clear for the time being. You'll see the taped area.'

'Okay, thanks. Enter DCI Flint on the log as well, please.'

'Will do, sir.'

Rob looked across at Danny as he drove down the long driveway. 'How's your head feeling?'

Danny growled, 'I'm getting there. Bloody retirement

dos. I won't be going to another one any time soon, especially when I've got work the next day.'

Rob chuckled. 'I bet Sue wasn't impressed. What time did you get home last night?'

'I think you mean, what time did I get home this morning? It was around two o'clock when I finally got home.'

Danny paused before adding, 'Never mind the time I got home. She was even less impressed when I asked her to drive me into work this morning.'

'I can imagine. That was a good call though, boss. The amount of people who fall foul of drink driving the morning after a night out is unreal.'

Rubbing his eyes against the sun's glare, Danny said, 'I'm just not used to drinking anymore. I suppose that's what old age does for you. Anyway, enough of my self-inflicted woes; let's see what we've got here, shall we?'

Rob parked the CID car behind the other police vehicles already parked on the side of the driveway.

After donning forensic suits, overshoes and gloves, the two detectives walked the last twenty yards towards the country manor house that was Hunters Croft. Danny could see the police tape that now cordoned off the area where vehicles would normally turn round. The only vehicle within that cordon was a mustard-coloured MGB GT.

Danny asked, 'Who owns the sports car?'

'From what Tina told me before we left the office, it belongs to Stan Jennings, the man who found the body.'

'Relationship to the deceased?'

'Stan Jennings was the deceased's agent and manager. From what I understand, he also lives here most of the time.'

Detective Inspector Tina Cartwright walked out the front door of the house just as Rob and Danny ducked under the blue and white police tape. There was another line of tape that led from the perimeter cordon to the front door. Danny and Rob walked adjacent to the tape until they stood on the stone steps that led to the front doors.

Tina said, 'Morning, boss. Good night?'

Wondering if he looked as obviously rough as he felt, and trying not to sound too grumpy, Danny said, 'Let's just say it was a long one. What have we got?'

'The deceased is the owner of the property, Harvey Jarvis. He was found in the main lounge of the property, just after ten o'clock this morning. The probable cause of death looks to be a single gunshot wound to the head. The police were called at ten fifteen, by the person who found him, Stan Jennings.'

'Any sign of the weapon near the deceased?'

'No, sir.'

'Tell me about Stan Jennings?'

'He normally resides here with the deceased but spent last night in Nottingham, after a row with Jarvis. He returned this morning and found the front door closed but not locked. He thought that was odd, as he had secured the front door prior to leaving the night before.'

'Rob tells me that Jennings was the dead man's manager. Who is Harvey Jarvis?'

'Harvey Jarvis is better known to the public as Guy Royal, the television entertainer. Jennings was both his agent and manager.'

'Guy Royal, the king of light entertainment, former star of the small screen?'

'The very same.'

'Bloody hell. Are the press aware yet?'

'Not yet.'

'Let's keep it that way for as long as possible. Even if Guy Royal hasn't been on television for years, he was so famous a few years ago the press will be all over this when it does break. Is the pathologist here yet?'

'Yes, boss. Seamus Carter arrived five minutes before you. He's already inside, examining the scene.'

Danny and Rob followed Tina inside the house and could instantly hear the pathologist's booming voice issuing instructions to his assistant.

Tim Donnelly, the scenes of crime supervisor, was standing in the hallway next to the double doors that led from the hallway into the main lounge.

Danny nodded to the experienced scenes of crime man and said, 'Are there any areas in here we need to avoid?'

'No, sir. We concentrated all our efforts in the hallway, prior to everyone else arriving. We've lifted several fingerprints in here, but have no idea who they belong to yet. We were just about to start in the main lounge when Seamus and Brigitte arrived. There's a single route into the lounge marked with tape, and platforms have been put down to walk on. There's a lot of blood on the floor, and I don't want anyone disturbing it until we've properly examined it.'

'Noted, Tim. I only need a quick look at the body; then I'll get out of your way. Has the scene been photographed yet?'

'Yes, boss.'

Stepping on the platforms that led across the parquet flooring of the sizeable lounge, Danny carefully made his way towards the prone figure of Guy Royal. Seamus Carter was examining the dead man, kneeling on another platform, which had been placed adjacent to the body.

As he approached, Danny asked, 'First thoughts?'

'Good morning, Danny,' Seamus replied. 'I can tell you that it's certainly foul play. There are two distinct head wounds that I can see. The first is the small entry wound on the forehead just above the eye, the second is the catastrophic exit wound at the back of the head. I have measured the entry wound, and it looks like a nine-millimetre calibre.'

Danny asked, 'Any idea on the type of gun used?'

'The small calibre suggests some kind of handgun; an automatic is probably the best bet. If Mr Donnelly can find the bullet or the shell casing, you might have a better chance of identifying the type of weapon used.'

Seamus paused before adding, 'Looking at the size of the exit wound, I don't think there's any chance of the bullet still being inside the skull of the victim, but it's not beyond the realms of possibility. I'll know better when I carry out a full examination later.'

'Any other injuries that are visible?'

'None that I can see.'

'How long will you need here?'

Carter glanced at Tim Donnelly. 'I shouldn't be more than an hour or so with the body. Then it will be down to Tim when he feels it's safe to remove the body without disturbing anything.'

Tim said, 'It will take us at least another couple of hours to process this room. I don't think we should risk moving the deceased until we've finished our examination.'

'There's no rush.' Danny nodded. 'It will take as long as it takes. What time do you think you'll be ready for the post-mortem examination?'

Seamus glanced at his watch. 'It's just gone twelve now. I'll make a call and book King's Mill Hospital mortuary for four o'clock this afternoon. That should give us plenty of time to do what's necessary here.'

'Okay. I'll see you at the mortuary later.'

Danny retraced his steps on the platforms and said to Tina and Rob, 'Let's talk outside.'

Once outside, Danny took a few deep breaths, filling his lungs with the cool, crisp air, before saying to Tina, 'Have you got all the staff you need to work the scene?'

Tina nodded. 'There are no obvious witnesses, apart from Stan Jennings, to speak to, and no house-to-house inquiries to carry out. I've got all the detectives here engaged in carrying out a thorough search of the property.'

'I saw cameras outside; do they cover the approaches to the property?'

'Unfortunately, not. There are dummy cameras on all four corners of the house, but they aren't linked to any recording device. Stan Jennings has told me they were put up three or four years ago, purely as a deterrent.'

'Might as well not have bothered. They wouldn't deter anybody.'

Tina shrugged. 'I know.'

'Do you need any assistance from the Special Operations Unit?'

'The grounds are quite extensive, so a section of SOU would be useful to search the property's exterior. There's also the car that Jennings owns. I think that should be taken to the forensic bay at headquarters for a full forensic examination. Jennings says he left by taxi last night and took another cab to get back here this morning. He couldn't tell us which taxi firms he used for either journey, so he could be bullshitting us. There could be forensic evidence inside the car.'

Danny nodded. 'Agreed. Let's get the car lifted and transported back to HQ.'

Rob said, 'I'll get that sorted, boss. I'll arrange for SOU and the vehicle examiners to attend.'

'Thanks, Rob.'

Danny looked at Tina and said, 'Are there any other vehicles registered to the house?'

'No. Royal didn't drive. He hasn't held a licence for over five years following a ban for drink driving.'

'Okay.'

He paused, trying to gather his thoughts. 'Are there any weapons registered to this address?'

'Not according to our licensing checks. There are no firearms or shotgun licences registered.'

'Have you spoken to Jennings yet?'

'I obtained a preliminary account from him when I first got here, but he needs speaking to properly.'

'Did you ask him about weapons?'

'Yes. He was adamant there are no guns anywhere in the house and never have been.'

'Has he given an account of his movements this morning?'

'A very brief one. He told me that he arrived by taxi at about 10 a.m., after leaving his car here overnight. As I told you earlier, he said the front door was closed, but not locked. The keys were in the lock on the inside. He walked in, saw the deceased on the floor in the lounge, and saw all the blood. He admits touching the body, feeling for a pulse in the neck. As soon as he realised that Royal was dead, he called the police from the telephone in the hallway. Then he went outside to wait.'

'Has that been confirmed?'

'I've spoken to the uniformed officers who were first on the scene. They confirmed that Jennings was sitting outside when they arrived. Apparently, in a very distressed state. He'd been crying.'

'What about the shoeprints in the blood?'

'Those are from Jennings. He claims he accidentally trod in the blood this morning when he found Royal.'

'Have we got his shoes?'

'Yes. He's wearing slippers now.'

'And where is he?'

'He's in the kitchen – at the far end of the hallway, past the lounge doors. DS Moore is with him.'

'Have we got swabs from his hands?'

'Yes. He was more than happy to provide that when I asked him. He did say that he had washed his hands before the police arrived, as he had Royal's blood on them.'

'I thought he said he'd stayed outside until the police arrived?'

'He washed his hands under the outside tap at the side of the house.'

'Okay. Jennings is going to have to stay somewhere else for a few days, until we've exhausted this place as a possible source of evidence. I'm going to invite him back to the office so he can give us a full and detailed account of his movements for last night. I also want to hear his version of the argument he had with the deceased. It's quite possible that Jennings was not only the person who found Guy Royal this morning, but also the last person to see him alive. And if he left last night as a result of a blazing row, he's got to be regarded as a suspect.'

'My thoughts exactly; that's why I've kept him isolated in the kitchen under supervision.'

'Good work, Tina. I'll leave you here to supervise the scene. If you need anything else while you're here, just call it in. At some stage, this incident will no doubt get out to the press. When that happens, you may need additional manpower to control the scene. Keep an eye on that situation.'

'Will do, boss.' Tina nodded as Danny wrapped up the conversation.

'I'll go and introduce myself and have a word with Stan Jennings.'

As he walked towards the kitchen, Danny used the tips of his fingers to massage his temples as yet another wave of alcohol-induced pain crashed through his head.

3
―――――

12.55 p.m., 30 September 1990
MCIU Office, Mansfield, Nottinghamshire

Danny looked carefully at Stan Jennings. Guy Royal's agent and manager was now sitting opposite him and Rob Buxton, in one of the interview rooms at Mansfield Police Station.

It was obvious the man was still deeply upset by what he had experienced earlier. He had offered no objection when Danny asked him to accompany him to the police station, to account for his movements the night before.

Danny observed the frayed cuffs of the man's tweed jacket and the grime-stained collar of his shirt. With uncombed hair and a few days' growth of stubble on his face, his general demeanour was scruffy and unkempt. Stan Jennings was either a man struggling financially, or someone who didn't worry about his appearance. A detailed examination of his finances would soon clarify the situation.

'My name's Detective Inspector Buxton, and this is DCI Flint.' Rob Buxton started the proceedings. 'We'll be leading the investigation into the death of Guy Royal. How long have you lived at Hunters Croft?'

'I moved in three years ago, when Guy was being hounded by the press. His second wife had left him by then, and he was worried about being at the house on his own. As you've seen, it's in a very secluded location.'

'So why did you spend last night away from the house?'

'Guy was having one of his tantrums. I've learned over the years that the best way to deal with him when he's in that state is to leave him to it and talk to him once he's sobered up.'

Danny said, 'Sobered up from what?'

'Booze. Guy's a big drinker.' Jennings paused, considering his next words. 'Some might say he's a functioning alcoholic.'

'Was it just drink? Or are we going to find drugs at the house?'

Jennings shrugged. 'I'm not his keeper. He's a grown man. Last night, I'm pretty sure it was just booze. He'd hit the whisky bottle hard all day yesterday.'

'What time did you leave the house last night?'

'I think it was around ten thirty.'

'Not late, then?'

'No, but Guy had started drinking early.'

'How did you leave?'

'In a taxi.'

'Why didn't you drive?'

'I'd had quite a bit to drink as well. I wasn't drunk, but I didn't want to risk losing my licence. Guy's already lost his. If I couldn't drive as well, we'd be well and truly fucked.'

'Which taxi firm did you use?'

Jennings scratched his head and squinted. 'This is what I'm having trouble with. I can remember I used A2B Cars this morning, but I haven't got a clue who I called last night. All the taxi firms I use are listed in the address book at the side of the phone in the hallway. It was a bit traumatic at the time, what with Guy shouting and bawling at me.'

'I see,' Rob said. 'And what were the two of you arguing about last night?'

'No. You've got it wrong. We weren't arguing. Guy just loses his shit and starts ranting. Half the time I can't understand what he's going on about. Last night, I just thought it was time I left so he could calm down and sober up. Like I said before, if he's got nobody to rant and rave at, he calms down and just drinks until he passes out.'

'Where did you go?'

'I still have a one-bedroom studio apartment in Mapperley Park. It's my bolthole for when he becomes too obnoxious.'

'How often do you go there?'

'Once in a blue moon. I love it at Hunters Croft, but sometimes I need my own space.'

'I can see why you love the house,' Danny said. 'It's a beautiful property. How does Guy Royal afford to keep it? It must be years since he was last on television.'

'It's been three years since he last had any regular work. It just seems longer. Guy paid cash when he purchased Hunters Croft; there's no mortgage. He's been paying the bills for the upkeep of the place from money he received from his book deal. He recently wrote his life story and made quite a lot of money from that.'

'And what about you? Where do you get your money?'

'Sometimes, when he remembers, I get paid what I'm due from Guy. I don't worry about it too much, as I still have plenty of money in the bank. I didn't squander the money I made when Guy's fame was at its height. Back then we both made a hell of a lot. Unlike Guy, I still have most of my money.'

'Did Guy have any enemies?'

Jennings looked down at the table. 'Detective, I'm sure you read the papers. It's no secret that Guy had his demons. Some of those demons come with a hefty price tag.'

'Go on?'

'He's always dabbled with hard drugs, and he did have a chronic gambling addiction.'

'What was his drug of choice?'

'He was addicted to Charlie. Let's just say, in answer to your earlier question, I wouldn't be surprised if you find cocaine in the house somewhere.'

'Do you know who supplied him?'

'Honestly, I've no idea.' Jennings shook his head. 'I think he scores from somebody in Nottingham.'

'What about the gambling?'

'Guy was a regular face at one of the casinos in Nottingham. The Black Aces, down Hockley way.'

'Is he in debt to them?'

Jennings simply shrugged at that.

'You're his manager as well as his agent,' Rob went on. 'Don't you know the state of his finances?'

'I have a rough idea, but Guy likes to spend money. It's very difficult to keep track of his current financial state. And at the end of the day, I'm not a bloody accountant.'

Danny could hear the growing irritation in Jennings's voice and decided to move on. He said, 'Anybody else you can think of who might want to do him harm?'

'There's the ex-wives club. Those two women hate him with a passion.'

'And what about you? What are your feelings towards Guy Royal?'

Shock at the question instantly registered on Stan Jennings's face. That shocked expression quickly changed to one of anger. 'How dare you ask me that? I've known that man since we were both sixteen, working at the holiday camps. He was like a brother to me. I loved him.

'I can't believe you asked me that.' Tears welled in his already bloodshot eyes, and he spluttered, 'I want to leave.'

Danny said, 'It wasn't my intention to upset you, Mr Jennings. I need to ask tough questions sometimes, but I'm sure you want to help us find the person responsible for your friend's death. You can leave, but Hunters Croft is now a crime scene, so you'll need to stay at your Mapperley Park flat for the time being.'

'Of course, I want to help you. I just don't appreciate you thinking I could be responsible for doing that to Guy, that's all. I'll help you in whatever way I can.'

'DI Buxton will drive you to your flat. I'm sure we'll speak again soon.'

Danny nodded at Rob, and both detectives left the room, leaving Jennings once again wiping tears from his face.

As soon as he closed the door, Danny said, 'Take him

back to his flat, have a good look round, and get a basic witness statement. I'm not buying that sudden torrent of crocodile tears in there. We need to take a very close look at Stan Jennings.'

4

4.00 p.m., 30 September 1990
King's Mill Hospital Mortuary, Mansfield,
Nottinghamshire

Danny slipped on the green surgical gown before joining Rob at the side of the stainless-steel examination table. Seamus Carter and his assistant stood the other side.

The now naked body of Guy Royal lay on the table, his shattered and bloodstained head resting at an awkward angle on the wooden block.

Seamus looked across the bench at Danny. 'I'm going to examine the head and neck first. I've already done a cursory inspection of the deceased and can see no other injuries apart from slight bruising forming around the right elbow. I think that injury was probably caused as he fell to the floor after being shot in the head.'

Danny nodded and involuntarily took a pace back, away from the examination table. He needed to be close enough to see what the pathologist discovered, but he didn't want to be too close. He had never managed to become accustomed to witnessing postmortems. After all these years as a detective, he still found the procedure an abhorrent but necessary part of the investigative process.

Carter continued to talk as he skilfully examined the head of the deceased, peeling back the scalp until the bone was exposed. 'I can now see the full extent of the injuries to the skull.'

Danny took a reluctant step forward to get a clearer look.

Seamus pointed to the wound on the forehead and said, 'You can clearly see the bullet hasn't fractured the skull at the entry point. This suggests to me that the assailant was standing quite close to the deceased. Not close enough to cause powder burns to the skin but close enough.'

Then the pathologist turned to his assistant and said, 'Can you help me turn him, please?'

This movement of the deceased exposed the back of his head, at which point the catastrophic nature of the exit wound became even more apparent.

Carter gestured as he said, 'The exit wound is larger than I first expected, which tends to contradict the relatively small size of the bullet. Have we found any ordnance at the scene?'

Danny nodded. 'DI Cartwright called me before I left to come here. Tim Donnelly has recovered both the casing and the remains of the actual bullet that was embedded in the wood surrounding one of the interior door frames.'

'Where was the casing?'

'That was found quite a way from the body, under a coffee table.'

'I'm no expert, but it may help you determine what sort of weapon was used if you can determine the trajectory at which the casing was expelled from the gun.'

'I thought all automatic handguns ejected the casing from the side.'

'Like I said, I'm no expert, and the majority of automatic handguns do have a side ejection port, but there are some older weapons that expel the casing from the top of the weapon.'

Danny didn't respond but quietly digested what he was being told. He knew there was a certain amount of conjecture on the part of the pathologist, but he had worked with the big Irishman enough times to trust his judgement and pay attention to his thoughtful theories.

The pathologist paused as he examined the injuries to the head again. He physically turned the skull to the left, examining its contents through the exit wound. 'Death would have been instantaneous. The amount of damage caused to the brain tissue is irreparable, and there would have been massive blood loss. There's no way he could have survived this injury.'

Silence fell in the room's clinical atmosphere then, and after another two hours, the pathologist finally completed his meticulous examination of the deceased.

Danny remained silent until the pathologist had completed his gruesome task. Seeing that he had now finished, he asked, 'Is there anything else we should know before your written report arrives?'

'Everything will be in much greater detail in my report, but there are a couple of things I need to bring to your attention now. It looks likely to me that the deceased was suffering from a venereal disease. Most probably syphilis. A blood test will confirm my suspicions, but there are definite signs of infection around his genitalia. The deceased also has severely damaged membranes inside both nasal cavities. The heart was enlarged, and there are minor burns to his lips and fingers. All these, when put together, suggest that the deceased was a drug abuser and that his drug of choice was most probably cocaine. His liver shows a large build-up of fats that could be signs of the early onset of cirrhosis. Your victim was obviously a heavy drinker.'

The pathologist paused to allow Danny to make a mental note of what he was saying before adding, 'It appears Guy Royal really lived up to the show-business lifestyle.'

Danny said, 'How far gone was the venereal disease?'

'It's hard to say, but from the look of it, I don't think it's ever been treated. If it is syphilis, it would have caused him a great deal of discomfort.'

'When will you have the toxicology results, to confirm your suspicions about the venereal disease and the substance abuse?'

'In the next day or two. As soon as I get them, I'll submit my full report.'

'Thanks, Seamus. As always.'

Danny and Rob removed the gowns and made their way out of the mortuary.

As they walked, Rob said in hushed tones, 'Bloody hell. A swollen liver, a raging cocaine habit and a bad dose of the clap. If that's the showbiz life, you can keep it.'

Danny nodded. 'It does beg the question though,' he said, 'if Guy Royal had such a raging cocaine habit, who was his supplier?'

'My money's on Stan Jennings, boss.'

Danny raised his eyebrows in agreement. 'Let's invite him back in for another word, then, shall we?'

5

6.00 p.m., 30 September 1990
MCIU Offices, Mansfield, Nottinghamshire

Danny, Rob and Tina made their way to the front of the briefing room.

The noise level coming from the detectives waiting in the crowded room was even louder than usual as they discussed the murder of such an infamous television celebrity.

Danny lifted both hands, and the room began to fall silent – but not quite soon enough for his liking. 'A bit of hush, please!' He raised his voice above the din. 'It's been a long day already; let's not make it any longer than we need to.'

In the immediate silence that followed, Danny looked at Tim Donnelly. 'Tim, I'll start with you. Have you completed your examination of Hunters Croft?'

'Not yet, boss. The ground floor has been completed, but we still have all the first floor to examine.'

'What about the crime scene itself? Have you found anything significant?'

'The main finds at the scene were the bullet and the casing. The bullet was recovered from the doorway immediately behind where the deceased had fallen. It means that when he was shot, the victim was standing between the assailant and the exit from the murder scene.'

'Okay, that could be useful.'

'What's the state of the bullet?'

'Obviously, it's damaged, but it's in one piece, and ballistics may be able to do something with it should we recover a suspect weapon.'

'Well, that's a good start. Where was the casing recovered?'

'The casing was found under a coffee table. It would have bounced well on the hard parquet flooring, so a direction of travel from the ejection port of the weapon will be hard to pinpoint. Generally, the direction was towards the right-hand side and behind the assailant.'

'What does that mean?'

'I've spoken to our firearms training staff, and they've suggested a weapon with a top ejection port is the most likely to give that trajectory. Obviously, the nature of the hard floor surface means this is not an exact science, not by any means.'

'I understand that, but did the firearms staff offer any opinions on likely handguns with such a top ejection port?'

'Their consensus was that it was more likely to be an older weapon. The most common example they could think of was the German Luger pistol that was widely used by the Wehrmacht during the Second World War.'

'That seems very specific.' Danny paused for a moment. 'And what's the likelihood of a Second World War German handgun still being around here in the UK today?'

'Apparently these guns were highly prized as souvenirs by Allied troops during the war, and many Lugers were smuggled back at the end of the conflict.'

Danny turned to Rob and said quietly, 'I want you to follow this up. Talk to as many firearms experts as you can find and see what we can establish as fact as opposed to conjecture.'

'I'm on it, boss.'

Danny looked back towards Tim and said, 'Anything else at the scene?'

'The only other thing of significance is a partial fingerprint found in a bloodstain on the doorframe that connects the lounge to the hallway. The bloodstain has been swabbed, and we're awaiting confirmation that the blood is from the deceased.'

'That's excellent. What's the clarity of the mark?'

Tim shook his head. 'That's the bad news; it's not great. It's badly smudged, and I'm not sure we'll get a positive identification. What I can tell you is that the mark is quite small. It could have been left by a man's little finger, or it could be a woman's finger that has left the mark. It's impossible to tell.'

A deflated Danny responded, 'What else of note?'

'We've found and lifted several fingerprints from the lounge. Some from the furniture and others from the fireplace where the deceased was found.'

'I saw shoeprints in the blood at the scene?'

'They are now confirmed as having been made by Stan Jennings.'

'I see.' Danny tried one more time, more in hope than expectation now. 'Anything else?'

Tim tilted his head slightly, as if in apology. 'We still have the first-floor rooms to complete, but so far that's it.'

'Okay, thanks.' Danny's eyes searched the room until he found DS Wills. 'Andy, how did the search of the grounds go?'

'Special Ops have carried out a full search. Although large, the gardens are mainly to lawn, so it wasn't a difficult task. SOU have carried out fingertip searches of the entire grounds and are satisfied there's nothing of any evidential value outside on the property.'

'Does that include the long driveway?'

'It does, boss.'

Danny nodded in acknowledgement, then paused before addressing the room. 'We know from Stan Jennings that he secured the front door when he left the property at ten thirty last night. That door was unlocked when he returned this morning. This means one of two things, either the killer had a key and surprised the deceased, or Royal recognised the killer and was happy to let them into the house.'

DC Baxter raised a hand. 'Forgive me for asking this, boss, but I haven't been to the scene. Do I take it there are no signs of forced entry anywhere at the house?'

'There's no forced entry, and the killer didn't bother securing the front door after Royal had been murdered.' Danny then addressed the room. 'Any other questions so far?'

The room remained silent.

'The postmortem has highlighted some interesting points that will necessitate further investigation,' Danny told them, his tone brisk. 'We know that Guy Royal was a drug user; physical signs indicate his drug of choice was cocaine. The man was also suffering from a venereal disease that the pathologist believes was syphilis. This will be confirmed when all the results from the toxicology tests have been received.'

Danny paused to look across at Tina before he said, 'As soon as we have confirmation of those facts, I want you to lead the investigation into his drug abuse. Let's see if we can identify any potential dealers, where he scored, and so on. You know the drill.'

Tina nodded.

'I also want you to make enquiries with his GP to ascertain if he was under any medication for the venereal disease.'

'Will do, sir.'

Danny continued, 'We're also aware that Royal was a heavy gambler. He was a regular at the Black Aces casino in Hockley.'

The gathered detectives took in this information with a general murmur and exchanges of glances.

Danny held up a hand and waited for the room to quieten again. 'So, although there are no house-to-house enquiries to carry out, and no witnesses to trace, there's still plenty of work for us to do. As a priority I want full background checks on both our victim, Guy Royal, and his manager, Stan Jennings. This will include their full antecedent histories, their lifestyles, the relationship between the two of them, and any relationships they had with others, personal or professional. I also want full financial checks that will include any recent life insurances that have been taken out, as well as the last will and testament of the deceased.'

He then looked at Rob and said, 'I want you to allocate four detectives to scrutinise Royal and Jennings. I'll expect them to have some answers this time tomorrow. Once you've allocated those teams, you and DC Lorimar are to concentrate on the Black Aces casino. Visit the casino tonight and speak to the owner. As a priority enquiry, we need to establish the extent of Royal's gambling habit and what debts, if any, he had outstanding.'

'Okay, boss.' Rob made some quick notes. 'And what about the firearms enquiries?'

'I'll allocate those to Fran Jefferies; that's an ideal enquiry for her to carry out. There's no one in this office more tenacious than Fran.'

Next, Danny searched the room until he saw DS Rachel Moore. 'Rachel, Stan Jennings has hinted he used a taxi firm, one that's listed in the address book next to the telephone in the hallway of Hunters Croft, to pick him up last night. I want you and DC Pope to recover that address book and go through it until you identify the taxi company that picked Jennings up.'

'I'll recover the address book after the briefing,' Rachel affirmed. 'We can make a start this evening.'

'Thanks. The sooner we can get an account from the taxi driver, the better.'

Danny paused before bringing the briefing to its conclusion. 'From what we already know about Guy Royal, it's clear he was a man who will have acquired many enemies over the years. The possibility that the killer was known to Royal makes it imperative that we systematically trace every single one of those enemies. We can only achieve this by thoroughly researching every aspect of his life. Finish up what you've got left to do this evening, but don't be too late off. I want everyone back on duty at seven o'clock tomorrow morning.'

6

3.00 p.m., 10 January 1989
Hunters Croft, Rufford Road, Ollerton, Notts

Guy Royal was pacing up and down the spacious lounge of his beautiful home. He was feeling irritated and didn't try to hide it.

He looked in disgust at his manager, Stan Jennings, who was sprawled out on one of the sofas, reading a book. With real venom in his voice, Royal snarled, 'When are you going to get off your fat arse and find me some work?'

Without looking up, Stan Jennings muttered, 'If only it were that easy. There's fuck all out there for you.'

'You've got to find me something,' Royal insisted. 'The bank refused to cash one of my cheques the other day. The situation's desperate. You need to find me something, even if it's only a fucking panto, for Christ's sake. I need some money coming in.'

Stan Jennings didn't respond; he just turned the page of his book, которая infuriated Royal yet further. 'This is serious!' Royal shouted, flying into a rage. 'What the fuck are you reading that's so important?'

Jennings closed the book and stood up. He used its spine to prod Royal in the chest and said, 'Stop shouting at me.' He paused before continuing, 'If you must know, it's Davy Rammer's autobiography; it's actually quite good.'

'How can a book about an ageing rockstar be any good? I bet it's a load of old shit!'

'It's not shit,' Jennings said, his voice calm. 'And I can tell you it's flying off the shelves. It's already sold thousands of copies. Maybe you should write a book about your life story. That's a book people would want to read, especially now.'

'What do you mean especially now? Are you trying to be funny?'

Ignoring Royal's comment, Jennings held the book up in front of his client's face. 'See the price? This book cost me ten quid. Work that out. Thousands and thousands times ten quid. I know the publishers take a cut, but I reckon you could make some serious money.'

Guy sat down heavily in an armchair, his anger and frustration dissipating. 'I couldn't write a book,' he said as he pushed his long, greying hair back off his face. 'It's a stupid idea.'

'I don't suppose for one minute Davy Rammer wrote this. I know him; the man has abused so many substances over the years he can barely string a sentence together when he's talking, never mind write an entire book.'

'So, if his head's mush, how's he written his life story?'

'He'll have paid someone to do it for him.'

'Can you do that?'

'Of course. Clever, educated people interview you and listen to your stories. They take notes and then write them down as your life story.'

'Who would do that for a living?'

'Plenty of people, I reckon. They're called ghost writers.'

'Could we hire a ghost to write my story?'

'Why not?'

'And all I'd have to do is sit and talk to them?'

'I think that's how it works, yeah.'

Royal shrugged. 'Do you think anyone would be interested in my story?'

'Are you joking? Of course people would be interested. You've still got an army of fans out there. They'd lap it up. It's only the television bosses who have an axe to grind with you.' Jennings leaned forward and looked his client in the eye. 'Guy, believe me, Joe Public still adores you.'

'I don't know if anybody would be interested now.' Royal shook his head with a kind of melancholic self-pity. 'It's been a few years since I was on the telly.'

'That's true.' Jennings nodded; his eyes were bright. 'But like you said, we're going to have to do something; the money's nearly all gone. Do you want me to investigate?'

'What have we got to lose?'

'Absolutely nothing,' Jennings said as he flicked to the back of the book. He held it up again and read aloud, 'This book was published by Bouldstone Press, London.' He paused, then said, 'I'll give them a call and see if they'd be interested. Let's face it, you're still a much bigger name than Davy Rammer will ever be. And they thought it worthwhile to publish his story.'

Royal still looked unsure. 'But how will you get in touch with this Bouldstone Press?'

'Leave that with me,' Jennings said with a confident shrug. 'That's what you pay your manager for, remember?'

7

3.15 a.m., 7 November 1989
Maid Marian Way, Nottingham

Almost six months had passed since Garry Poyser had fled the city of Newcastle. He'd led a hand-to-mouth existence ever since that fateful night, the one when he sold the shit ecstasy pills to Tyneside club-goers.

He had gradually moved south, never staying too long in any one place, aware he was now probably wanted by the police. He'd taken cash-in-hand jobs where he could find them, but he was now almost out of money. He had sold his car in Sheffield before catching a National Express coach to Nottingham.

He had slept rough for a week since arriving in the Midlands city, trying to save what little cash he had made from the car for food. He still had the ecstasy pills in his rucksack but hadn't dared sell any since Newcastle.

He pulled the sleeping bag closer around him and tried to edge his way further back into the shop doorway. The night was dry but extremely cold. A strong wind that had suddenly got up was blowing frigid air into the doorway.

He knew the freezing cold temperatures would stop him getting any sleep. Unblinking, he stared out at the now deserted road. It had been busy earlier, as there was a taxi rank thirty yards further down the road, where late-night revellers had queued up to make their way home. People passing the shop doorway never gave him a second glance; they were used to seeing unfortunate souls sleeping rough on the streets of their city.

Gradually, the party-goers, disco dancers and courting couples all disappeared, and slowly the passing taxis also became scarcer.

He heard her before he saw her.

In the distance, coming his way, he could hear the click, click, click of high heels on the pavement. The noise of the footsteps grew closer until she came into view. A woman, probably in her thirties and of mixed race, wearing a very short skirt and a fur jacket. A vision of loveliness.

Garry slowly sat up in the doorway to get a better look. As he'd initially thought, she was stunningly beautiful, and he couldn't understand why such a good-looking woman would be out alone, on these mean streets, at this time of night.

She leaned against a bus shelter virtually opposite his doorway, scanning up and down. She was obviously looking for a taxi, but the street was deserted.

He watched her closely as she pulled the collar of the fur jacket tighter around her neck as the wind buffeted her long dark hair. Mesmerised, he continued staring across the wide road at her.

A movement in the shadows to her immediate left caught his

eye, breaking his trance. He sought out the movement again and saw three men in the dark recess of a doorway. They were also staring at the woman, and he could see them gesticulating to each other about approaching her.

Fully awake now, he began to slowly ease himself out of his sleeping bag. He was careful not to make any sudden movements that would give away his position to the three men.

He looked back towards the woman and sensed she was completely unaware of the presence of the three men, who were now using the shadows to edge their way, unseen, along the street, towards the bus shelter.

Garry decided to act. He was about to shout a warning when one of the men, wearing a black leather jacket, lunged forward and grabbed the woman in a headlock, clamping his hand over her mouth. He began dragging the frantic, struggling woman out of the bus shelter, back towards his two accomplices. All three men then quickly overpowered her before they half dragged, half carried her towards the darkness of an alleyway.

Garry started to move as soon as the man grabbed the woman, and after sprinting across the road, he now stood in the entrance to the alleyway. It was dimly lit, but he could see that the man in the leather jacket, who had made the initial move, was now pressed up against her and was trying to kiss her. She was violently moving her head from side to side to avoid his attentions, and Garry could hear her snarling: 'Fuck off, you pig!'

Leather Jacket stepped back a pace and punched the woman hard on the cheek. Only the two men standing each side of her gripping her arms prevented her from falling. One of these men was short and fat; the other was taller and wearing a black beanie hat.

Leather Jacket gripped the woman's face and snarled, 'We can do this the hard way or the easy way. Stop being such an uptight bitch. You never know, you might enjoy it.'

The woman had regained her poise after the punch. Garry could see that her face was a mixture of fear and pure anger. The anger got the better of her fear, and she spat hard in Leather Jacket's face.

As the man drew his fist back to punch her again, Garry stepped forward and commanded, 'You blokes need to fuck off and leave her alone!'

Initially startled by the stranger's shout, Leather Jacket wheeled round to face Garry, forgetting all about punching the woman for a second time.

He reached inside his jacket pocket and withdrew a long-bladed knife, instructing his accomplices to, 'Keep a hold of that bitch; this won't take a minute.'

As he approached, Garry could see that he was holding the knife so the blade was pointed up, thrusting it out in front of him as he moved forward.

Working nightclub doors meant that Garry had faced men with knives many times before, and he knew this man didn't really know what he was doing. A proficient knife fighter will always hold the knife so the blade points down towards the floor.

Taking the initiative to surprise his assailant, Garry stepped forward, quickly closing the distance. As Leather Jacket thrust the knife towards his abdomen, Garry grabbed the man's wrist and pulled him in even closer, rendering the knife hand useless. As he struggled to free his knife hand, Garry delivered a devastating headbutt to the bridge of the man's nose. He heard the crunch as the blow from his forehead smashed into bone.

Garry instantly followed up that first headbutt with a second and a third, until he felt Leather Jacket go limp. He heard the knife clatter to the ground and released the man from his grip, allowing him to collapse to the ground.

Garry aimed a single vicious kick to Leather Jacket's temple, to incapacitate him further. As he now turned away from the unconscious man, Garry saw one of his accomplices hurtling towards him. He met the onrushing fat man with a ramrod-straight right fist, landing a hard punch between the man's eyes, knocking him backwards and down. He followed up the lightning-fast punch with a heavy kick to the man's head, effectively putting him out of the fight.

That just left the tall man wearing the black beanie to deal with.

This guy – who had earlier grabbed the woman, now released her from his grip – and was making a desperate grab for the knife.

Garry instinctively saw his intentions and beat him to the blade. Pointing it directly at the man's stomach, he said, 'You've got a choice, bonny lad. You either fuck off, and take your useless mates with you, or I'll gut you like a fish.'

Beanie Hat didn't need telling twice; he bolted from the alleyway, leaving his two accomplices bleeding on the floor.

Garry stepped over to the woman, who had slumped down on her haunches. He helped her to her feet and said, 'We need to get out of here before the police turn up. Somebody may have heard the commotion and called the cops.'

He helped the shaken woman from the alleyway, back out onto the street. Illuminated by the bright streetlights, he could now see the blood trickling from the side of her mouth and a livid purple bruise forming on her cheek.

She gripped his arm for support and whispered, 'Where did you come from?'

'I was trying to get some sleep over there and saw them coming for you.'

'Thank you for stepping in; not many would.'

'Nah. I'm not having that, pet. No woman deserves to be treated like that.'

The woman stared at Garry, and he could see she was assessing the scruffy bearded stranger who had helped her. Eventually she said, 'Why are you sleeping in a doorway?'

'Let's just say I'm between jobs at the minute, that's all,' he told her. 'I've a bit of a cash-flow problem. Anyway, never mind what I was doing; what were you doing out at this time of night on your own?'

'I normally have a cab pick me up outside the hotel where I'm working, but the manager at the Royal tonight was being arsey because I wouldn't give him more money as a kickback. He wouldn't let me call a cab and chucked me out, so I had to make my way down here to the taxi rank.'

Garry gave her a quizzical look.

She winced in pain as she half smiled. 'Oh, come off it. You look like a man who's been around the block a few times. What do you think I was doing?'

As a sudden look of realisation spread across Garry's face, the woman said, 'Don't give me that. I'm my own boss, and I make bloody good money.'

Garry smiled and said, 'Nah, I'm not judging you, pet. I bet you've never had to sleep in a freezing cold doorway.'

Heavy rain had started to fall as the woman waved down a passing taxi. She turned back to face Garry and said, 'Listen, I can't tell you how grateful I am that you stepped in and sorted those animals out. I don't want you sleeping rough on a night like this. Come back to my place and stay the night. It's the least I can do after you saved me from a world of pain. At least you'll be warm and dry, and you can have a bath.'

She paused before adding, 'And don't think anything else is on offer, because it isn't. Do we understand each other?'

'Totally. You're a lifesaver. Thank you. Hold the cab, and I'll grab my stuff from the doorway. Thanks again.' He paused. 'I don't even know your name?'

'Rebecca.'

'Pleased to meet you, Rebecca. I'm Jamie. Jamie Hart.'

8

9.30 a.m., 7 November 1989
7 Berkely Court, Church Drive, Carrington, Nottingham

Garry Poyser had slept well for the first time since he arrived in Nottingham. The bed in the spare room of the plush first-floor flat in Carrington was soft and comfortable and, more importantly, dry and warm.

When the taxi had dropped him and Rebecca outside the property in the early hours, they had both run up the concrete steps to the front door and straight into the flat, trying to dodge the worst of the teeming rain.

Rebecca had pointed him in the direction of the spare bedroom, saying, 'The bed's already made up. Don't make me regret inviting you back, Jamie. I meant what I said; nothing other than a bed for the night is on offer.'

She might have been one of the most stunning women he'd

ever seen, but he had no intention of making any sort of move on her; he was just glad to be in the warm and out of the rain.

The morning light as it streamed into the bedroom had woken him, but he remained in bed, savouring the comfort. He was surprised by a light knocking on the door.

He shouted, 'I'm awake.'

'Are you decent?' Rebecca asked. 'I've brought you a cuppa.'

Grabbing his boxer shorts from the floor, he quickly slipped them on and sat up in bed, saying, 'Yeah, I'm decent; come in.'

The door opened slowly, and Rebecca stepped inside carrying a large mug of hot coffee. Garry could see the livid purple bruise and swelling, which stretched from her cheekbone to the point of her chin.

He gratefully took the coffee and, after taking a sip, said, 'That looks nasty.'

She gingerly allowed her fingers to touch the swollen area and said under her breath, 'Bastards.'

He said quietly, 'I always use plenty of ice whenever I catch a punch. It takes the swelling down and makes the bruise heal faster.'

'Are you in the habit of catching punches?'

'I've worked on the doors quite a bit. Being a bouncer always carries that risk.'

'That explains how you handled yourself so well last night. I still can't quite believe you took all three of them on, and for somebody you didn't know.'

'Look, Rebecca, I'm no angel, but what they had planned for you was totally wrong. I've done plenty of bad shit in my time, but attacking women isn't what I'm about,' he assured her. 'I was glad to help, and I really appreciate the bed for the night. Like you said, I don't know you, and you don't know me, so I'm aware you took a risk to help me as well.'

'It was the least I could do. I need to go out later this morning, but the shower's in the room next to this one. There's some shaving stuff and shower gel in the cupboard under the sink that was left by a previous boyfriend; you're welcome to use that. I'll cook you a bit of breakfast while you get cleaned up.'

Garry wasn't at all surprised to be given his marching orders; he'd known all along it was a one-night-only offer. He was going to enjoy getting a hot shower and eating a proper cooked breakfast before he left, though.

Half an hour later, he'd showered, shaved and dressed. He followed the smell of cooked bacon through to the kitchen, where he found Rebecca plating up fried eggs, bacon and tomatoes.

He sat down at the table and said, 'That smells great. Thanks.'

She put the plate of fried food and another mug of hot coffee down in front of him and said, 'Jamie, I've been thinking about your situation. You told me last night that you were between jobs.'

Shovelling in a mouthful of bacon, he mumbled, 'That's right.'

'I was wondering if you'd consider working for me, for a while. I can't pay much, but I can offer you a roof over your head, plenty of food and hot water. Just until you get back on your feet.'

He took a sip of the hot coffee, swallowed and said, 'Doing what?'

'I know you can handle yourself; I saw that for myself last night. Sometimes my occupation also comes with risks. Too many times I've had to fight my way out of bad situations, like last night.' She shook her head and sighed at the memory. 'Usually, it's with clients who want more than I'm prepared to give, or hotel managers who won't take no for an answer. Basically, I need someone to watch my back and be there if I'm having a problem.'

Having wolfed down the food, he put the knife and fork on the plate, sat back and nodded slowly. 'I'm pretty sure I could do that for you.'

Rebecca looked serious. 'I'd have to smarten you up first,' she said with a small smile. 'It will mean long, boring hours sitting in the foyers of posh hotels. You'd need to be suited and booted, and a smart haircut wouldn't go amiss.'

'I don't have any smart gear,' Garry told her, suddenly despondent. 'And I haven't got the money for a haircut, never mind a smart suit, shirt and tie.'

'Don't worry about that.' She smiled at him properly now. 'I'll get you smartened up. Call it an advance on your first pay packet.'

'That sounds good to me, pet.'

'One other thing. Can you drive?'

'Yeah, I can drive.'

'I was thinking that if I got a car, you could drive me to appointments. That way I'll never have to be reliant on fucking taxis again.'

'Sounds like you've got it all worked out, Rebecca. I could give you driving lessons if you like, pet.'

She shook her head. 'I've never wanted to drive. I tried it once before, and it terrified me.' Then she took a deep breath before saying, 'It would be a totally professional arrangement. I can see that you scrub up okay, but I'm not looking for a new boyfriend. Is that clear?'

'As crystal, pet.' He laughed out loud and said, 'Actually, you're not my type, so that won't be a problem.'

'Cheeky sod.' Rebecca allowed herself a chuckle. 'Finish your coffee, and I'll take you into town. We need to get you groomed and kitted out. Once we've done that, we can go and look for a car. Do you know much about cars?'

'I'm no mechanic, but I know a good runner when I see one.'

'Perfect. Give me ten minutes to put some slap on to cover this bruise.'

Rebecca walked out of the kitchen, leaving Garry drinking his coffee.

He looked around the kitchen, then walked into the lounge of the smart flat and smiled. He hadn't been expecting anything like this when he woke up. This was a real opportunity for him to get back on his feet and keep himself under the radar. She didn't need to know his real name. He had no intention of causing her any problems. Her flat in Carrington was the perfect place to lie low. He knew that every night he spent sleeping rough on the streets, he was in danger of being name-checked by the police and arrested.

This new set-up wasn't ideal, but it would certainly do for now.

9

10.00 a.m., 2 October 1990
MCIU Offices, Mansfield, Nottinghamshire

Danny leaned back in his chair, facing his two detective inspectors. 'I want a quick recap on how we're progressing. It's been forty-eight hours, and we should be making significant progress.'

Tina Cartwright spoke first. 'We now have the names and addresses for both of Royal's ex-wives. I've allocated enquiry teams to visit them at their home addresses and make initial enquiries.'

'Are they local?'

'Fairly. One lives here in Notts, at Beeston. The other one lives just outside Derby at Darley Abbey.'

'Are there any children?'

'The only child is from Royal's first marriage. Brad Jarvis is eighteen years old and lives with his mother, Sharon

Jarvis, in Darley Abbey. Guy Royal never had any access rights to his son following the divorce and owes a substantial amount in alimony.'

'Sharon's still using Jarvis as her surname. I take it she never remarried?'

'Neither of the women have remarried. Only Sharon has retained the surname, possibly for the sake of her son. The other ex-wife, Nita Radford, reverted to her maiden name following the divorce settlement.'

'When are you due to see them?'

'Sharon Jarvis is being seen today. I've arranged to meet her at her home address after work. She was adamant she didn't want the police coming to her workplace.'

'Where does she work?'

'Derby Probation Office.'

'Okay, fair enough. What about Nita Radford?'

'Nita Radford is currently in Tenerife on holiday.'

'When did Radford fly to Tenerife? Can we rule her out?'

'Unfortunately not. Her flight was on the evening of the thirtieth. The day after Royal was killed.'

'Okay.' Danny frowned. 'When's she due back?'

'She's due to fly into East Midlands airport on the morning of the seventh.'

'I want to be kept informed when both women have been interviewed. We need to bear in mind the small, smudged fingerprint found at the murder scene, which could be from a woman.'

Tina nodded. 'I'll update you later today after I've seen Sharon Jarvis.'

'Good. Call me at home if you turn up anything suspicious. How are you progressing with the drug use inquiry? Are we any closer to identifying potential dealers?'

Tina shook her head. 'I've been in constant liaison with the drugs squad, and unfortunately, they're getting nothing from their informants. But they do have a list of suspected suppliers of cocaine who operate within the city. It will be a daunting task to systematically trace and interview each one, and with nothing to connect them to Royal, it's potentially a huge waste of time.'

'Keep at it. We need to identify Royal's dealer as soon as we can. It could be that he owed a significant amount of money for drugs already laid on. Drug dealers aren't renowned for their patience when it comes to collecting a debt.'

'I'll push the drugs squad to lean on their informants again.'

Danny turned to Rob Buxton and said, 'How is progress at the Black Aces Casino?'

'When I went there with Glen, on the night of the thirtieth, we were met with a wall of silence,' Rob said with a heavy sigh. 'That was mainly because the owner, Toni "Pap" Pappas, wasn't there. He's currently visiting family in Cyprus and won't return until the sixth of this month. He's been in Cyprus since the fifteenth of September, so wasn't in the country the night Royal was killed.'

'And do you expect Pappas to be forthcoming when he gets back?'

Rob shrugged. 'Hard to say. What we do know is that when we examined Royal's bank accounts, we've found several large payments going from his account into the casino's account. The last of those was three months ago. It's possible that Royal built up another substantial debt in that time. We do know there isn't much cash left in any of his accounts. If he does owe another large debt, he would certainly struggle to pay it. We'll have plenty of questions for Toni Pappas when he does return.'

'Okay. Keep me informed of any developments.' Danny paused before continuing, 'I received a telephone call from Seamus Carter this morning. The blood tests and toxicology results have confirmed a serious cocaine addiction and that Royal was suffering from venereal disease, namely syphilis. Tina, be sure to make enquiries with Royal's GP to see if we can establish how long the deceased had been suffering with this disease, and if any treatment had ever been administered.'

'Will do, boss.' She gave a half-smile. 'I'd not forgotten, sir.'

'One last update for you both.' Danny held their gaze, keen to impress upon them the import of what he had to say. 'I've been informed by the press officer this morning that several journalists are now aware of the suspicious death of Guy Royal. I'm working on a press release that will be aired on this evening's news channels. For now, it's only the regional press involved, but due to our victim's high profile, that interest could quickly escalate to national press attention. So expect the pressure for a result to start ramping up from now. Keep your inquiry teams working hard. We know Royal had plenty of potential enemies: we need to identify the one capable of carrying out his murder.'

10

5.30 p.m., 2 October 1990
8 Darley Street, Darley Abbey, Derby

Darley Street was a neat terrace row of three-storey cottages. Standing in the middle of the terrace, number eight looked particularly charming; it was obviously well cared for and looked in pristine condition for such an old building.

Jag let out a low whistle as he got out of the car. 'I've been to Derby loads of times and never knew this place existed. It's a beautiful area.'

Tina smiled her agreement. 'Nice house. Let's see if Sharon Jarvis has made it home from work yet.'

She used the ornate knocker to rap three times on the red front door.

There was a shout from within: 'Just a second.'

The door was opened by a middle-aged woman. Her wet

blonde hair was causing her towelling dressing gown to dampen at the shoulders.

Tina held out her identification. 'Sharon Jarvis?' The woman nodded, and Tina said, 'I'm Detective Inspector Cartwright; this is DC Singh. I spoke to you earlier and arranged to meet you this evening.'

A puzzled expression appeared on Sharon's face, so Tina added, 'So we could talk about your ex-husband, Harvey.'

Sharon Jarvis allowed a scowl to pass over her face and grumbled, 'What's that bastard done now?'

It was clear to Tina that Sharon Jarvis was unaware of her ex-husband's death.

'Can we come inside and talk?'

'Sorry. Of course, this way. You'll have to excuse the mess. I jumped straight in the shower as soon as I got home. It's been a long, hard day.'

Tina waited until everyone had sat down before she said, as gently as she could, 'I'm sorry to inform you that Harvey Jarvis was found dead at his home two days ago.'

Sharon sat open mouthed as the enormity of Tina's words registered.

Eventually she said, 'Well, I can't say I'm surprised. The last time I saw him, he looked dreadful. He'd obviously been hammering the booze and drugs again. Was it an overdose?'

Ignoring the woman's question, Tina asked, 'When did you last see him?'

'Three weeks ago, at my solicitor's office in Derby. I was trying to get some cash out of the tight bastard to help pay for his son's travel plans.'

'Were you successful?'

'Of course not. He made lots of promises, witnessed by my solicitor, but he still hasn't paid me a penny.'

'You mentioned your son's travel plans,' Jag Singh remarked. 'What travel plans?'

'Brad's got a place at Oxford University and wants to see some of the world first. He's gone backpacking in Australia. They call it a gap year.'

'Has he left yet?'

'He left a fortnight ago, why?'

'Do you know where he is right now?'

'He's working on a banana plantation near Cairns in Queensland.' Sharon Jarvis looked genuinely puzzled. 'Why are you asking about Brad?'

Tina said, 'We're having to ask these questions because Harvey didn't die of an overdose. I'm sorry to say that he was murdered.'

'I don't believe it.' Sharon's hands pushed her hair back as a look of shock passed over her face. 'I've seen nothing on the news. Are you sure it's Harvey? I can't believe the press aren't all over this.'

'Of course we would tell you before the news becomes public,' Tina told the woman. 'But I do have to ask you this. Can you tell me where you were on the night of the twenty-ninth and the morning of the thirtieth of September?'

'I went to work as usual on the twenty-ninth; then I was here.'

'All night?'

'Yes, all night,' Sharon insisted, a tone of irritation creeping into her voice. 'I had an early start at the office on the thirtieth. I was back in work by seven o'clock that morning.'

'Can anybody verify you being here that night?'

'No. Now that Brad's abroad, I'm here on my own.'

'When was the last time you visited Hunters Croft?' Jag asked.

'I've never been to Hunters Croft,' Sharon almost snapped, her face darkening. 'He bought that house to shack up with the tart he married after I walked out of his sorry life.'

'The press described your animosity towards your husband in minute detail after you'd split up. Was their account a true reflection of your feelings about your divorce?'

'Oh, it was true alright. When the reptiles from the press came calling after all the scandals broke, I told them the truth. Guy Royal had been a complete and utter bastard to me and my son. He was abusive, physically and mentally, to both of us and hadn't paid a penny of alimony for the upkeep of his son since the break-up. There was no reason for me to lie to save his sorry arse, even though that weasel manager of his asked me to.' She crossed her arms in a gesture of defiance and anger. 'No, I told them exactly what it had been like living with that monster.'

Tina nodded in recognition of the woman's words. 'And, apart from seeing him at your solicitor's, have you had any other contact with him recently?'

'No. I've had no reason to go anywhere near the man. I only arranged this last meeting because my solicitor thought it might work. I told her he would never part with any money, and I was right. I've had to take a bank loan out to help fund Brad's trip.'

'Okay. Thanks for talking to us, Sharon.' Tina rose, and Jag did the same. 'We may have to talk to you again to clarify things, as and when something comes up. For now, do you have any questions for me?'

'That's fine. I'm not planning on going anywhere.' She paused, as if considering her next words. 'I do have one question for you. How did Harvey die?'

'He was shot,' Jag told her, his voice neutral.

'Bloody hell. I hope you're having a good look at Stan bloody Jennings. I never trusted that weasel. He never really liked Harvey. He's only ever been interested in how much money he could make, riding on the back of Harvey's success.' Sharon showed them to the door before concluding, 'It was always about the money for Jennings.'

11

6.05 p.m., 2 October 1990
6 Comyn Gardens, St Ann's, Nottingham

Trudy Fraser was grabbing a last cup of tea before work began.

Work for Trudy meant another long, cold night standing on the corner of Forest Road East and Colville Street. She had worked that corner for over two years, and her regular punters knew where to find her.

At thirty years old, she had been a prostitute for over a decade, and now the years and the work's arduous nature were beginning to take their toll. For the last eighteen months, she had felt physically ill and had been surviving on paracetamol and gin to ease the pain.

She had recently noticed a massive reduction in the number of her regular clients. Times were hard enough without that, so she'd been grateful when she was picked up by Guy Royal's butler a few days ago. Royal was a pervert and could be a nasty bastard, but the money was always good. There were worse places to ply her trade than in Royal's flash house, out in the sticks.

But that day had been a near disaster. Royal, totally out of his head, had demanded weird, kinky sex from the outset. After spending an awful afternoon and evening pandering to his depraved demands, she had finally refused to carry on, and there had been an enormous row.

It had been a relief when the fat butler had finally paid her the money she was owed. At one point she'd almost resigned herself to just getting out of the house with her hands empty. It had been a tough gig, though, and she would have been gutted to leave without the cash. Royal had been relentlessly brutal, and her body was only just beginning to recover from the trauma of that afternoon and evening.

She had made her mind up that she would never trick for Royal again. The money just wasn't worth the pain and bruising she suffered afterwards. Guy Royal was a vicious pig, and she could understand why both his wives had left him. The newspapers were right, he was a monster.

As she applied the last touches to her rudimentary makeup, she glanced at the television that was playing to itself in the corner of the room. The local news was on, and suddenly there was an image of a country house on the screen. It was a house she knew well.

She abandoned her makeup routine, sat down in front of the television, and turned the volume up. Some podgy, overweight reporter in an ill-fitting suit was standing on the driveway of the house. He was talking about how Guy Royal had been found dead in his home two days ago.

Trudy leaned back in shock as she quickly worked out she had been with Royal the night before he died.

The reporter's next words made Trudy's blood run cold. He stared solemnly into the camera and said, 'At this time, the police are treating Guy Royal's death as suspicious and have launched a murder enquiry. They are appealing for anybody who may have information to contact the incident room.'

The reporter recited a telephone number, which was then displayed on the bottom of the television screen. But it disappeared from the screen before Trudy had a chance to jot it down.

She grabbed her tea and shovelled two heaped teaspoons of sugar in. Her hands were shaking as she gripped the mug. Her brain was in overdrive as she desperately tried to work out what she should do for the best. She knew her fingerprints would be all over the house, certainly in his bedroom and the adjoining bathroom. She had spent nearly a full afternoon and evening there. Her fingerprints were on the police database after being arrested for soliciting on several occasions, so the police would soon know that she had recently been there.

Somehow, she had to get ahead of the situation.

Guy Royal had been alive and well when she left in the taxi.

Then a wave of relief swept over her as she thought of the fat butler. He had still been in the taxi when it had dropped her off at Comyn Gardens. He would be able to confirm to the police that it couldn't have been her who killed Royal.

Grabbing her sheepskin coat, she hurried out of the flat, intending to make her way to the police station on St Ann's Well Road. She had information she urgently needed to tell the detectives there.

12

7.45 p.m., 2 October 1990
St Ann's Police Station, St Ann's Well Road, Nottingham

Rachel Moore and Jane Pope walked into the interview room and sat down opposite Trudy Fraser.

Trudy was holding a mug of tea in both hands, staring at the brown liquid, refusing to make eye contact with the two detectives. Rachel knew the woman had been waiting at the police station for over an hour and was probably starting to doubt the wisdom of walking inside.

To break the ice and alleviate some of the palpable tension in the small room, Rachel said, 'I'm sorry you've had such a long wait, Trudy, but we've driven from Mansfield, and the roadworks were a bit of a nightmare. Would you like a fresh drink?'

Trudy carefully placed the mug on the table, slowly

shook her head, then for the first time looked up at the detectives. Her blue eyes looked watery, and there was a worried expression behind them. Rachel knew she would have to tread carefully to avoid the woman refusing to talk to her.

The telephone call from the enquiry desk at St Ann's to the MCIU office had been a bizarre one. A woman, known to the local police as a prostitute, had walked into the station claiming to have significant information about the suspicious death of Guy Royal.

Rachel and Jane had left the MCIU immediately and travelled to the city. Countless roadworks into the city had caused them delay after delay, and when they finally arrived, it was a relief to find Trudy Fraser still at the police station.

'Thank you so much for your patience and for sticking around,' Rachel said. 'I understand you wanted to talk to us about Guy Royal.'

After a long pause, Trudy mumbled, 'I was at his house.'

It wasn't what Rachel had been expecting to hear, and the thought of the small, smudged fingerprint found in blood at the scene crashed into her brain. She recovered quickly and asked, 'Are you talking about Hunters Croft?'

Trudy flicked her long blonde hair back off her face and said, 'I don't know the name of the place. That big house in the countryside, the one that's been on the news.'

'When?'

'Three days ago. I was there most of the afternoon and evening, but I left that night. According to the news, that was the day before Guy Royal was found dead. Is that right?'

'What were you doing at Guy Royal's house?'

'I was there to party.'

'And how did you get there?'

'I was picked up on Forest Road by the fat bloke who lives at the house,' Trudy said. 'I think he's Royal's butler or something. Anyway, I've partied there a couple of times before, so I knew it would be worth going. I needed a good score.'

'So, you and this man, how did you get to the house?'

'In the butler's car. He's got a little yellow sports car, very flash.'

'I've got to ask you this, Trudy,' Rachel said. 'What do you mean by "party"?'

Trudy shrugged and said bluntly, 'I was paid to go there and have sex with Royal.'

'Was that with Royal on his own, or was the other man involved as well?'

'Fat man never wants to do anything.' Trudy shook her head, as if surprised. 'He doesn't even like to watch. He makes himself scarce, then sorts Royal's shit out when he gets too pissed or high.'

'In what way?'

'I don't know what you know about Guy Royal,' Trudy said, leaning back in her chair and crossing her arms, 'but he's nothing like the person on television. Forget all that cheeky chappie charm; Royal's a grade A pervert. He wants rough sex, the kinkier, the better. I'll put up with a lot, but there are some things I'm not prepared to do. Royal demands everything and doesn't like taking no for an answer.'

Rachel nodded, appreciating the woman's directness. 'Okay, Trudy. So, when you were at the house three days ago, what time did you arrive, and what time did you leave?'

'Fat man picked me up just after one o'clock in the afternoon. I don't usually go out for the lunchtime trade, but like I said, I needed the money. Lunchtime is always slow, and

I'm limited as to where I can take any punters that do come along.'

'And what time did you leave the house?'

'I'm not a hundred percent sure.' Trudy glanced about the small room, thinking. 'I reckon it was around half past ten. I know I'd had enough of Royal's shit by then, and I wanted out of there. The bastard wasn't going to pay me either.'

'I see.' Rachel couldn't help but raise her eyebrows at that. 'Did you get paid?'

'Eventually. But only because fat man sorted my money out.'

'And how much were you paid?' Jane asked.

A look of horror crossed the features of Trudy Fraser. 'Hey! Am I going to get done for this?'

'Nobody's looking to prosecute you for soliciting,' Jane quickly jumped in. 'We're only interested in what happened at the house.'

'You're going to have to trust us, Trudy,' Rachel pressed. 'As far as I'm concerned, you're here as a witness, nothing else. Okay?'

Trudy nodded, and after a long pause she muttered, 'A hundred pounds. I was paid one hundred pounds.'

'How did you get home?'

'A taxi arrived to pick me up. I was getting in when fat man decided he was going to get in the taxi as well. I think he wanted to get away from all Royal's shit, too.'

'Why was that?'

'Before the taxi arrived, Royal had really lost it. He was being vile and refusing to pay me the money I'd been promised. He even told me to fuck off and walk back to Nottingham. Fat man must have heard the row because he came downstairs into the hallway and asked what the hell was going on.'

'So, what happened after he came downstairs?'

'I told him I wanted the money I was owed and the fare for the taxi home.'

'I see.' Rachel nodded. 'So, when the taxi arrived, why did he get in as well?'

'Royal saw him give me the hundred quid I was owed, and he went mental. He completely forgot I was still standing there and started having a right go at the fat man.'

'Can you remember what was being said?'

'Fat man wasn't saying anything. He looked like he was just trying to ignore Royal's ranting and raving.'

'What was Royal saying?'

'I didn't understand most of it. He was so pissed and high. There was a lot of personal insults, but he did keep going on about his will and how fat man would end up with fuck all.'

'Did the other man respond to what was said about the will?'

'Not verbally, but I could see that he was really pissed off. That's when he decided to get in the taxi with me.'

'How was Royal when the taxi left?'

'He was off his head.'

'Drunk?'

'He'd been snorting coke and drinking whisky all the time I was there. The more coke he has, the worse he gets. The man's a pig anyway, but when he's smashed on drink and drugs, he's vicious and dangerous. That's why I wanted out of there.'

'Was he violent towards you?'

'In ways you don't want to know about, love.'

'I see.' Rachel let out a long breath, not wanting to make Trudy relive that sort of pain. 'So, Trudy, will this man you've described as his butler confirm your account of what happened, and how you left the property together?'

'I don't know.' Trudy wound a strand of hair around her finger, let it go in a curl, before she carried on. 'But I've been thinking while I was waiting here. Even if he doesn't, the taxi driver will. He'll remember driving out from Nottingham to that big house and the fact that he picked me and fat man up.'

'We haven't been able to trace that taxi yet. Was it from one of the firms listed in the address book?'

'I don't know if the number is in any address book. I called the cab. I just wanted the money for the fare from Royal or his butler. Neither of those two called the cab; I did. I used the phone in the hallway while they were rowing.'

'What taxi firm did you call?' Rachel asked, keeping her voice steady, as she realised this was a moment for a real breakthrough in the investigation.

'I use Sherwood Cars. It's the only taxi number I know off by heart, so I always call them.'

Jane caught Rachel's eye as she noted down the taxi company's name. But then she continued as if nothing of significance had been said. 'You mentioned how Royal was snorting cocaine. Have you seen him abusing drugs when you've been at the house before?'

'There's always loads of cocaine whenever I've been. I don't touch the stuff myself. It makes me want to throw up. I also need to keep a clear head when I'm with Royal, or things can easily get out of hand.'

'Okay, Trudy.' Jane tilted her head as she asked, 'Can you tell us where Royal gets his coke?'

Trudy shrugged and said nothing, looking down at the desk.

Rachel said, 'Earlier, you told me that the other man, the one you've described as Royal's butler, sorts all his shit out for him. Does that include supplying Royal with drugs?'

Trudy nodded.

'How do you know that?'

Trudy hesitated a moment. 'Because when he picked me up that afternoon, he showed me a massive bag of coke. I don't know if he thought I'd be partaking as well, but I remember him saying he'd scored for Royal and that it was going to be a hell of a party.'

'And are you sure it was coke?'

'It was the same bag of powder that Royal was shoving up his nose all afternoon, so yeah, I reckon it was coke.'

'Is there anything else about Royal's butler you can tell us?'

'Yeah. He's got a gammy leg and walks with a limp.' As she spoke, Trudy pointed to her own leg, a sympathetic look on her face. 'I remember because Royal, in that spiteful way of his, refers to him as the cripple.'

Jane made another note before she said, 'One last question about that night, Trudy. Apart from Royal and this butler, did you see anybody else at the house while you were there?'

'No.' Trudy emphasised her point with a definitive shake of her head.

As she worked to bring the interview to a close, Rachel added, 'Why did you come to the police station this evening, Trudy?'

'The news report said that a murder investigation had been launched. I know my fingerprints will be all over the bedroom, bathroom and probably other places inside that house. I also know Guy Royal was alive and kicking when I left that night.'

Rachel nodded; the woman's account made sense. 'Are you prepared to make a witness statement about what you've told us today?'

'Yes, I'll make a statement. Like I said, you lot need to know I've got nothing to do with his murder. If you ask me, the butler did it.' Realising what she'd said, Trudy let out a nervous giggle. She immediately apologised. 'Sorry. I didn't mean to laugh. You know what I mean.' She giggled again, not seeming to be able to help herself. 'The fat man did it. He was so pissed off with Royal, I bet he's done him in.'

13

8.30 a.m., 22 February 1989
Bouldstone Press, Eastcastle Street, London

Janice Millership stopped and looked in wonder at the ornate entrance before her. She could feel wave after wave of excitement coursing through her. It still all seemed so surreal. She couldn't quite believe she was about to walk through that door and start work in one of the most respected publishing houses in London.

The forty-one-year-old had been fascinated with books from an early age. A plain child, she had been teased and ridiculed at school. She was now a plain woman, not unattractive, but she never did anything to enhance her appearance. She wore unfashionable clothes that didn't complement her slim, almost boyish figure, and she never bothered with makeup or fancy hairstyles, preferring to keep her short mousy brown hair in a pixie cut.

One thing Janice did have was personality. She was a bubbly

character who smiled and laughed a lot. It gave her an appeal, especially to men, that she seemed totally unaware of.

For Janice, men had never been at the top of her priorities. She was happy in their company, but the prospect of marriage had never crossed her mind. Living and caring for her elderly parents had become her life. She had embraced the spinster life and concentrated all her thoughts of romance into the stories she wrote. It was her life's dream to have one of her romantic novels published and to be recognised as a bestselling author.

After years of rejections, she had decided to change tack, and rather than sending her manuscripts to publishing houses in the forlorn hope of getting one published, she started applying for jobs within those publishing houses, hoping that being on the inside of the industry would be a pathway to fulfil her dreams.

And today, two weeks had passed since she'd received written confirmation that she had been successful in her application to work as a secretary at Bouldstone Press in London.

Coming just two months after her elderly parents had both gone to live in a residential care home specialising in the care of dementia patients, the timing of the new job offer had been perfect.

It was the new start she had been praying for when she had made the tough decision to allow her parents to go into the home so they could receive the level of care and attention that their dementia diagnosis deserved.

Those two weeks since the postman had brought her the most significant letter of her life flew by. She had secured her parents' home, packed up her personal belongings, and driven to London, where she had been fortunate to find an affordable flat in a tower block in Camden, not far from the British Library. It was a reasonably nice area and only a fifteen-minute walk from the offices of Bouldstone Press.

As she stepped towards that ornate doorway, Janice could feel the excitement within her rising again.

She had to report to the typing pool initially, but would be seen later in the day by the personal secretary of Seymour Hart-Wilson, the owner of Bouldstone Press.

Somehow, she instinctively knew this was going to mark the start of a wonderful new chapter in her life.

14

2.30 p.m., 22 February 1989
Bouldstone Press, Eastcastle Street, London

Seymour Hart-Wilson was feeling a mixture of excitement and relief. The meeting with the television personality Guy Royal – and his manager, Stan Jennings – was going as well as could be expected.

He generally hated dealing with showbiz types, as he found it difficult to put up with their prima donna attitudes.

Guy Royal had a reputation as someone who was difficult to be around, and throughout the meeting he had more than lived up to that reputation. He was surly, borderline rude in the way he spoke, and was arrogantly dismissive of any suggestions made by his manager.

Hart-Wilson had been energised by the telephone call he'd received from Jennings, expressing the possibility of an autobiography penned by the disgraced star. He knew Royal's autobiography would be a story the public would lap up. He could see a huge market for a tell-all, no-holds-barred book detailing all the sordid details. The tabloid press had done a real hatchet job on Royal, running story after story, exposing the television star's predilection for drugs and prostitutes, as well as the abuse he was rumoured to have meted out to his two ex-wives.

Royal now had a deserved reputation as a monster, but interestingly he was also a man adored by large sections of the general public. With his long blond hair, he was someone who was still instantly recognisable and who had somehow managed to retain a huge fan base.

This was the enigma that was Guy Royal.

Hart-Wilson had been in publishing long enough to spot a goose about to lay a golden egg.

The three men had been in conversation for over two hours, and although Stan Jennings seemed to be totally on board with the deal being offered, Royal was proving to be stubborn and truculent.

The sticking point had been who would pen the autobiography. Royal was insistent that it was his story, and he wanted to write it. He wanted it to be a true autobiography. Ever since Jennings had first mooted the idea, the prospect of writing his own book had appealed more and more to Royal's overinflated ego.

Hart-Wilson realised that, for the book to be the success it undoubtably could be, it would require the skills of a top-quality ghost writer.

However, there was one more ace he could play to try to get Royal on board. He would appeal to the man's own monstrous ego.

In a smarmy, acquiescent voice, he said, 'There's no doubt in my mind that you could write your own story, Guy. But I want your book to be the absolute best it can be, that's all. How about a close collaboration working with my top ghost writer? And don't worry, you would always have the final say on what goes into your story. I have a superbly talented writer in our New York office who specialises in ghost writing the life stories of the very best actors, performers and politicians. Kingston Jones is a true master of his craft, and I'm sure he would relish the prospect of working with a huge TV star such as yourself. What do you think?'

'That sounds great,' Stan Jennings enthused. 'And he's your top man, you say?'

'The very best in the business. I'm as keen as you are for this book to be a stellar success. The bottom line is this. I know that with Kingston Jones's input, this book will absolutely fly off the shelves and make us all a great deal of money.'

'And this would be a genuine collaboration?' Guy Royal stroked his chin, musing. 'Not just me talking to him and him writing? I'd want to write most of the content and simply let him spruce it up a bit.'

'Totally.' Hart-Wilson beamed as he nodded. 'That could work beautifully.'

'I'm warning you now, if it doesn't work, I'll walk away and go somewhere else,' Guy Royal said, his tone switching again to a threatening, unpleasant timbre. 'I can see what you think this book will be worth. I'm not stupid, even if my porky manager is. I'd also prefer it if this Kingston of yours came to me. Getting to London these days is such a pain in the arse.'

Fearful of the lucrative deal slipping from his grasp, and even more horrified at the thought of one of his company's rivals landing the book, Seymour Hart-Wilson shuddered. Without thinking, he blurted out, 'Of course he can come to you. I'll provide your ghost writer with his own secretary, and they'll meet you wherever you want, to start the process. Come on, Guy. What do you say?'

After a long pause, Royal allowed a greasy smile to form on his lips. 'Call your man,' he said, 'and set up the first meeting. Let's make this happen.'

Stan Jennings punched the air. 'Yes!'

Seymour Hart-Wilson reached across his desk and shook hands with both men. The truth was, he needed this book deal as much as Guy Royal did. For the last six months Bouldstone Press had been haemorrhaging money. He needed a massive success to steady the business and prevent it going under. He genuinely believed this show-business autobiography could be that singular success and the answer to his company's financial prayers.

He didn't envy the ghost writer having to work alongside Royal, but that would be his problem. That was why Kingston Jones always got paid the big bucks.

The meeting over, Hart-Wilson pressed the intercom button on his telephone and asked his secretary to show Royal and Jennings out of the building.

As the two men left his office, Hart-Wilson followed them and introduced his secretary, who had been in conversation with another staff member.

Before the secretary could say anything, the other woman said in an overloud voice, 'Wow! My first day here, and I'm in the same room as Guy Royal.'

As Guy turned to face the woman, she gushed, 'You are simply amaaazing! I love everything you've ever done on the telly. You're just the best.'

Hart-Wilson was about to interject when he saw how Guy Royal was instantly lapping up the woman's attention. Instead of rebuking the new member of staff, he said, 'As you can see, all our secretaries and staff are huge fans of yours.'

Maintaining eye contact with the woman, Royal said, 'Is this young lady one of your secretaries?'

Hart-Wilson glanced at his personal secretary, who said, 'I'm sorry, Mr Hart-Wilson, this is Janice Millership. It's her first day with us today. Yes, she is a secretary.'

Royal continued to stare into Janice Millership's hazel eyes. 'I like you, Janice Millership,' he said. 'How'd you like to work with me on my book?'

From the look on Janice's face, she clearly couldn't believe her ears. 'I would love that, Mr Royal, but obviously it's not up to me.'

'What do you say, Seymour?' Royal asked as he spun round to face Hart-Wilson. 'Can Janice be assigned to work on my book?'

'I don't know,' Hart-Wilson spluttered, entirely wrong-footed.

'You said your ghost would have his own secretary; I want the lovely Janice here to be that secretary.'

'Okay, okay.' Hart-Wilson knew when he'd been backed into a corner. 'I'll get everything arranged to get Kingston Jones over here and set up a meeting. And Ms Millership can be his secretary; that won't be a problem at all.'

Royal stepped forward and pecked a kiss on the back of Janice's hand. 'I look forward to seeing you again soon, Janice.'

'This way, please, gentlemen,' Hart-Wilson's secretary said, leading them away as briskly as she could.

As the trio departed, Hart-Wilson hissed at Janice, 'What the hell were you doing, young lady? You don't talk to potential clients like that.'

'I'm sorry, sir.' Janice looked crestfallen. 'I was only being friendly. I'm not actually such a big fan of Guy Royal. I was just shocked at seeing somebody so famous.'

'Well, big fan or not, you're going to be seeing a lot more of him. I've got a special job lined up for you, Ms Millership. I hope you don't regret being so friendly. From what I've seen this morning, Guy Royal isn't the easiest man to work with. Can you drive?'

15

8.00 a.m., 23 February 1989
West Fourth Street, Greenwich Village, New York

Kingston Jones couldn't understand what had gone so catastrophically wrong with his relationship. He had lived with Ralph Hooper, at the artist's apartment, for almost a year. The first ten months of their romance had been idyllic.

The two men had met at an art gallery where Ralph was displaying some of his latest artwork. The middle-aged artist was finally gaining the recognition his art deserved, and he was being touted as one of the most influential artists to emerge from America since Andy Warhol had first trailblazed the concept of 'pop art'.

Ralph Hooper was a gay man who'd never made any secret of his attraction to other men, and he had made a beeline for

Kingston Jones as soon as he saw the tall, elegant black man enter the gallery.

Kingston Jones was not an overtly gay man, but he didn't try to hide his sexuality either. He found himself instantly attracted to the rugged good looks, long ash-grey hair and neatly trimmed beard of the artist with the sparkling blue eyes.

The two men had spent a wonderful afternoon chatting about art. Ralph had shown a real interest in Kingston's work as a writer, and both men were happy to discover they were creatives with such a lot in common.

Neither man had wanted that first afternoon to end, and their connection had gone from strength to strength over the following weeks. After five weeks of dating every night, Ralph had asked Kingston to move into his spacious studio apartment in the fashionable Greenwich Village district.

Kingston had gladly accepted the offer, seeing it as confirmation that the love they felt for each other was a genuine, lasting one. Over the ensuing months their relationship had only encountered one problem. The extensive travelling Ralph had to do to promote his artwork meant he was forced to spend a lot of time in California, leaving Kingston alone in New York to pursue his own career as a writer.

However, although they were sometimes apart for weeks, when they were eventually reunited, the two men never had a problem rekindling their love.

Until four weeks ago.

For no apparent reason, Ralph had started to become agitated and resentful. He was short tempered and verbally lashed out at Kingston over the smallest disagreements. It was totally out of character for the quiet, mild-mannered artist.

That morning, things had come to a head as Kingston was getting ready to leave for work. He'd kept any noise to a bare minimum as he prepared and ate breakfast. He was aware Ralph was still in bed, after yet another late night watching television on his own. Twice during the night, Kingston had asked his lover to switch off the set and come to bed. Both times he had been blanked, as Ralph just stared at the flickering screen.

Just as Kingston was leaving for work, Ralph had woken in a foul mood and stormed into the kitchen to confront his lover. 'Why the fuck do you have to make so much noise?'

'If you came to bed at a reasonable hour, you wouldn't be so grouchy,' Kingston countered in a jocular fashion.

He recoiled physically in alarm at the sudden venom and spite of Ralph's answer. 'I don't come to bed because you're in my fucking bed! I want you out of here today! You can collect your shit after work. Now, fuck off!'

Kingston was so shocked by the outburst that he slumped onto one of the kitchen bar stools as his briefcase slipped from his grasp, clattering to the floor.

Gathering himself, he made full eye contact with his lover and said, 'You don't mean that, Ralph.'

As he waited for a response, he maintained eye contact with Ralph. Kingston could sense a rage behind his lover's eyes that he had never seen before.

He said softly, 'What's wrong, Ralph?'

Unblinking, Ralph stared hard at Kingston and said, 'Nothing's wrong. We're just done, that's all. I meant what I said. Get your stuff after work. I'm going back to bed.'

'Don't walk away from me,' a distraught Kingston murmured. 'We need to talk this through. I love you.'

Ralph spun round and snarled into Kingston's face, 'Well, I don't love you. There's nothing more to say. You need to leave right now.'

As the tears started to sting Kingston's eyes, he grabbed his briefcase, stormed out of the apartment, and slammed the door behind him. His head was spinning. He truly thought he had found his soulmate. His relationship with Ralph Hooper had been an affirmation of his sexuality. He had always held niggling doubts before meeting Ralph, but as soon as they started living together, Kingston realised that what he had found with the talented artist was true love.

As he looked up and down West Fourth Street, searching for a cab, he couldn't understand how Ralph could turn his feelings off so abruptly. And all that anger and rage, so visible in his lover's sad blue eyes. What was that all about?

Something didn't sit right, but Ralph had spitefully made his feelings clear, and Kingston wasn't going to stay with a man who didn't love him.

He decided there and then that he would in fact move out that evening. He still had the keys to his old apartment in Queens. He would get his stuff after work and move out that night.

Those initial feelings of upset and sadness were quickly being replaced by very different emotions. Anger and outrage now filled his head at the callous and brutal way Hooper had ended their relationship.

'Well, fuck you, Mr Ralph Hooper,' he muttered under his breath. 'Who needs your shit at eight o'clock in the morning.'

At the sight of a yellow cab, Kingston raised his arm and yelled, 'Taxi!'

16

10.00 a.m., 23 February 1989
Water Street, Financial District, New York

A crestfallen and increasingly bitter Kingston Jones nursed yet another small paper cup of strong coffee. The waste basket at the side of his desk was almost full of empty paper cups. He had consumed so much coffee since arriving at his office at Bouldstone Press in the Financial District that his head was now buzzing.

He hadn't managed to complete any of the work he had intended doing. His mind was still racing from the events of that morning. He just didn't understand what had changed so dramatically in his relationship.

The telephone ringing on the desk tore him away from his self-indulgent thoughts.

He snatched up the handset and said wearily, 'Kingston Jones.'

The person on the line said, 'Kingston. The very man I need to speak to. How the devil are you?'

Instantly recognising the quintessentially English accent, Kingston replied, 'I've had better days, Seymour. What can I do for you?'

Seymour Hart-Wilson was never one for small talk, so he got straight to the point. 'I need you to get on the next plane to London. I've an extremely important ghost-writing assignment for you. I need my best man to assist in writing the biography of one of Britain's greatest ever television stars. It will be a massive coup for Bouldstone Press to publish this book. So, when can you get here?'

Kingston knew he had a talent for ghost writing; he had made a successful career writing on behalf of other people. Although very skilled at it, it wasn't a process he enjoyed. The financial rewards were good, but there was none of the recognition other authors received for their endeavours.

'Not sure I like the sound of "assist in writing". What does that mean exactly?'

'The client believes he can write his own book. Having seen a small sample of his writing, I know he can't. It would be a disaster. I need you to work your magic and make this book a roaring success. Bouldstone here in the UK are overdue a bestseller, and I'm sure this could be it.'

Kingston was thoughtful. He had worked on books before where the client was invested in writing a genuine autobiography. Where they had kicked hard against the expertise being offered.

'I'm not sure I like the sound of "assisting". Either I write it, or I don't. These collaboration pieces never really work, and they come with all kinds of grief and upset. I don't know if I need all that right now. Who's the big star, anyway?'

'I doubt you'll have heard of him. It's a man named Guy Royal. He was massive on the small screen over here a few years ago. At one time, he seemed to be on every TV show that was aired. He was one of the UK's highest earners in the world of show business.'

'Yeah,' Kingston said with heavy sarcasm in his voice. 'He sounds a huge star. How come I've never heard of the dude?'

'Trust me. He was a real TV phenomenon over here, but it's his backstory that will make this book a bestseller. Guy Royal's a fatally flawed character with more than his fair share of demons. The punters will lap up his story. This book will be massive in the UK.'

'I don't know. I've a lot of personal shit going on here right now.'

Desperate to engage Jones for the job, Hart-Wilson said, 'Look, Kingston, this book is important, so I'm prepared to pay you double your normal rate. I think it will take at least six months to complete. That's worth a small fortune to you. Do you really want to turn this lucrative offer down over some shitty melodrama happening in your personal life?'

After the upset he had endured since the row that morning, to hear his problems described in such a brutal way made up Kingston's mind.

After a brief pause, where images of the anger in Hooper's blue eyes flashed through his mind, Kingston said, 'Okay, Seymour. You're right. I'm in. I'll catch the next flight to Heathrow. I could do with a break from this town.'

'Good man. Call me with the details of the flight, and I'll arrange to have you picked up at the airport.'

'Will do,' Kingston said as he replaced the handset, his head spinning with questions.

Will London ease my pain?

Who needs Ralph Hooper?

And who the hell is Guy Royal?

17

9.00 a.m., 3 October 1990
MCIU Offices, Mansfield, Nottinghamshire

Rob Buxton was met by DC Fran Jefferies as he walked in. 'The boss wants to see you in his office straight away, sir,' she said.

'Okay, Fran, thanks. Do you know why?'

'He didn't say, but he's got DS Moore and DC Pope in there.'

Rob knocked once on the door and walked into Danny's office. Rachel Moore and Jane Pope were already sat down.

'Grab a seat, Rob,' Danny said. 'You need to hear this.'

As soon as Rob sat down, Rachel said, 'We saw Trudy Fraser last night at St Ann's. Trudy's a working girl; she was hired to entertain Guy Royal at Hunters Croft the day before he was found dead.'

Rob let out a low whistle. 'When you say hired, I take it she wasn't picked up by Royal himself?'

'No, she wasn't.' Rachel shook her head. 'She was picked up by Stan Jennings from Forest Road East, in the city. Then Jennings drove her out to Hunters Croft in his MGB GT.'

'Why hasn't Jennings mentioned any of this?'

Danny said, 'Tell him the rest, Rachel.'

'Probably because when Jennings picked her up, he showed her a bag of cocaine that he had just scored,' Rachel said. 'Trudy states she later witnessed Jennings give that bag of drugs to Royal. She also gave us details of the argument between Royal and Jennings, which she overheard as she was leaving the house. She's told us that during that row, Royal was making threats about cutting Jennings out of his will.'

Rob asked, 'What time did she leave Hunters Croft?'

'At the same time as Jennings,' Rachel told them. 'They left in the same taxi. The reason Jennings was so vague about which taxi firm he called was because he never called the cab. It was Trudy who called the taxi from the house. She called a taxi firm from memory, not from the address book next to the telephone.'

'Has this been confirmed?'

'Yes, boss.' Jane Pope nodded. 'After we obtained a witness statement from Trudy, we went to the office of Sherwood Cars on Mansfield Road. The dispatcher remembered the call from Trudy because he had to quote her a one-off fare for the driver to travel out to Ollerton and back. He said it was twenty pounds because of the distances involved.'

'Did you speak to the driver to confirm that Jennings left at the same time, and whether or not he saw Royal?'

'The driver, Shivansh Patel, wasn't working last night, but we've arranged to talk to him later this morning.'

'We also need to establish who he dropped off first.'

'Trudy states she was dropped off at her home in St Ann's first,' Rachel said. 'But that's slightly strange because they would have had to pass Jennings's flat at Mapperley Park on their way.'

'We need to establish where the driver took Jennings after dropping Trudy off, then.' Danny looked thoughtful. 'For all we know, he could have driven Jennings straight back to Ollerton.'

Rob glanced over at Danny and said, 'It's no wonder Jennings hasn't been straight with us. We need to talk to him again.'

'I agree.' Danny nodded. 'I want him arrested and questioned under caution. I want you and Glen Lorimar to arrest him for supplying Class A drugs to Royal and see where that takes us. It's interesting to hear that Royal was making threats towards Jennings, about his will. Have we had sight of Royal's last will and testament yet?'

'Andy's got that enquiry. I believe he's arranged to pick up a copy from Royal's solicitor later this morning. I'll check exactly when.'

'Okay. Let's hang fire until we have sight of the will. We need to know what's in there. We need to see how, were he to be cut out of it, it would affect Jennings.'

Now Danny looked at Rachel. 'What time are you seeing the taxi driver?'

'When I spoke to him on the telephone last night, we agreed to meet him at his home address at ten thirty this morning. He wanted time to drop his kids off at school first.'

'That's great. By the time you've got his account and a statement, we should have a copy of Royal's will.'

He paused before turning to Rob. 'As soon as we know exactly what we're dealing with, I want you and Glen to fetch Jennings in. He's lied to us about so much already, and now he's in deep shit for potentially supplying Royal with Class A drugs. Hopefully, arresting him will focus his mind, and he'll start giving us some straight answers.'

'Do you really think he could have shot Royal?'

'I always keep an open mind, but in my experience, money is often the biggest motive for murder. Let's see where we are after we've spoken to the taxi driver and seen Royal's will.' Danny turned to look at Rachel and Jane. 'You did great work last night. The statement from Trudy Fraser is both comprehensive and damning, for Jennings. It will be interesting to see how he reacts when he's arrested.'

'Oh, and sir,' Rachel said, blushing slightly, 'I felt I needed to inform Trudy about the health problems Royal was suffering, after we'd taken her statement.'

Danny raised an eyebrow. 'That he had syphilis?'

Rachel nodded, still seeming a little awkward.

Danny continued, 'How did she react to that bombshell?'

'Let's just say if Royal weren't already dead, she'd be first in the queue to kill him.'

18

3.00 p.m., 3 October 1990
Mansfield Police Station, Nottinghamshire

Rob Buxton stared at Stan Jennings as Glen Lorimar made the introductions of the people present in the interview room. As well as the two detectives and Jennings, the only other person present was the show-business agent's solicitor.

Stan Jennings looked unwell. His face was pale and sweating at the prospect of being questioned by the detectives. But Rob was also aware that Jennings had a medical condition that could be a problem if he put the man under too much pressure.

When he'd been booked in by the custody sergeant following his arrest, Jennings had mentioned that he suffered from a heart condition, which meant he needed to always keep his medication for angina with him.

Erring on the side of caution, the custody sergeant had arranged for Jennings to be examined by a police surgeon to ensure it was safe for him to be detained and questioned.

This and the subsequent disclosure to Jennings's legal representative had caused long delays. Jennings had been arrested at one o'clock and had already been in custody for two hours.

Rob and Glen had used that time to formulate their interview strategy. They now knew that the taxi driver, Shivansh Patel, had dropped Jennings off at his flat in Mapperley Park after dropping off Trudy Fraser. The driver recalled how Jennings had asked him to drop the woman off first and him second. Jennings had paid him, then given him an extra five pounds as a tip, asking him not to mention that there'd been a woman in the car with him to anybody, as he didn't want it getting back to his wife. Patel had thought nothing of it and gladly accepted the extra money. He also recalled seeing another man looking out the window of the big house near Ollerton as he'd driven away. His description of the man at the window fitted that of Guy Royal. The detectives could now assume that when Stan Jennings and Trudy Fraser left Hunters Croft, Guy Royal was still alive.

The two detectives had now also read Guy Royal's will.

And the will's biggest beneficiary was Stan Jennings. In the event of Royal's death, he stood to inherit Hunters Croft and all its contents. The solicitor now responsible for the will had explained to DS Wills that this had been a recent amendment, and that Stan Jennings had been present when Royal had signed to agree to the amendment.

The detectives knew that if Royal had carried out his threat to revoke that amendment and cut Jennings out of his will, it would have huge financial implications for the middle-aged agent. If money was a motive for murder, then Jennings certainly had motive.

Now, with the introductions over, Rob looked directly at Jennings and said, 'I arrested you earlier today on suspicion of supplying Class A drugs to Guy Royal. I'm now also arresting you on suspicion of the murder of Guy Royal.' Rob then repeated the caution and said, 'Have you anything you want to say about the reasons for your arrest?'

There was silence, and Rob wondered if Jennings's solicitor was going to interrupt to protest the further arrest, or to hand the detectives a prepared statement, or if Jennings himself would answer, 'No comment.'

After a very long pause, Jennings said softly, 'It's shameful that you've arrested me for the murder of my lifelong friend. I didn't kill Guy; I could never hurt him. On the other matter, all I have to say is that I'm not a drug dealer. Guy was having bad withdrawal symptoms and needed to score. He asked me to get gear for him, as he was scared to collect it himself. I drove into Nottingham and picked the drugs up from his dealer. I didn't buy it; it was laid on. I didn't take any money from Guy when I gave it to him later at the house. Like I said, I'm not a dealer. I was just doing my friend a favour.'

'What was Royal scared of?'

'I'm not sure.' Jennings shrugged. 'The dealer was extremely aggressive towards me when I collected the drugs, saying it was the last time it would be laid on. He threatened that if Royal didn't settle his debts soon, there would be repercussions.'

'Did he elaborate on what those repercussions would be?'

'No. But it doesn't take a brain surgeon to work out they wouldn't be pleasant.'

'Do you know how much Guy owed?'

'No. But the way the dealer was acting, it must have been substantial. To be honest, he scared the shit out of me. When I first showed up, he told me to fuck off. He said there would be no more snow until he was paid.'

'How come you ended up with a bag full of cocaine, then?'

'I talked for ages,' Jennings admitted. 'I just mouthed off any old shit so I could get the gear and get out of there. I told the dealer Guy would be good for the money soon, and that he would be down in a few days to settle the debt.'

'And the dealer went for that?'

'I can be very persuasive when I need to be.' Jennings gave a wry smile. 'I fed him some bullshit story about a new television deal Guy had just signed, one that would mean a lot of money coming his way. At the end of the day, this drug dealer is like any other, a greedy bastard who wants to make as much money as he can. I know how they think, so I can manipulate them.'

'That's a dangerous game to play.'

Again, Jennings shrugged. 'It got me out of there with the drugs though, didn't it.'

'So…' Rob paused for a few seconds before asking, 'who's the dealer?'

'Seriously? I can't tell you that. I'd be dead meat.'

'At the moment, you're the dealer.' Rob made sure to look Jennings straight in the eye as he said this. 'You're the person who's been seen handing drugs to somebody else for them to use. Unless we can talk to the person who supplied you with those drugs, we only have your word that this other dealer exists at all.'

Before Jennings could answer, his solicitor leaned forward and whispered something in his ear.

Jennings responded by whispering something back to the solicitor, who then sat back and said, 'You know my advice.'

Rob could see the inner conflict raging behind Jennings's eyes and waited.

Eventually, Jennings said, 'You know I could get killed or seriously injured if I give you a name, right?'

Rob remained silent, simply waiting for Jennings to come to a decision.

After another lengthy pause, the agent said, 'What if I tell you that I went to a house on Noel Street at Hyson Green. The front door is painted bright red, and the house is opposite the Boys Club. There can't be that many cocaine dealers living there.'

'I don't need games from you; what I need is a name.'

Jennings sighed in exasperation, held his head in his hands, and said under his breath, 'I just know the man as Jimmy Beans. He's a big West Indian guy with dreadlocks and lots of gold teeth.'

'Okay. We'll check out this Jimmy Beans. Now, what can you tell me about Trudy Fraser?'

'The prostitute?'

'Yes.'

'I saw her as I was driving back from Hyson Green. I drove along Forest Road East, and she was standing there, plying her trade on the usual corner. Guy had asked me to fetch a woman back for him if I saw anybody I knew. I recognised Trudy, she's been out to the house before, so I picked her up.'

'Did she understand why you were taking her out to the house?'

'Of course she did; she's a tart.' Jennings sneered. 'She knew it would be a good payday for her. She was quite happy to get in the car.'

'Why didn't you mention Trudy had been at the house when we spoke to you before?'

'I didn't think it was important.'

'Your friend had been murdered, and you didn't think someone else being at the house the night before was important?'

'No. Because I knew she'd left at the same time as me. It couldn't have been Trudy who killed Guy.'

'Okay.' Rob leaned forward on the table. 'Tell me about the argument you and Guy had that night...'

'I've already told you; he was ranting, saying all kinds of shit.'

'Ranting about what?'

'He was pissed and high as a kite. I wasn't really listening to what he was ranting about.'

'Trudy Fraser was listening,' Rob told him. 'She's let us know about some of the specifics she heard.'

'I don't believe you.'

'She's made a written statement that says she heard Guy Royal threaten to remove you from his will.'

'So what? Whenever we argue, he threatens stuff like that. It doesn't mean he's going to do it. You must understand that the sober Guy is a completely different person to the pissed-up, high-as-a-kite Guy.'

'We know that you would stand to lose a great deal financially if Guy had followed through with his threat to cut you out of his will.'

'Yes, I would, but I knew he would never do that.'

'I understand that leaving you Hunters Croft in the event of his death was quite a recent amendment. Whose idea was it?'

'It was Guy's. I've gone without pay, off and on, for months. Leaving me the house was his way of paying me back for everything I've done for him. It had always been a verbal agreement, but he decided to put it in writing with a solicitor.'

'He decided that?'

There was a long silence before Jennings blustered, 'All right, all right. It was my idea, but Guy readily agreed to it.' The man wiped tears from his eyes and continued, his voice cracking with emotion. 'You've got this all wrong. I would never harm Guy. I looked after him. I did everything for him. I loved that man.'

Rob ignored the outburst, waiting in silence for Jennings to compose himself, then pressed on with his questions. 'After being dropped off by the taxi at your flat in Mapperley, did you get another taxi back out to Hunters Croft so you could have it out with Guy once and for all?'

Jennings sank his head in his hands. 'No,' he murmured, his voice muffled.

'And when he insisted that he was going to carry out his threat, you decided to kill him before he had the chance to do it. You decided to ensure you would inherit Hunters Croft.'

Rob paused to allow Jennings to digest what he had said, then continued, 'Did you take a gun with you when you went back to the house?'

'What? No, of course not. I don't own a gun or have access to one, and there aren't any guns at the house.'

'Did you use that weapon to ensure that there was no chance you could lose the house? Did you go back there and shoot Guy Royal?'

'No, no. That's not what happened. I didn't go back until the following morning. By then Guy was already dead. I didn't kill him; I couldn't do that.'

Jennings started to sob, clutching at his head in his hands.

'I've no further questions for you. Do you want to speak to your solicitor?'

Without looking up, Jennings nodded.

The solicitor asked, 'What are your intentions now, Detective Inspector?'

'I'll talk to the custody sergeant, but my intention is to bail your client pending further enquiries. I will be asking for stringent conditions on that bail, though.'

'Whatever you think appropriate. I won't be contesting any bail conditions at this time.'

The two detectives left the interview room so Jennings could consult in private with his solicitor.

'What are your thoughts, Glen?' Rob said as the door closed behind them.

'I don't think Jennings killed Royal. I think he would have been quite happy to continue living the life he shared with Royal, without resorting to murder. I just don't see him as a cold-blooded killer, and he looked genuinely surprised when you spoke about guns.'

'I agree. But right now, I want you to make enquiries with every taxi firm in the city. I need to rule out the possibility that Jennings took another cab back out to Hunters Croft that night.'

Glen nodded. 'I'll get onto that. I'll also talk to the drugs squad and see if they've any intelligence on Jimmy Beans. Drug dealers aren't renowned for their patience when it comes to large debts, and it sounds like Jimmy Beans knew exactly who Guy Royal was, and possibly where he lived. I see him as a much stronger suspect than Stan Jennings.'

'I might agree with you there,' Rob said with a nod. 'I'll run it by the boss first, and if he approves, I'll arrange bail for Jennings on all charges pending further enquiries. It will be the custody sergeant's decision if he thinks bail for the murder charge is appropriate in this case. He may want to push for a remand in custody.'

19

8.00 a.m., 4 October 1990
MCIU Offices, Mansfield, Nottinghamshire

Rob knocked once before walking into Danny's office. Danny looked up from the report he was reading. 'How was Stan Jennings when you took him home last night?'

'Feeling sorry for himself over the pending drugs charge and regretful that he wasn't straight with us from the outset.'

'I see.' Danny nodded. 'So, did you make any progress on the taxi enquiries last night?'

'Glen has spoken to almost all of the cab firms in the city, and so far, there's nothing to suggest Jennings went back to Hunters Croft the night Royal was killed.'

'So that eliminates that possibility. You did the interview,'

Danny said. 'Are you convinced that Jennings isn't responsible for Royal's death?'

'I just don't see it, and Glen Lorimar is of the same opinion. There's no evidence, and apart from his evasive attitude, which may have been down to the drugs, there's no reason to think he's personally involved. The custody sergeant is happy that Jennings doesn't pose a risk to anybody else and was happy to bail him with conditions on all charges.'

'Could he have got someone else to do the actual killing?'

'Set it all up, you mean? It's a possibility and was another reason we went for a long bail date. To give us time to explore that angle.'

'Good.' Danny crossed his arms and leaned back in his chair. 'It did cross my mind that he could have set something up. And we both know stranger things have happened.'

'They have, but I just don't see it in this case.'

'Let's keep a close eye on Jennings. I haven't ruled him out completely yet.'

'I know.' Rob shrugged. 'Hence the heavy conditions on his bail, boss.'

'And what are those exactly?' Danny asked.

'A condition to reside at the Mapperley Park flat, surrender his passport and sign on at Radford Road police station every day.'

Danny made a note of the conditions and said, 'Good. I want to know if he doesn't sign on. Which leaves us with the drug dealer at Hyson Green. What's his name, Jimmy Beans?'

'Jimmy Beans is his street name. Apparently, he has a taste for the bourbon Jim Beam. His real name is Tyrone Armstrong. The address that Jennings visited to collect the cocaine has been confirmed as 8 Noel Street, Hyson Green.

Drugs squad have that as one of the addresses regularly frequented by Armstrong. We've had the property under surveillance from the sixth floor of Braidwood Court since seven o'clock last night. So far there's been no sightings of him.'

'What's Armstrong's history?'

'He was born in Jamaica, but moved to the UK with his family fifteen years ago, when he was ten years old. He regularly travels back to Jamaica and is strongly suspected of having links with gangs on the island. He has previous cons for importing and supplying Class A drugs. He was released from Leicester Prison twelve months ago after serving two and a half years of a five-year sentence following his last drugs conviction.'

'Anything for violence?'

'He has two previous convictions for actual bodily harm; neither were dealt with by way of a custodial sentence. All the drugs squad intelligence suggests that Armstrong is an individual who is feared on the street. He has a reputation for extreme violence that his previous antecedent history doesn't bear out. There are markers on the PNC for weapons, as a knife was involved in one of the ABH offences.'

'Any intelligence on use of firearms?'

'There are reports linking Armstrong to various firearms, but it's all low-level intelligence. There's nothing concrete that definitively states he has access to firearms, just rumours on the street.'

Danny sighed in exasperation. 'Bloody hell. A knife is involved when he assaults somebody, and he receives no custodial sentence. Then he serves two and a half years of a five-year sentence before he's released. Is it any wonder he's gone straight back to dealing?'

Rob shrugged, expressing his shared feeling of helplessness. 'The judicial system's getting worse, boss. All we can do is put these people before the courts. Everything is out of our hands after that.'

'I know, Rob. It's beyond a joke. You mentioned the Noel Street address is one of the addresses known to be frequented by Armstrong. Where are the others?'

'There's good drugs squad intelligence placing Armstrong at several addresses around the city. Like all heavy dealers, he never stays in one place for long. He also has links to London and Birmingham.'

'Have you circulated him as wanted yet?'

Rob couldn't help but raise his eyebrows at that. 'Do you think there's enough of a connection to Royal's murder to warrant him being circulated as wanted on the Police National Computer?'

'Probably not for the murder,' Danny conceded, 'but we suspect him of supplying Class A drugs to Stan Jennings, so let's circulate him for that offence. I want Armstrong in custody so we can question him about his connection to Guy Royal. If he's backed by the gangs, as intelligence suggests, it makes him an even stronger suspect. The Yardies never allow bad debts to spiral upwards, and bad debtors only ever end up one way when they are involved.'

'I'll get him circulated, boss,' Rob agreed with a grim half-smile.

'That's a top priority, and keep the observations running on Noel Street. We need to locate Tyrone Armstrong as soon as we can.'

20

1.30 p.m., 24 February 1989
Bouldstone Press, Eastcastle Street, London

Kingston Jones knocked once and walked into Seymour Hart-Wilson's office.

Seymour stood and extended his hand. 'Come in, come in. Grab a seat.'

As the two men sat down, Seymour said, 'How's the hotel? Comfortable?'

'It's very nice for now. If I'm going to take this job on, I'll need to find more permanent accommodation. I've never liked living out of hotels, even ones as grand as the Cardinal.'

'There's plenty of time to address your accommodation needs; let me tell you about this exciting project.'

'I'm all ears, Seymour. Who is this Guy Royal fella?'

'Guy Royal was the biggest star on British television up until *three years ago when his show-business life completely unravelled.'*

'How can that happen?'

'Royal rose to stardom at a meteoric rate,' Seymour began. 'He went from performing as an average stand-up comic in small working men's clubs to being the host of virtually every new television talent show, game show or talk show. He became extremely hot property almost overnight.'

'So what went wrong?'

'There had been unsubstantiated stories of Royal's wild private life for years,' Seymour said, in a confidential, salacious tone. 'By all accounts he'd always had a horrendous ego and was reputed to be a pain in the arse to work with. Anyway, one of his ex-wives started the ball rolling by selling her story to one of the red tops. It was a dreadful tale of spousal abuse. She gave lurid details about her ex-husband's lust for prostitutes and hinted at wild drug-fuelled orgies in hotels.'

Kingston raised an eyebrow. 'Was there any truth in the stories?'

'Enough truth for television executives to start having a closer look at their most highly paid star. At the same time as the TV channels were having second thoughts, the rest of the tabloid press all turned their attention towards Guy Royal. There wasn't a day went by without yet another tawdry tale of the star's outlandish behaviour.'

'His fall was as dramatic as his rise, by the sound of it.'

'Exactly that. After ten years of being at the top, he last appeared on television three years ago and hasn't worked much since.'

'Why do you think his story would sell?' Kingston said, not yet won over.

'You must try to appreciate just how big a star this man was

here. He still has legions of fans out there. I know they would love to read his version of events. I'm confident this book will fly off the shelves. It's just what this firm needs, an instant hit, something that will shift millions of copies.'

Kingston was thoughtful for a moment. 'Are you proposing for me to write only about his fall from grace?'

'That's the idea, why?'

'I'm thinking maybe we should rekindle the affection the public had for this man, by charting his rise to success too. Remind people of the Guy Royal they all loved, not the monster they have become used to reading about in the newspapers. The way I see it, I should write about his rise to stardom first; then we publish a second book charting his downfall.'

'That's genius.' Seymour leaned forward in his eagerness. 'How long do you think it would take?'

'Depending on how available and cooperative Royal is, it shouldn't take too long.' Kingston appeared to be doing some calculations in his head. 'A few months, perhaps.'

'Excellent. I've already arranged for you to have a permanent secretary at your disposal for any shorthand or typing you require. Janice Millership only recently joined the company, but her references were impeccable, and she's already met Guy Royal. He seemed to take a bit of a shine towards her, so she'll be useful easing you into those first meetings.'

'Easing me in?'

'Trust me,' Seymour said, with a slight grimace. 'Guy Royal isn't going to be an easy man to work with, but if you tell him what he wants to hear and then just do your thing, it will be fine.'

'And this character has taken a shine to Miss Millership, has he?'

'She flattered him when they met. That was all it took. He

insisted I make her your personal secretary to help you work on the book.'

'That's great.' Kingston nodded, convinced by Seymour's plan. 'I'll need her to take shorthand notes at all my meetings with Royal. I can type at a good speed myself, so once she's transcribed her notes, I'll be able to create the first draft.'

'Guy Royal is based near Nottingham and has requested that you travel to him to conduct your interviews. I know you don't drive, but Ms Millership has a clean licence, so she'll be able to drive you to all the meetings.'

'Sounds like you've got everything in place. Is there anything else I need to know?'

'Two things,' Seymour said, counting them off on his thumb and first finger. 'The first one being I've already paid Royal a substantial sum as an advance on sales, so I need you to make this work. The second being, and I've already alluded to this, it's only fair to warn you that Guy Royal has an ego the size of a small country and probably won't be the most relaxing person to work with.'

Kingston nodded, seemingly unperturbed. 'I don't see a problem with either of those issues. I'm sure that, with Janice's help, I'll get along famously with this Guy Royal character. I'm also confident that I'll be able to knock out a first draft reasonably fast. Now, how about you introduce me to Janice Millership, then make an appointment later this week for us to drive up to Nottingham and meet Royal.'

21

3.00 p.m., 24 February 1989
Dickens Café, Eastcastle Street, London

Janice Millership couldn't quite believe what was happening in her life.
Less than an hour ago she had been summoned to the office of Seymour Hart-Wilson, where she was introduced to the man tasked with writing the life story of Guy Royal.

Kingston Jones was, in her eyes, nothing short of perfection. She had been smitten at first sight, by his tall, elegant frame and handsome face. Not only was he devastatingly handsome, but he was also warm and friendly. When he spoke, his soft New York accent was delivered in a voice that was irresistibly deep and rich in tone.

Hart-Wilson had told her to take the rest of the day off to help Kingston acclimatise to the city, and now here they were sitting in her favourite café, surrounded by portraits of famous writers.

Kingston took a sip of his coffee and said, 'I understand you haven't been at Bouldstone long, Miss Millership?'

'Please, Mr Jones, if we're going to be working together, I insist you call me Janice.'

'Janice it is, and I don't want any of this Mr Jones nonsense. Call me Kingston.'

'I haven't been at Bouldstone a week yet,' Janice gushed. 'I still can't quite believe what's happening.'

He smiled, revealing perfect white teeth. 'Oh, it's happening all right, but from what Seymour was telling me, it's not going to be an easy ride. This Guy Royal character sounds like he could be hard work.'

'He does have a reputation for being difficult, but when I met him, he seemed perfectly charming.'

'So, Janice,' Kingston said, switching subjects easily, 'I don't know London too well. Do you live near here?'

'I have a flat in Camden; it's about a fifteen-minute walk away. Perfect, really – it's a nice quiet area and close to the office.'

'That does sound perfect,' Kingston said with another of his smiles. 'I'm stuck in a hotel in the city for now, which I hate. I can't stand living out of a suitcase. I'll need to find myself somewhere a bit more permanent.'

'I can help you with that.' Janice leaned forward in her enthusiasm. 'There's always flats coming up for rent around me.'

'Flats?'

'Sorry, apartments.'

'Oh yes, please, if you could. It would be nice to have some company close by. I don't know London at all.'

'You can probably tell by my accent that I'm not a Londoner,' Janice said. 'I've only been here about a month, and to be honest, I've felt a little nervous about exploring the city on my own.'

'Well, we need to remedy that. You help me find an apartment, and I'll gladly escort you around the sights of London. It's always so much better checking out cool places with someone else.'

Blushing slightly, Janice assured him, 'Oh yes, I'll start looking for a flat, sorry, apartment, as soon as I get home.'

The thought of exploring London with this tall, handsome – and so very charming – American was the stuff her dreams were made of. She felt like she was occupying the pages of one of her own romance stories.

Finishing his coffee, Kingston said, 'Come on, Janice, I'll walk with you to Camden. If I'm going to be living there, it will be good to check out the area before I make my way back to the hotel.'

'That would be lovely, thanks,' Janice said as she stood from the table, where she abandoned her own half-drunk coffee as they left the Dickens Café together.

22

1.00 a.m., 5 January 1990
Crown Plaza Hotel, Nottingham

Rebecca Marney was panicking.
She hadn't expected there to be any problems with this trick.
How wrong could she be.
The client was a nineteen-year-old university student who had been goaded by his housemates to pop his cherry. When he and his friends had arrived four hours ago at the foyer of the Crown Plaza, a few eyebrows had been raised by the staff working the front desk, and Rebecca was pleased she had backup in the shape of her minder, Jamie.
Rebecca had also been relieved to see the client's friends all leave the hotel after dishing out a series of exuberant back slaps to their painfully shy friend.
Throughout all the initial mayhem of their arrival, her

minder had remained seated in the foyer, a disinterested observer nursing a malt whisky as he read through documents.

Garry Poyser – the man known to Rebecca as Jamie – looked every inch the bored businessman going over reports generated by the day's business meetings. He was in fact reading a copy of Shoot football magazine hidden within a beige-coloured folder.

He had been ready to intervene if any of the other lads had attempted to gatecrash what had been booked as a private party.

That was four hours ago.

Meanwhile, the client had gradually become more and more emboldened – and less and less painfully shy – throughout his time with Rebecca, and she wondered if he had taken some other stimulant on top of the spirits he'd consumed from the minibar.

The client had paid to spend the entire night with her, but as the hours went by, he became more and more aggressive. He started by being verbally abusive, calling her disgusting names, and this soon escalated into threats of physical violence. Rebecca wasn't prepared to put up with his shit and wait until he became violent. She called time and started to get dressed.

That was when things started to go horrifically wrong. The student pinned her to the wall, trying to prevent her from putting her clothes on. She had pushed him backwards, and he had fallen over, striking his head on the bedside drawers. The blow to the back of his head had stunned him long enough to enable her to throw her clothes on.

She was waiting for the lift at the end of the corridor when she saw the client emerge from the room, wearing just his jeans and trainers. Clearly raging, he started to run towards her with an expression of hatred writ large on his face.

She abandoned the idea of waiting for the lift, removed her high heels, and bolted down the stairs, carrying the strappy, black patent shoes. She could hear the young student chasing her. He *was bellowing, making awful threats as they both hurtled down the concrete fire escape stairs.*

Rebecca burst into the calm of the foyer, looking around, desperately seeking her minder.

He was nowhere to be seen.

She continued to run, heading straight for the revolving doors of the hotel, the bare-chested youth still behind her.

She bolted through the door and was relieved to see Jamie leaning against the wall opposite, smoking a cigarette.

In a voice fuelled by panic, she yelled, 'Jamie! Get this nutter off me.'

Garry looked up and immediately took in the scene.

Discarding his half-smoked cigarette, he raced across the road and intercepted the youth, grabbing him by his right arm. The youth instantly turned and threw a punch towards Garry's head.

He ducked and avoided the blow before punching the youth hard in the stomach. Instantly following that up with a punch to the side of his face, which dropped the student to the floor.

Garry leaned over him and growled, 'Stay down, you idiot, or I'll really fuck you up.'

The two hard punches had knocked all the aggression out of the youth, and with blood pouring from the cut on his left cheekbone, he remained curled up on the floor in a position designed to protect his body from any further harm.

Garry turned to look for Rebecca and saw her a few yards away. She was breathing hard after her traumatic flight through the hotel.

He grabbed her arm and said, 'Come on, let's go. The hotel staff will be calling the cops.' He walked her towards the car park to retrieve the car. 'Are you okay?'

She nodded but didn't speak, wiping the messy tears from her face.

'What happened in there?'

'What happened was Mr Shy Boy turned into Mr Junior Fucking Psycho.' She turned and gave him a half-smile, calmer now she was out of danger. 'One minute he was a bumbling idiot struggling to get it up, the next a raving sex maniac who wouldn't take no for an answer.'

'Did he hurt you?' Garry asked, genuinely concerned. 'I'll go back and sort him out proper like if he has.'

'I'm okay. Let's just get out of here. I won't be able to work in the Crown Plaza again anytime soon, that's a fact.'

As he opened the car door, Garry grinned at her. 'You need to find a new line of work, flower.'

'Oh, yeah. Right you are, Jamie. And who's going to pay all the bills to keep a roof over your head, then?'

'Point taken, pet,' he said as he started the car. 'Let's get you home for a stiff drink.'

'Reckon I need more than one after that shit show.'

23

2.00 p.m., 4 October 1990
Nottinghamshire Police Headquarters

Danny had been surprised to receive the telephone call from HQ. He had been expecting the new head of CID to take up his post the following week, so to be called in to see him for a meeting today had been a shock.

He'd heard a lot about the man replacing Chief Superintendent Adrian Potter, and now he was about to meet him for the first time. He would have preferred to be better prepared for their first meeting.

And after working alongside Adrian Potter for so long, he wasn't sure what to expect from the new man. As he walked towards the headquarters building, he reflected on what had often been a difficult working relationship with Potter and wondered how this new relationship would pan out. More specifically, would it be a case of better the devil you know?

Detective Chief Superintendent Mark Slater was almost ten years younger than Danny and a product of the Bramshill Police College accelerated promotion scheme. He had a reputation as a moderniser, keen to embrace the latest techniques in forensics and crime investigation. He also had a reputation as a strict disciplinarian who had served time on the complaints and discipline department of the West Yorkshire force.

Danny climbed the stairs to the command corridor and muttered out loud, 'Keep an open mind.'

He knocked once on Slater's door and waited.

There was no shout from within, instead the door opened, and he was standing face to face with his new boss.

Slater was a similar height and build to Danny. He had close-cropped dark hair and looked fit and tanned. He was dressed in a dark blue business suit, a white shirt and a tie that carried the FBI logo.

With a smile, he extended his hand and said, 'Chief Inspector Flint, it's good to finally meet you.'

A little taken aback by the warmth of the welcome, Danny took the hand offered, and the two men shook hands.

Slater said, 'Come in, come in. Grab a seat.'

Danny walked in, and as he sat down, he thought, *Could this be any different to my first meeting with Adrian Potter?*

As Slater sat down, he said, 'Apologies for the bolt-out-of-the-blue phone call, but I got back from the States a week earlier than I had planned, so I thought rather than sit at home twiddling my thumbs, I might as well get in here and make a start. And you were the first person I wanted to talk to.' He paused before continuing, 'When Jack Renshaw spoke to me about this job, he told me that he expected you to take up the role, but if for any reason you didn't, would I be interested.'

Awkward, thought Danny. This was not the line of conversation he'd been anticipating on his way to HQ.

Slater continued, 'Can I ask why you decided not to take on the role?'

Danny coughed once and said, 'I just didn't think I would be best suited to the role. I prefer to be a bit more hands-on.'

Slater sat back in his chair and steepled his fingers as though deep in thought.

Eventually he said, 'I didn't mean to put you on the spot, Danny. I was just curious as to why anyone would turn down what in effect would have been two promotions in quick time?'

'It was a decision,' Danny started, knowing that he was copping out, 'that both my wife and I thought long and hard about, but in the end I value being happy in my work more than promotion.'

'Fair enough. I know it's not for everyone. So, Danny, tell me about the MCIU?'

'What do you want to know, sir?' Danny asked. 'Current cases?'

'No. Tell me about the concept. I've just had a month in the States, where they allocate an entire murder enquiry to two detectives. Whereas here we have an entire team.'

For the first time Danny could feel himself bristle at the new boss's comments.

'Thankfully, the murder rates here in the UK are lower than in the States,' he said. 'The MCIU was first established by Jack Renshaw's predecessor, Miles Galton. When Jack Renshaw came in as chief constable, he saw the merits of having a dedicated team of detectives to work on the highest-profile cases, rather than extracting them from all over the county, thereby depleting every CID office. It has worked well ever since.'

'Don't get me wrong, Danny,' Slater assured him. 'I think the concept of such a unit is a great one. I also know that more and more provincial forces are taking up the idea of having major crime investigation teams. What's the turnover of staff like?'

'It's not high. Detectives tend to stay on the unit once they arrive.'

'Promotion?'

'I have one detective sergeant who was promoted and remained in post, as I had a vacancy for a DS at the time.'

'Makes sense, I suppose,' Slater agreed. 'I just wondered about giving an opportunity for other detectives to broaden their skills by spending time on the MCIU.'

Danny was thoughtful as he spoke. 'I don't think constant turnover would benefit the unit. My detectives tend to carry out tasks without being asked, and that sort of initiative and confidence only comes with experience.'

'I can understand that.' Slater nodded. 'How would you feel about detectives joining on a temporary basis?'

'On attachment, you mean?'

'Yes.'

'Would they be on attachment as additional staff, or would I lose people to accommodate them?'

'Additional.' Slater held Danny's gaze steady as he continued with his thoughts. 'I was thinking possibly two detectives at a time on six-month attachments. I'd have to run this by the divisional detective inspectors as well, but I'll only do that if you think the idea has merit.'

'I think that could work well,' Danny said with a nod. 'The attached detectives would certainly pick up skills they could then transfer back to division upon their return, and if it was an ongoing scheme, then those skills would eventually disseminate throughout the force.'

'And, Danny, do you think newcomers would be accepted on the unit?'

'As long as they conducted themselves in a diligent and professional manner, I'm sure they would be.'

'That's great.' Slater leaned back in his chair, satisfied. 'I'll set up meetings with the divisional DIs. Now, tell me about this case that's all over the newspapers.'

'You mean the Guy Royal investigation?'

Slater nodded, again steepling his fingers.

Danny gave him a quick resumé of the case and the investigation.

Slater listened intently before saying, 'Why haven't you charged Stan Jennings? He has motive, he can't really account for his whereabouts, and the footprints in blood linked him to the scene.'

'That is all true, sir,' Danny admitted. 'Jennings hasn't been entirely ruled out as a suspect. He's currently on bail. Until we've exhausted all other enquiries, that's how he'll remain. The evidence against him is nowhere near strong enough yet to support a charge or attain a conviction.'

Slater nodded, then stood up, indicating the meeting was over. He said, 'Well, keep me posted on all developments, please, Danny. I like to be kept fully abreast of everything. Any new suspects, any arrests, everything. You'll find that I'm supportive of your department, but I need to be kept in the loop. Is that fair?'

'More than fair, sir. I haven't got a problem with doing that.'

'Excellent. One last thing, I've never been one for formalities.' Slater smiled and gave a slight shrug. 'When it's just the two of us talking, call me Mark. I haven't been knighted by Her Majesty, yet.'

'No problem.' Danny returned the grin. 'Mark.'

Slater walked Danny to the door and once again extended his hand. 'Good to see you, Danny.'

As Danny walked back to his car, he was deep in thought. Not once had Mark Slater mentioned budgets. He had also suggested more staff, albeit on a temporary basis. It was obvious from his naïve comments about charging Jennings that Slater lacked experience as an investigator.

Still, after the battles he had endured with Adrian Potter, Danny felt that the meeting had been positive. He found himself grinning as he unlocked the car door.

Working alongside Mark Slater looked set to be a breath of fresh air.

24

11.30 a.m., 2 March 1989
Hunters Croft, Rufford Road, Ollerton, Notts

Kingston Jones sighed. Working with Guy Royal was proving more difficult than he would ever have imagined. He was an experienced ghost writer, while this man was an egotistical fool who stubbornly refused to listen to any of his suggestions.

The meeting had got off to the worst possible start when Kingston mooted the idea of writing about Royal's rise to fame first. Even when first Stan Jennings and then Janice Millership had voiced their support for the plan, Royal had been adamant that he didn't want to go over that old ground.

It was only when Jennings pointed out that two books could mean two lots of royalty payments instead of one that Royal had begrudgingly relented.

Royal's arrogance towards Kingston was typified by his

behaviour when he abruptly walked out of the meeting, saying that Jennings could provide all the details of their path to the top, as he had been the one who had orchestrated it.

His parting shot, as he flounced through the door, was, 'Just get on with it!'

As the door slammed shut, Stan Jennings smiled at Kingston Jones. 'Please don't take his behaviour personally. Guy had a bad night; he hardly slept. He struggles to think things through when he's tired. I think writing the first book's a great idea. It will remind all those punters why they fell in love with Guy Royal in the first place.'

'Exactly,' Kingston said. 'We need to dampen the public's recent impressions of him. All those horrendous accounts pushed out relentlessly by the newspapers will have taken their toll on their affection for him, however popular he was a few years ago.'

'I totally get that,' Jennings said with an understanding nod.

'But do you think Guy will eventually get it?' Kingston asked. 'I need him to talk to me.'

'I don't know.' Jennings shrugged. 'It's true what he said, though. I can provide all the details you'll need to write the first book. We don't need his input that much. We've worked together for over twenty years. I was the one who masterminded his rise to the top. It was my connections in the business that helped him achieve his big break.'

'Let's make a start, then, shall we?' Kingston said with a sigh. 'Janice can take shorthand notes of our conversations. We're going to need several meetings to get enough material for me to draft something out. But, for now, we simply need to sketch out a basic timeline. Key moments that helped Royal's career to progress and flourish. Times and dates of the various television shows he's presented over the years. Any industry awards, that sort of thing.

*This first book has got to be all about positivity. I want anything that shows him in a good light. Charity work, anything.'

'I can do that.' Jennings nodded. 'But I don't fancy coming down to London for meetings all the time.'

'No problem. We can meet wherever you like. Janice is happy to drive.'

'Okay,' said Jennings, looking pleased. 'Unless Guy really kicks off, let's carry on meeting here. You never know, he may even come round to the idea and help with the book.'

'You never know.' Kingston smiled. 'Right, time to make a start on those key dates.'

'Let me grab my diaries.'*

25

6.30 p.m., 2 March 1989
Watford Gap, Northamptonshire

It had been a very long day, and the stop at the motorway services for something to eat and drink had been very welcome. It had been Kingston who suggested they pull in, and Janice had been only too happy to take a break from driving through the dark in heavy motorway traffic.

The food – and the coffee – had been a major disappointment to the tall American.

He pulled a face as he placed his cup back in its saucer. 'I can't believe they pass that black sludge off as coffee; it's disgusting. How can you drink it, Janice?'

'I'm used to it, I suppose, and I was gasping.'

'You need to come over to New York and experience the food and the coffee in one of our diners. You'll understand why I'm complaining then.'

'I can't believe Jennings never offered us a drink all the time we were there.'

'I know. Those two guys are something else, aren't they. Neither of them would ever qualify as the host with the most, that's for sure.' He laughed at his own joke and said, 'So, Janice Millership, tell me a little bit about yourself. What are your dreams?'

Janice took a sip of her coffee and said, 'My dream has always been to be a published writer. It's all I've ever wanted. Ever since I was old enough to read, I've immersed myself in books. Trying to escape my humdrum everyday life, I suppose. I virtually lived at our local library. Then, as I got older, I started to think about writing something of my own.'

'Have you started that journey and written something?'

She suddenly felt self-conscious, almost embarrassed to be talking about her work to the successful American, so she just nodded shyly.

'You have?' Kingston beamed. 'That's amazing. Good for you, Janice. What do you write?'

She looked into the man's soft brown eyes, trying to gauge if he was mocking her, or if he was seriously interested in her work.

She decided it was the latter and said quietly, 'I've written five romance novels. I've set them all during the turn of the century in the cathedral city of Durham. All five follow a young woman struggling to make her way in life.'

'That's great.' Kingston's voice was warm, his praise heartfelt. 'Have you had any of them published yet?'

'I've tried. Sadly, all to no avail. I've got countless rejection letters that can attest to my efforts.'

'Well, maybe I can help you do something to change that. Let me see your work, and maybe, between us, we can get it to a stage where a publisher will give it serious consideration. If Bouldstone aren't interested, I'm sure I'll be able to find another publisher who's looking for something new in that genre. It's always very popular.'

'You'd do that for me?' Janice said, taken aback at his offer.

'Sure I will. You'll have to let me read your work first, though.'

The thought felt a little daunting, but Janice knew an opportunity when she saw one. 'Of course you can read it, thank you.'

'It would be an honour,' Kingston said as he pushed his hardly touched coffee cup to one side. 'I suppose we'd better get back on the road. How long until we're back in the city?'

'It's about another hour or so, depending on the traffic.'

'Are you okay? Not too tired?'

'I'm fine,' Janice assured him as they made their way back to the car. In fact, she was more than fine; she was buzzing. She had never felt happier. Her mind was now filled with thoughts of being a successful author, and a life spent together with the handsome American.

As she started the car, her mind repeatedly asked an unspoken question.

Is this what love feels like?

26

8.00 p.m., 4 October 1990
Mansfield, Nottinghamshire

Danny swirled the ice cubes in his whisky glass before taking a sip. The noise of the ice clinking made Sue look up from the book she was reading. She slipped a bookmark between the pages and said, 'A penny for your thoughts?'

Danny placed the glass on a coaster on the coffee table and said, 'I was just thinking about the meeting I had with Mark Slater today.'

'The new head of CID? I didn't think he was starting for another couple of weeks?'

'He's started early. Didn't want to sit at home twiddling his thumbs was his expression.'

Sue stood up from the armchair and sat down next to her

husband on the sofa. 'That sounds very keen. I couldn't imagine you giving up your leave so easily.'

Danny scoffed and said, 'I don't know how you can say that. You know how many times I've gone in to work on rest days and leave days.'

Knowing she had touched a nerve, she laughed and said, 'You are so easy to wind up, Mr Flint. I swear it's like shooting fish in a barrel.'

Danny grabbed her waist and tickled her, saying, 'I'm that easy. Am I?'

Sue playfully fought off her husband and said, 'Seriously, what's he like?'

Danny grinned. 'Who?'

Laughing, Sue said, 'You don't get me that easy, mister. Just answer the question.'

Danny picked up his glass and took another sip before saying, 'Well, he couldn't be any more different to Adrian Potter, that's for sure.'

'In a good way?'

'It's early days, but yes, I think so. He's young and extremely ambitious. I know he sees himself as a future chief constable. Having said that, he was extremely complimentary about the MCIU and even asked for my thoughts on a scheme that would see the unit getting more staff, albeit on a temporary basis.'

'That all sounds very positive.'

'It was. Not once did he mention finance or how much the unit was costing the force. I think we could get along well.'

'So no regrets about not taking the job?' Sue asked, looking directly at her husband.

'None at all.' Danny shook his head. 'It was the right decision for me, the right decision for us as a family. Anyway, that's enough about work; tell me about your day. What mischief have you and Hayley been getting up to?'

27

6.00 p.m., 2 September 1989
Bouldstone Press, Eastcastle Street, London

There was an atmosphere of muted excitement in the large reception area of the publishing house. It was a spectacular space with marble floors, a high vaulted ceiling and ornate chandeliers that spoke of a bygone era. The perfect place for a book launch.

It was where Bouldstone Press always held their parties. Many a bestselling novel, biography or autobiography had been launched from this very room.

The carefully selected audience from the world of show business were sipping flutes of champagne and eating canapés, alongside the men and women of the nation's media. All were awaiting the arrival of the star of the show, Guy Royal.

Tonight was the launch party for A Rising Star, *the much-anticipated memoirs of the disgraced television celebrity.*

Like a cat on a hot tin roof, Seymour Hart-Wilson was nervously pacing the floor. Across the crowded room, he saw Kingston Jones chatting happily with Janice Millership. He pushed his way through the crowd until he was standing next to them. He hissed, 'Where's Royal?'

Kingston whispered back, 'Don't worry. He's on his way. Jennings called me earlier to say they were safely on the train and that they would get a taxi from St Pancras straight here.'

'When they arrive, I want you two to look after them. Once he's done his prepared speech, it's imperative that you don't allow Royal to get drunk and make any unsolicited comments to the press. Those bastards would lap it up if he went on a pissed-up tirade at his own book launch.'

'We'll do our best, but the man's a loose cannon. You know that.'

Seymour nodded, but whispered back fiercely, 'I can't afford for him to do or say anything that will jeopardise sales. The early figures from the pre-release advertising look fantastic. If we handle it right, this could be huge. I've spent a small fortune on his advance and on advertising, so I need this to go big.'

'Time will tell on that, Seymour,' Kingston murmured. 'I'm just happy I got it in some sort of readable shape. It hasn't been easy. Guy Royal's a fucking nightmare to work with. To tell you the truth, if it hadn't been for the input of Stan Jennings, this book would never have been written.'

'Yes, yes, but none of that matters now,' Seymour said urgently. 'I'm sure his fanbase will lap it up. And if they do, the sequel, A Fallen Star, *will go stratospheric. Let's be honest here, that's the part everybody's really interested in. The British public love to build up their heroes, but they love tearing them down even more.'*

'We need to have a conversation about Fallen Star,*' Kingston*

said urgently, trying to catch Seymour's eye. 'I'm not happy about spending even more time in the company of that egotistical lunatic.'

But just then the noise of chatter and buzz in the room suddenly went up as Guy Royal, flanked by Stan Jennings, strode in through the front doors of the publishing house.

'Come on, let's get over there and get this done before he says something that screws us all,' Hart-Wilson hissed. 'We can talk about the sequel when we've got tonight out of the way.'

As they pushed their way through the crowd towards Royal, the American ghost writer said, 'I mean it, Seymour. I'm not sure I can work with this man again. The only thing Royal about him is that he's a right royal pain in the ass.'

Hart-Wilson ignored the comment. He was already in meet-the-press mode, smiling broadly as he guided Royal towards the small stage area. He had no intention of allowing Royal to answer any of the questions being hurled at him by the assembled press. There was a prepared press release that all members of the press would be handed at the end of the night, along with a complimentary signed copy of A Rising Star.

As they reached the stage, he handed the prepared speech to Royal and hissed, 'When you get up there, it's vital you stick to the script. Don't give these bastards an excuse to ruin your launch. Tonight could be the difference between us making a loss and turning an incredible profit.'

Don't worry, Seymour,' Royal said with a grin. 'I've played this game all my life. Trust me, I know what I'm doing. I'll be charm personified. These scumbags want me to fuck up. Well, I'm not going to oblige them tonight.'

28

10.00 p.m., 2 September 1989
Thames Embankment, London

Kingston Jones and Janice Millership walked slowly side by side as they strolled along the Thames Embankment. The lights of the city reflecting off the inky black waters of the river combined with the ornate white lamps at the side of the path to cast a magical glow.

There was an unexpected extreme chill in the air for the time of year, and both were glad of the long coats and scarves they wore. Their warm breath formed white clouds as it met the frigid night air.

'I just don't understand how Guy Royal can be like that,' Kingston observed. 'He was so charming and engaging tonight. Unless you really knew him, it would be so easy to think that's what he's like all the time.'

Janice said, 'I'm just glad he was like that. It would have been *a disaster if the press had seen even a glimpse of what we've witnessed over the past three months.'*

'I just don't get it.' He paused before pointing at the House of Commons on the far bank and said, *'I swear, Guy Royal has more faces than Big Ben!'*

Janice chuckled; she adored these times when it was just her and the handsome American.

But since hearing him voice his displeasure to Seymour Hart-Wilson about ghost writing the sequel to A Rising Star, *she had been worried. The last thing she wanted was for this beautiful man to go back to New York and disappear out of her life forever.*

She slipped her arm in his as they walked, and said in a voice barely above a whisper, 'Did you mean what you said to Mr Hart-Wilson about not writing the sequel?'

'I'm just not sure I want to commit myself to several months of Royal's shit. It's so depressing being around him. The man's a bone fide monster.'

'I know what you mean,' Janice said, *'but we've had some fun as well, haven't we?'*

Sensing the melancholy note in her question, he said cheerily, 'Sure we have.'

'And Hart-Wilson seems pretty hell-bent on you staying. He made it sound like you may not have much of a choice.'

'I've always got a choice, Janice,' Kingston said, a sharper edge to his voice. *'He might not like it, but there are plenty of other ghost writers.'*

She stopped walking and turned towards Kingston, so she was looking directly at him. 'Personally speaking, I hope you stay. If not for Guy Royal or Seymour Hart-Wilson, then for me.'

As he looked into her eyes, Jones could hear the depth of feeling in her voice.

After a long pause he said, 'Janice, you're so sweet. I suppose I could stand a few more months of Guy "royal pain in the ass" Royal if we get to work on his crappy recollections together.'

Beaming, she stood on tiptoe and reached up, planting a soft kiss on his cheek.

He smiled, but he didn't return the kiss. He placed his arm around her waist and began walking again. 'I swear it's getting colder. Let's get you home, Janice. You can tell me how your latest romance novel is progressing. Let's get Royal's mess of a life story out of the way; then I'll make it my mission to get you published.'

As the two of them walked arm in arm alongside the river, her heart felt fit to burst.

29

8.45 a.m., 6 October 1990
Albert Grove, Radford, Nottingham

Rob Buxton and Andy Wills parked at the end of a row of parked cars on Albert Grove and walked to the battered Ford Escort van that contained the two drugs squad officers.

Rob tapped lightly on the passenger window and held his warrant card close to the glass. The window was wound down, and the man inside said, 'Morning, boss. I'm DS Steve Crane, and this is DC Tim Spencer. Are the firearms team on their way?'

'They estimate they'll be here in the next half hour. Any movement at the address?'

'Nothing so far. It's the house with the black door and the net curtains on the windows, number thirty-two.'

'Anybody watching the back of the house?'

The detective nodded his completely bald head. 'I've got DC Reagan and DC Baker at the rear of the property. The rear yard only gives access to a shared walkway that emerges at that alley over there.'

He pointed to an alley entrance that was three properties away from their target address.

Rob squatted down at the side of the van, looked at the detective sergeant and said, 'When you called our office, you mentioned an informant had given you the tip that Armstrong was at this location. How good's your info?'

'I wouldn't have called you if I didn't think it was accurate information. The guy who phoned it in is usually bang on the money.'

'Did he mention any weapons?'

'I specifically asked if Beans was armed, and he said definitely not, but I can understand why you want to wait for the firearms team to get here. I just hope he stays put, because if he does come out before they get here, you'll have a decision to make, or he'll be in the wind again.'

'DC Baker to DS Crane.' The sergeant's radio crackled into life. 'There's movement at the rear of the target address. Curtains have been pulled, and I can see people moving about inside the house. Over.'

'Shit,' DS Crane muttered under his breath before speaking into his handheld radio. 'Okay. Let me know as soon as anybody leaves the house. Over.'

Suddenly, the front door of number thirty-two opened, and a tall black man, with his dreadlocks stowed beneath a woollen hat in the colours of the Jamaican national flag, emerged with a young woman. Both were laughing and joking on the doorstep.

Rob and Andy ducked down behind the van out of view of the suspect.

Steve Crane whispered, 'That's Jimmy Beans, boss. He's going to blow any second. What do you want us to do?'

Rob had a decision to make and only seconds to make it. Without hesitation he said, 'If he starts to walk away from the house, we take him.'

All eyes were now locked on the couple as they kissed and cuddled on the doorstep. They shared one last passionate kiss before Tyrone Armstrong stepped away. Rob heard him say, 'Bye, doll,' as he started to walk briskly away.

'He's off,' Rob hissed. 'Let's go.'

Instantly, Rob and Andy began running towards Armstrong, followed by Steve Crane and Tim Spencer.

Albert Grove was a long narrow street that had a mixture of terraced housing and bigger semi-detached houses. There were no front gardens, just stone walls that fronted small yards. Cars were parked half on and half off the pavement. The street felt quiet; there were no other pedestrians around.

When Andy started running, Tyrone Armstrong was about fifty yards away and walking briskly.

He must have heard boots on the pavement, because when Andy Wills was no more than ten yards away, he suddenly looked over his shoulder. Andy was close enough to see Armstrong's eyes widen as he saw four men all running towards him.

Armstrong tried to start running too, but Andy's momentum meant he was on him before he could really get going. As Andy grabbed the drug dealer, both men went crashing to the floor.

But before Andy had the chance to grab both of his quarry's arms, Armstrong started to swing punches. One punch landed heavily on Andy's cheekbone. The DS grimly maintained his grip on Armstrong's coat and was pleased to hear the other officers approaching fast. Both Steve Crane and Tim Spencer had overtaken Rob in the foot chase, and they were first to arrive and help Andy.

With the assistance of the others, Andy managed to restrain Armstrong while avoiding further punches. As Steve Crane put the man in handcuffs, Andy said, 'Tyrone Armstrong, I'm arresting you for the supply of Class A controlled drugs.'

Armstrong snarled, 'What ya talking about? I ain't got no gear on me, Babylon.'

A breathless Rob Buxton took Steve Crane out of Armstrong's earshot and said, 'We'll take Armstrong back to Radford Road. Are you going to search the address?'

'Yeah. I'll make it look like we're executing a warrant, which will safeguard my informant a little, and you never know, we might get lucky and find some gear inside.'

'Thanks for your help, gents,' Andy said. 'He's a bloody handful all right.'

Tim Spencer was going through Armstrong's pockets and pulled a flick knife from one of the inside pockets of the combat jacket he was wearing. He held it up and said, 'Yeah, a handful all right. Good job he didn't have the chance to get this bad boy out.'

He handed the knife to Andy, who muttered, 'For fuck's sake. That was a bit too close for comfort.'

30

11.30 a.m., 6 October 1990
Radford Road Police Station, Nottingham

Rob Buxton and Andy Wills walked into the CID office, having just completed their first interview with Tyrone Armstrong. They had questioned him about his drug dealing generally, while making no specific allegations.

Armstrong's solicitor had advised his client to answer every question with a standard 'no comment' response and had complained to the detectives after the interview that he thought the whole thing was a fishing expedition and that his client should be released forthwith.

Rob had told the solicitor there would be at least one further interview before any consideration was given to the release of Armstrong.

As they walked into the office, Andy said, 'I can see

where the solicitor's coming from; unless we start talking in specifics, it does look like we're fishing.'

'I know.' Rob nodded. 'I'm going to run it by the boss first to get his approval, but my plan is that when we go back into the interview, we arrest him on suspicion of the murder of Guy Royal. We then question him specifically about his supply of drugs to him. If he's not involved in Royal's death, it might make him start talking to protest his innocence. Have you seen the state of your cheekbone, by the way?'

'No, but I can certainly feel it. While you're on the phone to Danny, I'll get the search for Armstrong cancelled on the Police National Computer.'

Andy started to walk away as Rob picked up the nearest telephone and dialled the number for the MCIU. 'And get some ice for your face,' he shouted after Andy.

31

12.30 p.m., 6 October 1990
Radford Road Police Station, Nottingham

The atmosphere in the small interview room had totally changed. Tyrone Armstrong fidgeted nervously and shot fleeting glances towards his solicitor, who sat stern faced, poised with pen and notepad, ready to take notes of the interview.

When Rob had arrested Armstrong in front of the custody sergeant on suspicion of the murder of Guy Royal, the big man had looked totally shocked.

His solicitor had muttered something under his breath and then insisted on a further consultation with his client.

That had been thirty minutes ago, and now Rob and Andy faced Armstrong across the desk in the smoke-filled interview room.

Rob said, 'How well did you know Guy Royal?'

'I know the man; he's a customer. But I've got nothing to do with him dying, man. I ain't no killer.'

'A customer?'

'Yeah, you know.'

Rob shook his head. 'No, I don't know. Can you explain what you mean?'

'He was a user; you know what I'm saying, man.'

'Are you telling me you sold product to Guy Royal?'

'On occasion, yeah. It's business.'

'Exactly what product are we talking about?'

'That dude liked his snow. He was always on the sniff for Charlie.'

'Guy Royal purchased cocaine from you?'

'Sometimes, I would drive out to the big house and pass it to Royal himself, or sometimes he would send his fat flunky to find me. I'm telling you that Royal fella couldn't get enough primo product.'

'I see,' Rob said, his tone neutral. 'And does he owe you money?'

Armstrong turned to his solicitor and exclaimed, 'You see. That's what I'm talking about, right there!'

He looked back at Rob and said, 'That Royal fella, he owed me a lot of cash. Why would I want to kill the man before he's paid me what he owed me? That don't make no sense, man. I ain't killed that guy. No way.'

'When was the last time you supplied Royal with cocaine?'

'I don't know. I haven't been out to the house for a long time.'

'We know that you supplied cocaine to Stan Jennings the day before Royal was killed.'

'Yeah. The fat flunky came to me and scored. That's the

last time.'

'Did he pay you?'

'No, it was laid on. Flunky told me Royal was getting hooked up for another TV show, that he would be rolling in cash real soon and would easily clear his debt then.'

'And you believed that?'

'Yeah, I believed the fat man. Why? Was he giving me shine?'

'There was no TV deal.'

Armstrong slammed his fist on the table. 'Raasclaat! Damn that fat fucker's bullshit!'

'So how much have you laid on Guy Royal?' Rob asked as he observed Armstrong's reactions. 'What was his debt?'

'He owed me two large, man.'

'Two thousand pounds?'

'Yeah. I didn't want the man dead. I needed that cash; there's no way I'd do somebody for that. I'll never get that cash now. This is well and truly fucked up, man.'

'Where were you on the night of the twenty-ninth of September?'

'A week ago?' Armstrong said.

'Yes. One week ago.'

'That's easy. I was with Martha. Where you caught me this morning, that's Martha's place. I see her two nights every week before moving on. I was with her last night and was planning to spend the night with her tonight as well, but I had to nip into town for a little business. Last week was the same. I spent the night at Martha's. She'll tell you the same, if you ask her, man.'

'We'll be checking that.' Rob looked Armstrong straight in the eye, and the man gazed back at him for a long moment. 'So, tell me, are you in any way involved in the death of Guy Royal?'

'No fucking way. I keep telling you, I haven't killed that dude.'

'Do you know if Royal or Jennings ever scored off other dealers?'

Armstrong shrugged. 'Don't know, don't care if they did. Not my business.'

'But your business was to regularly supply both Guy Royal and Stan Jennings with class A drugs, namely cocaine.'

'Yeah. But go and speak to Martha; she'll tell you where I was on the twenty-ninth and the thirtieth.' The man's deep voice was calm as he made his point. 'I ain't no killer. That's all bullshit, man. I ain't killed nobody.'

32

10.00 a.m., 23 April 1990
7 Berkely Court, Church Drive, Carrington, Nottingham

'Are you awake?' Rebecca Marney said as she knocked lightly on the bedroom door. A weary voice replied, 'I'm just getting dressed; be out in a minute.'

Rebecca walked back into the kitchen, where she paced up and down, nervously chewing her nails.

Garry Poyser came into the kitchen and filled the kettle with water. As he put a spoonful of coffee in the mug, he looked at Rebecca's worried face and said, 'Everything okay? You look awful.'

'No, I'm not okay. Something dreadful's happened. My mum's seventy-two and lives alone in Norwich. The old man who lives next door to her phoned me this morning. He told me Mum had a bad fall last night and that he'd found her this morning after hearing her crying for help. She'd been on the kitchen floor all night.'

'Bloody hell.' Garry felt his stomach lurch in shock. 'Is she okay?'

'Her neighbour called an ambulance, and Mum's been taken to hospital. The ambulance man told the neighbour that he thought she'd broken her hip.'

'That's bad. Do you know which hospital they've taken her to?'

'Yeah, I wrote it down.' She glanced at the piece of paper in her hand and said, 'The Norfolk and Norwich University Hospital.'

Garry finished making his coffee, then made a mug for Rebecca too. 'What are you going to do, pet?' he said, passing her the hot drink.

'I'll call the hospital first, but whatever they say, I'll have to go to Norwich. I'm the only one Mum's got. I need to go and look after her and the house.'

'Do you want me to come with you?'

Rebecca was thoughtful for a moment, then said, 'I'd prefer you to stay here and look after this place. I hate the thought of it being left unoccupied. It wouldn't take the thieving little shits round here long to suss nobody's home. I'd come back to a robbed and empty house. I can get the train down to Norwich.'

'Pack your stuff first; then make that call to the hospital. As soon as you're ready, I'll drive you to the station.'

Rebecca nodded and walked into her bedroom, returning a few moments later clutching a wad of banknotes.

She thrust the bundle of cash towards Garry and said, 'There's five hundred there. I've been meaning to put it in the bank for ages, but you might as well have it. You'll need some cash to run this place and get food while I'm away.'

Garry took the money and said, 'That's a lot of cash. How long do you think you'll be gone?'

Rebecca shrugged. 'I don't know. I need to see for myself how she is, and if she has broken her hip, I'll need to assess how she's going to cope. She lives alone, so I may have to think about getting some permanent carers in for her.'

'I don't want to pry, but can you afford that?'

'I've got money in the bank. I'm trying to save enough to start my own beauty business. I don't want to be doing this all my life.'

She suddenly became tearful and said in a choked voice, 'I don't know, Jamie. I just need to get down there and see her.'

Garry put his powerful arms around her, held her close, and said, 'This place will be fine, pet. You know I'll look after it, and I won't take the piss with your money. Finish packing, and I'll drive you to the station. You need to be with your mam. Take as much time as you need down there.'

She wiped her eyes with her fingers and said, 'Thanks, Jamie.'

33

10.00 a.m., 7 October 1990
Black Aces Casino, Hockley, Nottingham

Danny Flint and Glen Lorimar walked into the reception area of the Black Aces Casino. A young woman was busily stacking chips behind a Perspex screen. She had her back to the detectives and seemed to be unaware of their presence.

Danny tapped his car keys against the screen, causing the young woman to turn and face them. There was a mixture of surprise and alarm on her face.

She spluttered, 'I'm sorry, gents, but we're closed.'

Danny held up his identification card and said, 'My name's Detective Chief Inspector Flint. I need to speak to the owner. Is he around?'

Recovering her composure, the young woman said, 'Mr Pappas is in his office. I won't be a minute; wait here, please.'

And then she disappeared through an interior door behind the screen, leaving the detectives alone in the foyer.

Glen said, 'Well, at least we know the main man's back from his trip.'

Less than a minute later, the doors into the casino were being unbolted, and a man mountain beckoned the two detectives inside. He grunted a barely audible, 'Follow me.'

Danny and Glen followed the very large and very silent man through the casino and up a single flight of thickly carpeted stairs until they were standing outside heavily varnished double doors. The silent giant knocked once and then opened the door, pointing for the detectives to go inside.

Danny walked in first, followed by Glen. The man mountain followed them both inside and closed the door. He positioned himself in front of the doors, immediately behind the two detectives.

Danny was met by a man in his mid-sixties, with deeply tanned skin and a full head of steel grey hair. He wore a powder blue lounge suit and a white open-necked shirt. Several heavy gold chains hung around the man's neck, and his fingers were adorned with gold sovereign rings.

The man was leaning against the large desk that dominated the room. The desk was the same colour as the mahogany wood panelling on each of the walls. There were no windows in the office; the only source of illumination was the long strip light on the ceiling.

The man pushed himself away from the desk and stood directly in front of Danny. He extended his hand and said, 'I'm Toni Pappas. I take it you are Chief Inspector Flint?'

Danny accepted the casino owner's hand and said, 'I am, and this is DC Lorimar. We're from the Major Crime Investigation Unit, and we're currently investigating the suspicious death of Guy Royal. Our information is he was a customer of yours.'

'I heard Mr Royal had died,' Pappas said in a neutral voice. 'That was a very bad day for me. He had a substantial outstanding debt due to his misfortune at my roulette wheel.'

'So I understand. What is your policy on debt? How do you go about retrieving money owed?'

Toni Pappas smiled and extended both his hands in a gesture of appeasement. 'I appeal to the better nature of the client. That way they always pay.'

'Is that what you did with Guy Royal, appeal to his better nature?'

'I believe Mr Royal had recently received a written notice of his outstanding debt. That notice would have informed him that he would receive no further credit here, not until his debt was paid in full.'

'What would happen to a client who had no intention of paying what they owed?'

'That's a hypothetical question, Detective.' Pappas's voice took on a harder edge. 'It's a scenario I've never had to deal with myself. What I can tell you is this, I would never do anything to a debtor that meant they were ultimately unable to pay. That's just not good for business.'

'So nobody has ever failed to pay a debt owed to you?'

Again the appeasing smile, accompanied this time by a shrug. 'What can I tell you? People always pay. Sometimes it takes a little more time, but I can be very persuasive.'

'Let's talk about Guy Royal specifically. How much did he owe you?'

'Come, come, Detective.' Pappas let out a chuckle, but

there was no mirth in the sound. 'I couldn't possibly divulge that kind of information. I have my client's confidentiality to think about.'

The casino owner's smug answers were starting to grate on Danny. Through gritted teeth, he said, 'Listen, Pappas, this is a murder enquiry. You can and will tell me what I want to know, or I'll have uniformed cops, the vice squad and licensing officers all over this place for a month. Which I don't think will be conducive to your clients' confidentiality or your business. Do we understand each other?'

Danny sensed the man mountain take a step towards him and Glen. He whirled around to face the giant and said, 'Back up.'

Pappas shouted something at the man in a language that Danny assumed was Greek, and instantly the giant stepped back away from the two detectives.

'Ignore my friend Theo,' the casino owner said. 'He gets a little overprotective at times.' He paused before adding, 'I think we may have got off on the wrong foot, Chief Inspector. Of course I want to co-operate with the police in their enquiries. There's no need for you to feel it necessary to interfere with my business.'

Danny nodded, then asked again, 'So how much did Guy Royal owe the casino?'

'Theo,' Pappas instructed, 'go and find Stav. I need him in here.'

The giant left the room, and while they waited, Pappas explained, 'Stav Georgiou is my godson. He deals with all outstanding debt owed to the casino.'

A moment later, the giant returned with another man.

When the two men walked in, Pappas said, 'There's no need for you to stay, Theo.' He waited for the giant to close the door, then said, 'Detectives, this is my godson, Stav. He's my chief of security and deals with all outstanding debts owed to the casino. Ask him anything you need to know.'

Danny looked at Stav; he was like a smaller version of the man mountain who had just vacated the room. In his late thirties, he was a lot shorter, but stocky and obviously very powerful.

For the third time, Danny repeated the question, 'How much does Guy Royal owe the casino?'

Without looking at any paperwork to refresh his memory, Stav instantly said, 'Royal owes twenty-nine thousand, five hundred and fifty pounds.'

Danny almost let out a low whistle, but he tried not to show how taken aback he was. Instead, he turned to face Pappas and said, 'Why was he allowed to run up a debt that size?'

Pappas said, 'Granted, I normally set a ceiling of twenty grand for credit, but Royal was a special case. He's been in debt to us before for similar amounts and has always paid. He was good for business. He was always very funny when he was in the casino; the other punters loved it when he was here. Celebrities are good for business.'

'Not so much when they're dead.'

'That's very true, Detective. Now you understand why I said it was a bad day when I found out he was dead. Let me assure you, nobody from this casino is involved in any way in Guy Royal's death.'

'You mentioned a written notice to Royal earlier,' Danny said. 'Who gave him that?'

'I did,' Stav said. 'It was a standard letter we send out to debtors. I felt the debt had become high enough, and we needed to get some of it marked off.'

'How was it given to him?'

'I drove out to his house and delivered it personally.'

'When was this?'

'Towards the end of last month. It was about a week before he died.'

'Did you go inside the house?'

'No. There was nobody home, so I just dropped it through the letter box.'

Danny turned to face Pappas. 'That's all for now. We may have to speak again in the future.'

As the two detectives started to leave, Danny looked at Stav and said, 'I take it you won't mind providing a set of elimination fingerprints?'

'Yes. I would mind,' Stav growled. 'Am I a suspect or something?'

Pappas said, 'Do as he asks, Stav. We have nothing to hide.'

'They are elimination prints,' Danny said matter-of-factly. 'We need them to compare against fingerprints found at the deceased's home. After your prints have been checked against any outstanding marks, you can witness them being destroyed if you wish. My colleague here will arrange a time for them to be obtained.'

A subdued Stav nodded. 'No problem.'

34

6.00 p.m., 7 October 1990
Fletcher Road, Beeston, Nottinghamshire

Jag Singh parked the car outside the red-brick semi-detached house. It was a neat and tidy house with a single bay window next to the front door and two windows on the first floor.

Jag said, 'This is the house, boss. The light's on.'

Tina Cartwright said, 'Let's see what the second Mrs Guy Royal thinks of his death.'

The two detectives knocked on the front door and waited.

Eventually, the door was opened by a woman in her early forties. She looked as though she had just woken up. Her shoulder-length fair hair was a tousled mess, and she was rubbing sleep from her eyes.

Tina could see two suitcases in the hallway. She took out

her identification card and said, 'I'm Detective Inspector Cartwright, and this is DC Singh. I need to speak with Nita Radford.'

The woman stifled a yawn and said, 'I'm Nita Radford. What's wrong?'

'Can we come in, please? I need to ask you a few questions about your ex-husband.'

Nita Radford now appeared instantly awake. Her eyes widened, and she folded her arms across her chest before snarling, 'I've got nothing to say about that prick.'

Tina persisted. 'Guy Royal was found dead a week ago at his house. He was murdered. We need to ask you some questions. It shouldn't take long.'

A still disgruntled Nita opened the door wider and said, 'I suppose you'd better come in. You'll have to excuse the state I'm in. I only arrived back from Tenerife a couple of hours ago, and I was just flaked out on the sofa.' She paused and gestured. 'Take a seat. Can I get you a drink? I need a coffee.'

Tina shook her head. 'We're fine, thanks. Grab yourself a coffee, and we'll have that chat.'

A few minutes later, Nita returned to the front room and sat down on the armchair opposite the two detectives.

She took a sip from her mug and said, 'I've got to be honest with you both. I really couldn't care less that piece of shit is dead. He made my life a misery for the eleven months we were together. I hope he rots in hell.'

'I understand the divorce was extremely acrimonious,' Tina said, trying not to respond to the undisguised venom in the woman's reaction. 'Why was that?'

'Living with that man was a complete nightmare. He would regularly subject me to physical beatings and depraved sexual assaults. By the time I managed to leave him, I was a mess. It took me two years to fully recover, and that's when I took my revenge.'

'Revenge?'

'I set my stall out to kill his career, and that's what I did. I sold my story to the *News of the World*. They loved it. The revelations ran every Sunday for six weeks. By the time I'd finished dishing the dirt on Guy, he was a total has-been who couldn't get work anywhere.'

Tina could see the glint of satisfaction in the woman's eyes as she recounted her story. She said, 'Why didn't you go to the police about the abuse you suffered during the marriage?'

'Because once I was away from him, I knew that killing his career would hurt him harder and longer. Let's face it, Detective. He's done nothing worthwhile since the newspapers printed my story. Other people have jumped on the bandwagon and sold their own stories about Guy as well. Including that sanctimonious cow who was married to him before me. She could have warned me what he was like, but chose not to, so fuck her too.'

'Can you tell me where you were on the night of the twenty-ninth and the morning of the thirtieth of last month?' Tina said, to bring the conversation back on track.

'At eleven o'clock on the morning of the thirtieth, I was on an aeroplane coming in to land at Tenerife. I'd spent the night before at the Holiday Inn next to East Midlands airport, as it was an early flight. I don't drive, so staying at the hotel was the sensible option. I've got all the details of the hotel in my handbag. You can check with them; they'll have all my check-in details.'

'Thank you, Nita; we'll do that,' Tina said. 'Can you think of anybody who would want Guy Royal dead?'

'Christ! How long have you got?' Nita exclaimed, becoming animated again. 'The man was a total shit, and the world's a better place with him gone. I tell you, love, when you find out who murdered that bastard, pin a medal on them from me.'

35

8.00 a.m., 8 October 1990
MCIU Offices, Mansfield, Nottinghamshire

'This investigation is so bloody frustrating,' Danny said as he sat in his office with his two detective inspectors, discussing the state of the Royal inquiry. 'Two good suspects in Stan Jennings and Tyrone Armstrong, who have ultimately taken us no further forward. I really thought Armstrong was our man, but now he's been alibied by his girlfriend, Martha Patterson.'

'How strong is that alibi?' Tina said.

'Good point,' Rob said, 'but it's not just her. They ordered pizza that night at her address. We've tracked down and spoken to the pizza delivery guy. He's told us that when he delivered the pizza around midnight, Martha and Tyrone answered the door together wearing nothing but a duvet.

Martha has said they spent the entire night in bed, making love and eating pizza.'

'Right,' Danny said, not wanting to know any more about that particular scenario. 'And Stan Jennings. Have we unearthed any solid evidence to tie him to the murder? I know we have plenty of circumstantial stuff, but is there anything concrete to report?'

Tina shook her head. 'I've got staff working around the clock, delving into his background, and they've come up with a big fat zero so far.'

'Any concerns over the ex-wives?'

Tina answered again. 'As you know, Sharon Jarvis was interviewed a while ago, and Nita Radford was interviewed last night. Jarvis doesn't have a concrete alibi, but neither woman can be connected in any way to the murder scene. It's fair to say both women loathed Royal, and from what we've gathered so far, it seems both had good reasons to wish him harm.'

'So can we rule these two women out as suspects?' Danny said. 'Is that what you're telling me?'

'Unless there's some dramatic new information, yes.'

'And Sharon Jarvis has a son. Have we looked at him?'

'Brad Jarvis was out of the country at the time of the murder. He's in Australia backpacking for a year before he starts university.'

'They might not have killed him,' Danny said as he sat back in his chair, 'but I'm amazed at just how many people really despise this man. Have we found anybody with a good word to say for him so far?'

Both inspectors remained silent.

It was Rob who broke the silence. 'I can remember watching Royal on the television. At the time, everyone thought he was amazing. A funny, funny man who had a common touch when he engaged with the audience. You would never have guessed what he was really like.'

'I've never been a big fan of these light entertainment shows,' Danny replied, 'so I don't really have any memory of what he was like on TV.'

'If you want to get a sense of the man, you should read his two autobiographies,' Rob said. 'They make interesting reading. The first book charts his rise to fame, and the second one, *A Fallen Star*, sets out his fall from grace. I read them when I was on leave recently. They are genuine riches-to-rags stories; they don't pull any punches.'

'Have you still got the books?'

'Yeah. I'll bring them in. I say they don't pull any punches; that's not true. The more this investigation reveals about Guy Royal, it's obvious he was far worse than how he's portrayed himself. I'm amazed somebody hasn't bumped him off before, to be honest.'

'Well, they have now, and it's down to us to find out who and why.' Danny paused before continuing, 'I want every witness seen again and reinterviewed. We may have missed something vital.'

The two inspectors nodded and stood to leave.

'Talking about these books,' Danny added, 'find out who published them and what contact they had with Guy Royal.' Then he looked at Rob and said, 'Rob, take Rachel and go and see the publishers. I want you to establish anything you can about the contact they had, and what the process was with these books. If Royal's true nature surfaced when they were being written and published, it's possible he upset somebody else along the way.'

36

1.00 a.m., 27 May 1990
Nottingham City Centre

Garry Poyser swore under his breath as he walked out of the Black Aces Casino, in the Hockley district of Nottingham.

He had endured another torturous night of loss in the casino.

Over a month had passed since Rebecca left to visit her sick mother in Norwich. On that day, she had given him five hundred pounds to spend on household bills, food and drink.

Then, the second week on his own in the flat at Carrington, he had felt so bored that he dressed smartly and went into the city centre for a few beers. He had ended the night in the Black Aces, and everything had been perfect. That first night he had won big on the roulette wheel, almost doubling the two hundred pounds he'd taken out with him.

He cut a desolate figure as he trudged through the city now.

He walked with his head down and his hands in his pockets, reflecting on how it would have been better to have lost all his money on that first night.

After that first big win, he became a regular visitor to the casino. As the nights went by, he steadily lost all the money Rebecca had left for him. The losing streak continued as he gambled on in a vain attempt to recoup his losses.

Until tonight. As he lost on yet another spin of the roulette wheel, the casino security staff had pulled him roughly to one side and told him his credit had been withdrawn. He would be barred from the premises until his debt of three thousand pounds was cleared in full.

He had protested at first, demanding they allow him the opportunity to win his money back. But then, surrounded by five burly security men, he had decided against taking his protests further.

It had been impressed on him that unless he paid his debt in full, he would experience a world of pain. He had been left in no doubt that the security guards, and their supervisor, meant business and were no strangers to administering violence.

He had stormed out of the casino, vowing never to return. They could whistle for their money.

As he walked, the cold air cleared the alcohol and cigar smoke from his brain, and he realised that, on his first visit to the casino, he had signed up to be a member. No membership meant no play at the tables. He now recalled how he had given the casino staff the name Jamie Hart and Rebecca's address.

He swore under his breath. He knew he couldn't ignore the debt. At some stage, those meatheads would visit Rebecca's flat to demand their money.

As he walked through the theatre district, he saw a queue of people waiting impatiently to be allowed access to a nightclub.

People at the back of the queue were pushing, causing pressure at the front. He could see a single bouncer at the head of the queue, trying to control things.

There was a bright green neon light above the door, intermittently flashing the name Manhattan Junction.

A germ of an idea formulated in Garry's brain. He suddenly knew exactly how he could make enough money to pay off the casino before Rebecca returned from Norwich.

He walked up to the front of the queue and faced the burly doorman, who was struggling to hold back the impatient crowd. He was working alone and looked stressed with the situation.

'Looks like you could do with a hand, mate,' Garry said. 'Are there any jobs going on the door here?'

'Are you serious?'

'Yeah. I've worked nightclub doors in Newcastle, Liverpool and London. I've a hell of a lot of experience.'

'You couldn't have come at a better time, pal,' the giant said. 'Two staff have walked out on me tonight. I'm seriously understaffed here. When can you start?'

Garry ducked under the velvet rope, zipped up his black bomber jacket and said, 'How does right now suit you?'

The man beamed and said, 'I'm Frankie Daniels. Head doorman. Welcome aboard. We'll talk cash and hours at the end of the night. Usual dress codes apply. No training shoes or football tops. Pretty much everything else goes. We have a zero drugs policy. If you see anyone smoking weed or popping pills, they don't get in. Understood?'

'Understood.'

'What's your name, Geordie boy?'

'Jamie Hart.'

A smiling Daniels said, 'Nah. I prefer Geordie Hart.'

'Whatever you like. You're the boss. Where do you need me?'

'Work the front entrance until the queue's gone down a bit, then come and find me inside.'

'Okay, no problem.'

Frankie Daniels made his way inside the club, leaving Garry alone working the front door. It was easy work for him, and he soon had the queue – of mainly attractive young women – in order. In no time at all, the impatient pushing from the back had stopped altogether.

He had been pleased to hear the Manhattan Junction had a zero drugs policy. It would make demand for the ecstasy tablets he intended pushing at the club even higher. He would just have to be careful when he was around the other staff.

He knew that selling the MDMA tablets he had brought with him from Newcastle was the only way he could get his hands on the three grand he owed the casino.

He knew the risks involved in selling the little white tablets with the red dragon motif, but he also knew it was his only hope.

37

10.00 p.m., 18 February 1990
Bouldstone Press, Eastcastle Street, London

The crowded room was finally starting to empty as the invited guests and members of the press started to drift away. Many bottles of champagne had been drunk and trays of fancy canapés consumed during the launch party for the sequel to A Rising Star.

A beaming Seymour Hart-Wilson sashayed across the ornately tiled floor towards Kingston Jones and Janice Millership. He had clearly overindulged in the complimentary fizz and placed a conspiratorial hand on the tall American's arm before whispering, 'Thank God, I've just put Royal and Jennings in a taxi, so we can all breathe again.'

Janice nodded. 'Although, Guy's been no problem again tonight. He really does know how to play the game. As soon as there's an audience, any type of audience, he knows exactly how to work them.'

Kingston muttered, 'Unlike when there isn't one, and then he's just a pain in the arse.'

But nothing could dampen Seymour's high spirits, and he gushed, 'I knew this would be the big one. Everybody's been waiting for A Fallen Star. This is the book everyone wants to read this summer. The numbers for pre-orders make for amazing reading.'

'That's great news, Seymour. Personally, I'm just pleased it's all over.'

'Let's celebrate in style now we can relax. Who wants more champagne?'

Janice replied, 'Not for me, Seymour, I'm bushed. Think I'll call it a night.' She turned to Kingston and said, 'Do you want more fizz, or do you want to share a cab?'

He drained the last of his champagne and put the empty glass on a nearby table. 'No more for me,' he said. 'I'm ready when you are. It's been a long day.'

They both said their goodbyes to Seymour and made their way outside. A row of black cabs was parked directly outside the publishing house. The local cabbies were all aware of the event, and they knew people would be needing a ride home.

They walked to the next available cab, and Janice gave the cabbie directions as she got in. Kingston was feeling the effects of the champagne and was a little tipsy. As they were driven through the busy streets, Kingston said, 'I like this city at night. It reminds me of home. New York is always so vibrant at night.'

Janice gripped his arm and said, 'I'd love to see it one day.'

'You'll have to come over and visit. I could show you all the sights, the Statue of Liberty, Ellis Island, Brooklyn Bridge, the works.'

Janice could feel her heart racing and desperately wanted to tell him exactly how she felt about him. The love she felt was so strong, it was almost painful. Something had always stopped her from telling him exactly how she felt, but maybe tonight was the night.

She was just about to say something when he said, 'Now that the books are launched, I'm seriously thinking about going home. I was only supposed to be here for the one book, not two, and I'm ready to see New York again.'

Janice suddenly felt like there was a steel band constricting her ribs, and she struggled to draw breath. Open mouthed, she gasped for air, desperately trying to quell the surge of panic she was experiencing.

Kingston shot her a worried glance and asked, 'Are you okay, Janice?'

She managed to splutter, 'I'm fine. It's just a bit stuffy in here.'

Kingston rapped on the dividing glass and said to the driver, 'Hey, man! Have you got any aircon in this cab? It's hot back here.'

The cabbie shouted, 'No aircon, mate, but the windows will wind down if you need some fresh air.'

Kingston instantly leaned across Janice and turned down the window on her side as far as it would go. As the cold air rushed into the cab, he said, 'Is that any better?'

She nodded and said quietly, 'You wouldn't be going straight back, would you?'

'Not straight back, why?'

'There's still so much of this city, this country, that you haven't seen. It would be nice to show you before you leave. I'd love to show you around my home, in the northeast. It's so beautiful up there and so very different from London.'

'That sounds great, Janice. Thank you.'

He was so charming, so courteous, but she knew there was no way she could tell him how she felt now.

She should have realised that once the books were finished, he would return home. That didn't help the feeling of devastation that now engulfed her.

Janice felt only relief when the cab finally stopped outside Clifford Towers and Kingston got out. He paid the full fare and said, 'See you in the morning, Janice.'

She found that she couldn't speak and just waved at his retreating silhouette from the back of the cab as it sped away.

Hot tears were now streaming down her face. And they had nothing to do with the cold air blasting in through the window.

38

10.00 a.m., 19 February 1990
The Dorchester, Mayfair, London

It had been Stan Jennings who had proposed the idea of a breakfast meeting at the Dorchester Hotel, with Seymour Hart-Wilson, to discuss what could be done to cash in on the success of A Rising Star *and* A Fallen Star.

Hart-Wilson had readily agreed, as he was keen to use the success of the two autobiographies to possibly launch further books written by former television star Guy Royal.

After a late night at the launch party, and now suffering from a massive hangover, Hart-Wilson was beginning to doubt the wisdom of talking business so early in the day.

Looking at the mountain of fried food on Stan Jennings's plate, it was obvious why he had suggested the idea of holding the business meeting in the restaurant over breakfast. Seymour Hart-Wilson had never been one for starting his day with fried food.

After a night drinking excessive amounts of champagne, that held even truer this morning.

He teased the fresh blueberries and raspberries through the low-fat yoghurt with his spoon and tried hard not to look at Guy Royal and Stan Jennings as they devoured the Dorchester Hotel's famous traditional English breakfast.

He caught a glimpse of Royal's fork as it burst the yolk of the fried egg on his plate, causing the yellow liquid to run over the fried black pudding. He experienced a wave of nausea so strong that for a moment he thought about bolting to the lavatory.

Abandoning any prospect of eating the food in front of him, Hart-Wilson placed his spoon in the bowl and waited patiently for Royal and Jennings to finish their meals.

After a torturous fifteen minutes for the publisher, it came as a relief when he heard Stan Jennings signal that he'd finished eating – with an enormous belch. The ugly sound drew disgusted looks from other diners in the exclusive surroundings, where manners were supposed to be paramount.

Next, Guy Royal's overweight manager wiped a smear of egg yolk from his chin with a white linen napkin and said, 'Right, let's get down to business, Seymour. We've got a train to catch in an hour.'

Seymour regained his composure to ask, 'Have you or Guy come up with any ideas?'

'I've already scribbled down a few possibilities,' Royal said. 'My favourite is for a series of three books. All three would be centred around the story of a young woman from a very poor background who's forced, through traumatic circumstances, to leave home at a young age and find work at a huge country mansion. It would be the bawdy tale of a beautiful, buxom parlourmaid fighting off the usually unwanted, but sometimes wanted, attentions of the landed gentry. Gradually, this woman would climb the social ladder, using all the weapons at her disposal, until she becomes a powerful woman in her own right. A real rags-to-riches story, but one that's full of raunchy sex scenes. Sex always sells. Am I right, Seymour?'

Hart-Wilson nodded, slightly surprised by the direction Royal had gone in. 'And you've got enough ideas for three books?'

'Yeah. No problem. This writing lark's easy,' Royal crowed. 'I've been working on these stories while Kingston Jones was messing about with his text. The first one's almost done. What do you think?'

Hart-Wilson was thoughtful.

Royal's idea was by no means an original one, and by the sound of it, it was never going to be a literary classic. But with Guy Royal's name on the cover, Hart-Wilson believed that such a series of books could sell well; that is, make Bouldstone a lot of money.

The thought of money banished his hangover a little and caused a smile to break out across his face. 'I like the idea,' he admitted. 'I think readers would buy into the fact that the storyline somehow reflects your show-business personality, Guy. And three books really could generate some significant revenue.'

'That's great,' Jennings said as he clicked his fingers for the waitress to bring more coffee.

'But,' Hart-Wilson quickly added, 'I would insist on Kingston Jones having an input into these new titles, just to ensure the quality of writing is maintained.'

Royal pulled a disapproving face. 'I'm not bothered about working with Jones again. He's such a boring sod. Does it have to be him?'

'It's vital. We really need to hook your readers into the first book so they're willing to invest in all three. That's the beauty and selling power of a trilogy.'

'Do what Seymour says, Guy. After all, he's paying,' Stan Jennings chipped in. 'I like Kingston, and he does know his stuff. Let's face it, Guy. It was Kingston who made a success of those first two books.'

Royal grimaced. 'All right, all right. Jones can work on them, but he'd better not piss me off, or he's gone.'

'I can see you like Guy's idea,' Jennings said as he made full eye contact with Hart-Wilson, 'so let's talk numbers. With Rising Star and Fallen Star still riding high, you know these three books will sell well just because Guy's name will be on the cover. We want a bigger advance than last time, one that's substantial and non-returnable.'

'How substantial?' a nervous Hart-Wilson spluttered.

'Five hundred thousand.'

'What? That's ludicrous. There are never any guarantees a book will sell that well, regardless of what the author's written before.'

'I've been doing my research, Seymour. We both know there are plenty of other publishing houses ready to cash in on the success of Guy as an author. I'll simply take his trilogy idea to one of them. In fact, I've already spoken to two publishers who are more than willing to pay the advance we're asking – not unreasonably – for.'

A feeling of dread washed over Hart-Wilson at the prospect of losing out on what could be a very lucrative deal.

After a long pause he said, 'There's no need to go elsewhere, Stanley. I'm prepared to pay half a million pounds as an advance, but that sum will cover all three books.'

'Non-returnable?'

'Yes. I'll have my lawyer draw up the contract within the next three working days, ready for you and Guy to sign.'

Jennings stood up and leaned across the table, extending his hand. 'It's a deal. As always, it's been a pleasure doing business with you, Seymour. I'll get the breakfast bill.'

A disgruntled Hart-Wilson wasn't smiling as he stood and accepted the greasy handshake. Half a million pounds! That kind of money was capital his company could ill afford to lose right now. Even with the success of Royal's first two books, Bouldstone Press was on the brink of financial ruin. To pay such a huge advance against the future sales of a three-book deal was a massive risk, to make that advance non-returnable was downright dangerous, but with nothing else on offer, Hart-Wilson felt it was a risk he had to take.

The creditors were already hovering. He desperately needed all three of the new series of Guy Royal books to follow the lead of the first two and become huge, unprecedented successes in their own right.

39

9.30 a.m., 20 February 1990
Bouldstone Press, Eastcastle Street, London

A nervous Janice Millership met Kingston Jones just outside the entrance to Bouldstone Press. She said quietly, 'Any idea why Mr Hart-Wilson wants to see us this morning?'

As they walked in the main entrance, Kingston Jones laughed. 'Haven't a clue, Janice. Don't look so worried. Maybe he wants to give us both a bonus for doing such great work on Royal's books.'

Five minutes later, they were both standing in front of Hart-Wilson's desk in his office.

The head of the publishing house told them to take a seat and said, 'The sales for the two Guy Royal books are already fantastic and projected to get even better. You both did a great job on them.'

Kingston shot Janice a knowing look and silently mouthed, 'Told you.'

Hart-Wilson continued, 'That's the reason I asked you both to come in this morning. I wanted to tell you what we propose to do next with Guy Royal.'

The half-smile disappeared from Kingston's face, instantly replaced with a scowl. He said in a voice that barely contained his anger, 'How about I propose we don't do anything with that jackass. I'm really pleased the two books are doing well, Seymour, but I'm even more pleased I don't have to work with that egotistical maniac again. He's a total nightmare.'

'I'm afraid it's not going to work like that, Kingston.'

'What are you talking about?'

'Royal's books are doing so well right now that we need to capitalise on that success. I had a meeting with Royal and his manager yesterday. As a result, I've signed Royal up to write three more books.'

'What kind of books?' Kingston demanded. 'We can't spin his life story out any longer than we already have.'

'He's going to write three bawdy historical novels.'

'Why would you ask him to do that, Seymour? It's a crazy idea.'

'Don't worry. His name on its own will sell the books. Look how well the first two are selling.'

'That's totally different,' Kingston insisted. 'People were interested in the man's life story. Nobody will care less about any second-rate fiction he writes.'

'You're wrong, Kingston,' Seymour said in a voice of steel. 'The contracts are already being drawn up.'

Frustrated, Kingston blew out his breath. 'Trust me. This man has no idea how to write any kind of book. It amazes me he can even sign his own name.'

'Don't you get it? It doesn't really matter if Royal can or can't write. All that matters is that you can. We let him scribble down a first draft of his rubbish. You take that first draft and make whatever changes are required until we've got three readable bodice rippers.'

'And what makes you think I can write sexy romantic fiction. If that's what these so-called books end up being.'

'I need you to make this work, Kingston. I've already agreed to pay a substantial advance on the three books.'

'This is madness. I won't do it.'

Hart-Wilson raised his voice and almost shouted, 'If you want to remain employed by this publishing house, you'll do it!'

Kingston shouted back, 'You can't blackmail me like that!'

At which point, Hart-Wilson realised he'd pushed the American ghost writer too far. He held up his hands in a gesture of appeasement and said quietly, 'It's only three books, Kingston. I need you to make them a success. Let me be candid with you; it's vital these books do well. The proverbial wolf is at our door, dear boy.'

Janice had remained silent until now, but now she said softly, 'I'll be there with you, Kingston. I'm sure we can put up with Royal's tantrums if we work together. It's not going to be for ever, is it?'

The writer paced around the room, allowing his anger to subside. Then he said, 'Three books and that's it. And don't even think about pulling any more of this bullshit on me, Seymour.'

With that, he stalked out of the office, followed quickly by Janice.

As she tried to match the tall American's long strides, she promised him breathlessly, 'It will be okay, Kingston. It's only three books.' As she spoke, Janice allowed a smile to form on her lips. She was secretly pleased that Hart-Wilson had manoeuvred

Kingston into staying. Anything that meant she could spend more time with the American was sure to make her happy.

As she followed him out of the main entrance, she thought about the two of them working together over the coming months. She wondered if she'd be able to pluck up the courage then to tell him exactly how much she loved him.

40

1.15 a.m., 9 October 1990
Nottingham City Centre

For the first time in four months, Garry Poyser felt happy as he strolled through the almost deserted city centre streets. The door supervisor had let him get a flyer, as the nightclub wasn't that busy.

He could feel the wad of banknotes in his jacket pocket. The club hadn't been that busy, but there had been a lot of interest in the product he'd been selling on the door.

As soon as he'd left the club, he dived straight into the kebab shop next door and ordered a doner kebab to celebrate.

After months of dealing with drunken louts at the Manhattan Junction, he had finally managed to sell enough ecstasy tablets to pay his debt at the casino in full and still have a couple of hundred pounds to spend.

In the end, it had taken just over four months to make the cash he needed, as he had to be extremely careful how he sold the tablets. Even being hyper vigilant, there had been at least two occasions when other doormen had seen what he was selling.

He'd taken each of them to one side and impressed on them how it would be in their best interests not to say anything to the door supervisor.

There was something about the way he made the subtle threats to each man. They both understood that if they grassed him up, it would cause them a world of pain.

He had one small bag of the pills left to punt out, around thirty in all. They were still in the loft at Rebecca's flat in Carrington.

He'd found that he missed his flatmate, but he expected her back from Norwich any day soon. The last time he had spoken to her, Rebecca was busy sorting out carers for her elderly mum so she could get back to Nottingham and start earning some cash.

He would try to flog the last of the pills next weekend and then quit working the doors at the nightclub. He couldn't stand the aggravation of dealing with drunken idiots wanting to fight each other any longer.

He cursed as chilli sauce from the kebab dropped onto the front of his jacket. In disgust, he hurled what was left of the greasy food into a bin and hailed a passing cab. As the taxi sped through the dark Nottingham streets, Garry's thoughts turned to the Black Aces Casino. He would make those bastards wait for their money.

41

8.00 p.m., 9 October 1990
MCIU Offices, Mansfield, Nottinghamshire

It had been a long day, and Danny was still working on a new press appeal asking for information on the murder of Guy Royal. He was finding it difficult to put freshness into this new appeal.

In frustration, he grabbed the sheet of paper he was making notes on and screwed it up before hurling it with the others into the waste bin.

He knew the enquiry was floundering, and without a breakthrough soon, there was a real possibility that the shooting of Guy Royal would remain unsolved.

Which was not the start Danny wanted for the MCIU under the new tenure of Detective Chief Superintendent Mark Slater.

The knock on his door startled him a little, as he thought

he was alone in the office, and he was surprised to see Glen Lorimar walk in.

Glen said, 'Have you got a minute, boss?'

Danny was shocked at how tired his detective looked. He said, 'You look terrible, Glen. What's happened?'

'It's my daughter, Sandra. She's in the ICU at Queen's.'

'How?'

'She was out in Nottingham with a group of friends. They're all at college together, and they were celebrating one of the girls' birthday.'

'How the hell did she end up in the ICU?'

'From what I can gather from her friends, she's been an idiot and taken ecstasy.'

'How is she?' Danny said, immediately concerned for his colleague.

'It's not good, boss.'

Glen brushed tears from his eyes, and his voice broke a little as he said, 'The doctors don't know how she's going to react to the treatment they're giving her. It's horrible to see her in there like that. She's got tubes everywhere, and beeping machines are keeping her alive.' He paused. Then with real anger in his voice, he said, 'I can't believe she's done something so stupid.'

Danny asked, 'Do her friends know where she got the ecstasy?'

'No. They'd been to a few clubs during the night, and it was only when they were waiting at the taxi rank that Sandra started to feel unwell.'

'What was the last bar they were in? Ecstasy usually causes a quick reaction – if it's going bad.'

'Usually, but not always,' Glen said. 'From what I can

gather, the last place they were in was the Manhattan Junction.'

'I'll need a list of all the pubs and clubs she went to,' Danny said, switching into business mode. 'I'll get Rob and Andy onto this first thing in the morning. You need to be at home with your family, not here.'

'I wanted to let you know what's happened, but I didn't want to tell you over the phone.'

'I appreciate that, Glen. Is anybody else involved?'

'There were four girls taken to the Queen's Medical Centre last night. Two recovered quite quickly and have now been released from the hospital. It's just Sandra and another girl who are still being treated in the ICU.'

'Tell Rob and Andy I've already fired a call in to the drugs squad,' Glen told him. 'The detective I spoke to told me that over the last three months they've seen an increase in bad reactions of clubbers who have taken ecstasy. This is the first time anybody has ended up in the ICU, though.'

'Have they any ideas who the supplier might be?'

'No.' Glen shook his head. 'They can't even pinpoint which club or pub is involved.'

'You can leave it with me now, Glen,' Danny assured him. 'I'll make sure the rest of the team know what's happened. We'll find the bastard who's pushing this shit. Now go home and be with your wife and family.'

'I'm going back to the hospital; my wife's still there with Sandra. I just wanted to let you know in person.'

'Take whatever time off you need, Glen. Don't even think about work, and please keep me informed if anything changes with Sandra. Fingers crossed she'll start responding positively to the treatment soon.'

42

8.00 a.m., 10 October 1990
MCIU Offices, Mansfield, Nottinghamshire

Danny had called the entire MCIU staff to a morning briefing so he could inform them of the current dire family situation of their friend and colleague Glen Lorimar.

He impressed on the gathered detectives that they were to spend the first hour of their day gathering as much information and intelligence about drugs sales in Nottingham pubs and clubs as they could.

He said, 'Every one of you in this room has their own contacts within the drugs squad, and most of you have registered informants that cover the city centre. I want you all to start getting stuck into those sources. Somebody out there knows exactly who's peddling this shit. Glen has phoned through the list of clubs and pubs his daughter visited last night.' Then his eyes searched the room for Rob Buxton. When he saw him, he said, 'Rob, I want you and Andy to start visiting every pub and club on that list. Get into their ribs, and if you don't get one hundred percent cooperation, I want you to make their lives extremely uncomfortable.'

Rob nodded and said, 'I was due to travel to London today to visit Bouldstone Publishers with Rachel. Do you want me to cancel that?'

Danny paused. He was conflicted over finding out what had happened to the daughter of his friend and colleague and moving the murder enquiry forward. He suddenly felt exhausted. He took two deep breaths and said decisively, 'I want you and Andy working on this today.'

Next, he searched the sea of faces again until he saw DC Pope. 'Jane,' he said, 'I want you to go with Rachel today for the Bouldstone Press enquiry. Will travelling to London cause you any domestic strife?'

'I'll need to make a quick telephone call,' Jane said, 'but then I'll be good to go.'

'Good. Okay, everybody, let's get cracking.'

43

11.30 a.m., 19 August 1990
Hunters Croft, Rufford Road, Ollerton, Notts

Almost six months had passed since Kingston Jones had been press-ganged into helping Guy Royal write his debut romantic novel. For Kingston it had been six months of hell. He had put up with endless tantrums from Royal, and the idea of collaborative working, as proposed by Seymour Hart-Wilson, had failed spectacularly.

Royal contradicted every suggestion and argued against any advice he'd been given by the experienced ghost writer. Kingston had spent countless fruitless hours cajoling and trying to guide the hapless Royal.

At last, Royal had completed his first draft and sent it to Bouldstone. After reading it through, Kingston couldn't believe that Royal had removed every section he had rewritten and had sent the manuscript to the publishers in its original, unpolished and desperately bad form.

At which point, a frustrated Jones had made the decision to travel to Royal's Nottinghamshire home; his plan was to make one final attempt to talk some sense into the former television star.

The book in its current state would be a disaster. The experienced American knew it would take the major rewrite he had already completed to get it anywhere near ready for publication. Knowing the size of the ego he was about to confront, he wasn't hopeful that Royal would agree with his plan.

The journey from London to Royal's home had been a fraught one. The traffic was heavy, causing major delays, and the conversation in the car with Janice Millership on their long journey north had been stilted and strained. By the time he reached Royal's home, Kingston was already dog-tired.

And now, the meeting with Royal and his manager was going terribly.

As always, Royal had been arrogant and dismissive of any ideas and advice from Kingston.

In frustration, Kingston held up the typed manuscript and said, 'I'm sorry, Guy. This book is nowhere near the standard needed to publish. You have removed all the sections I worked on with you, and you've totally disregarded everything I've said. The character profiles are a joke, and there are holes in the plot so big you could drive a couple of your red London buses through them.' He drew in a deep breath before continuing, 'The whole thing is garbage. You need to listen to what I'm telling you, or this book will bomb when it's released.'

Sprawled out on a luxurious sofa, Guy Royal waved his hand in a condescending manner and said, 'Piss off, Jones. You're just jealous because I've been paid the big money by Seymour, and you're still scratching around for peanuts.' Then he sat up and pointed aggressively towards Jones before almost snarling at him, 'I don't need any lousy input from you. What I need is a new ghost writer.'

Janice Millership leapt angrily to Jones's defence. 'You are so wrong. It was only Kingston's hard work that made the first two books a success. Why won't you listen to him?'

'I'm not taking advice from someone like him.'

All the simmering tension and frustration suddenly boiled over, and Kingston stepped up and grabbed Royal's shirt front, pulling him up off the sofa.

'What do you mean someone like him, you racist prick!'

Incensed, Royal pulled himself out of Kingston's grasp and yelled, 'Get your hands off me, you...'

Kingston stepped forwards again and yelled back, 'You what? Go on, say what's really on your mind, you piece of shit.'

As his face turned deep red, Royal growled, 'I'll have your fucking job for this; you can't lay hands on me. Get out!'

Stan Jennings hastily got his bulk between the two men and pushed them apart. 'I think you'd better leave, Kingston.'

'Don't worry, I'm going. I can see I'm wasting my time here.'

As Kingston stormed out, followed by Janice and Jennings, Royal screamed after him, 'There's nothing wrong with the book as it is! I'm calling Seymour right now. You're history, Jones!'

Kingston simply said through gritted teeth, 'Fuck off.'

Stan Jennings followed them out of the house and walked with them along the driveway. As Kingston got in the car, Jennings said, 'Don't do anything hasty, Kingston. Can't you just do the rewrite anyway? Guy doesn't need to know the first draft's been altered. He'll never read the book once it's back from the printer.'

'Not this time,' Kingston spat. 'I've put up with enough of Royal's bullshit. Seymour can publish the bloody book just as it is.' He slammed the car door shut in Jennings's horrified face and snapped, 'Come on, Janice. Let's get back to London.'

44

10.00 a.m., 20 August 1990
Bouldstone Press, Eastcastle Street, London

Seymour Hart-Wilson was pacing up and down in his office. 'What the hell were you thinking?'

Kingston Jones was sat in one of two chairs that faced Hart-Wilson's desk. Janice Millership sat in the other.

Kingston said, 'I'd had enough of Royal's bullshit. Not only is this prick arrogant, he's a racist. He showed his true colours yesterday, and I'm done working with him.'

'Oh, you're definitely done working with him. You can't lay hands on a client, whatever they say. He's talking about involving the police.'

'Fuck him.'

'You've left me no choice, Kingston. I've got to protect the publishing house. I've got to let you go.'

'You're firing me because of that arrogant piece of shit?'

'What else can I do?' Seymour lifted his hands in despair. 'I can't risk police involvement. My competitors would love the damage that would do to our reputation.'

'That's totally unfair and you know it,' Janice said, bold in her defence of the man she loved. 'Kingston was provoked. You weren't there, sir. You can't fire him over this.'

Hart-Wilson simply dismissed her comments with a wave of his hand.

Kingston said, 'You can fire me if you like, Seymour. But you need to know that without the major rewrite I've already done, Royal's book will bomb spectacularly. It's pure garbage.'

Hart-Wilson sat down heavily in his chair. 'There's no time for that. The book is already coming off the presses at the printers now.'

'What? The manuscript Royal sent?'

'Yes. The launch date is scheduled for the first of September in eleven days' time. The press releases have gone out. Why did you have to argue with him? Why didn't you quietly make the changes needed, just to make it readable?'

'I tried that. Every section I wrote, Royal changed back to the original. He's started to believe his own hype. He refused to let me make any changes. That's why we argued. I was just trying to make him see sense.' Then Kingston stood and said, 'If I'm fired, I'm out of here.'

As he walked out, Janice stood too and said to Hart-Wilson, 'What do I do now?'

'You start back in the typing pool tomorrow.'

As Janice followed Kingston out of the office, Hart Wilson said bitterly, 'And make the most of it, Miss Millership. None of us may have jobs for much longer.'

Janice ignored Hart-Wilson's comment and raced after Jones. She caught up with him on the steps outside the main entrance. Breathless and panicked, she said, 'What will you do now?'

'Look for another job.' He shrugged. 'I guess. I need time to think.'

Hardly daring to ask the question, she said quietly, 'You're not going back to New York, are you?'

'Not immediately. Like I said, I need time to think. I've got to understand what just happened in there.'

There was a long pause as they walked together towards the Embankment.

Kingston said, 'The rent on my apartment is paid for the next three months, so there's no need to rush a decision. I do miss New York, though.'

Janice saw a glimmer of hope in his last comment and said, 'Do you fancy a coffee?'

'That would be good. And don't worry, Janice, I haven't forgotten about your book. Let's make sure we work on that and get it sent to a few publishers.'

45

10.00 a.m., 3 September 1990
Bouldstone Press, Eastcastle Street, London

Janice Millership felt nervous as she walked into Seymour Hart-Wilson's office. The head of the typing pool had informed her that the owner of the publishing house wanted to see her in his office immediately.

Hart-Wilson said, 'Sit down, Miss Millership. I understand from some of your colleagues that you and Kingston Jones are still close. Is that correct?'

'We're friends. Is that a problem?'

Hart-Wilson allowed an unpleasant smile to form on his lips. 'No, no, no. Of course it isn't.' He paused before continuing, 'I'm sure you're aware, but the launch of Guy Royal's new book was two days ago. The early sales figures are nothing short of disastrous. The critics have panned it, calling it an affront to literature and asking how on earth it was ever published. I'm afraid Bouldstone Press is a bit of a laughingstock right now.'

It was now Janice's turn to allow herself a small smile. Everything Kingston had said about the book had been proved correct.

She said, 'Mr Jones did try to warn you, sir.'

'Yes, yes. I know he did. I need to speak with Jones today, as a matter of urgency. For the sake of this publishing house, I need to try to rescue this disastrous situation. Do you think Jones will listen?'

'I don't know. He was pretty upset when you sacked him.'

Hart-Wilson shook his head at the memory. 'That was all a horrible misunderstanding. I need him back here. He might listen to what I've got to say if you're here too.'

'I doubt I'll make any difference to his decisions, sir.'

'Even so, I want you to call Jones and arrange to meet him for a coffee, this morning.'

'I'll see what I can do, sir.'

46

11.30 a.m., 3 September 1990
Dickens Café, Eastcastle Street, London

The small café was almost empty.
 The breakfast rush had finished an hour ago, and it was still a bit early for customers wanting lunch. The only other customer in the place was a scruffy, unshaven old man. He was sitting alone at a table in the corner, nursing a lukewarm mug of tea, trying desperately to make it last as long as he could so he didn't have to go back to his cold, lonely flat.

Janice Millership and Seymour Hart-Wilson sat at the table nearest the window.

Hart-Wilson said, 'Do you think Jones will come?'

She shrugged. 'I think so. I just asked him if he fancied a quick coffee.'

Her boss nervously glanced at the pictures of brilliant writers that adorned the walls of the café. Seeing him looking, Janice smirked and said, 'Have you seen Guy Royal's picture yet, sir?'

Hart-Wilson pulled a disapproving face, but before he could comment, the door to the café opened, and Kingston Jones walked in.

Seeing Hart-Wilson sitting with Janice, he said, 'What's going on?'

Hart-Wilson gushed, 'Please do sit down, Kingston. We need to talk.'

'I think you said everything last time. I know I've got nothing to say to you, Seymour.'

Janice said, 'You're here now. At least sit down and have a coffee.'

Reluctantly, the tall American removed his overcoat and sat down.

Janice said, 'I'll get the coffees while you two talk.'

'I owe you an apology, Kingston,' Hart-Wilson said. 'I should never have listened to Royal. I was wrong to fire you, and I'd like you to come back to Bouldstone.'

'It's bombed, hasn't it?' Jones said.

'Excuse me?'

'Royal's book. It's a disaster, isn't it?'

Hart-Wilson glared at Jones for a long time before saying, 'Yes, it's bombed. The whole situation is nothing short of a catastrophe. Sales are next to nothing, and on top of that, I've paid Royal an enormous non-returnable advance that I now have no chance of recouping. That's capital the publishing house can ill afford to lose right now. The bottom line is this, that stupid contract I agreed with Royal could finish Bouldstone Press.'

'I'm truly sorry at how things have worked out for you, Seymour, but I don't see how I can help you. I don't work for Bouldstone anymore, remember?'

'That was all a terrible misunderstanding,' Seymour simpered.

'I don't understand what you're saying. Are you offering me my job back?'

'Sort of. I need you to work on the second and third novels once Royal's written them. It will be off the books, and he'll never know you're involved. I'll make sure that he doesn't see the finished books until after they're published.'

'I don't see how that will work?'

'Royal's used to seeing Janice. She can still drive to his home and pick up the work as he completes it. She can deliver it to you; then you can turn his scribblings into something decent. That way I might be able to at least recoup some of the advance he's been paid.'

'And if I refuse?'

'If you refuse, I'll make it my mission in life to stop you ever working in the publishing industry again.'

Kingston scowled. 'And there he is. The same old Seymour. Only ever interested in one thing, himself.' He stood to leave just as Janice returned with the coffees.

Seymour held up both hands and said, 'I'm sorry, Kingston. I didn't mean that. All I'm asking is that you work off the books until Royal's contract has finished; then you'll have your job back. Can't you see I'm desperate here. I gambled everything on this trilogy. I can see now that I've made a grave error. I have jeopardised the very future of Bouldstone.'

'Surely it's not that bad.'

Hart-Wilson didn't answer. He looked broken, and Kingston could see the tears welling in the man's eyes.

Kingston sat back down next to Janice and said, 'Have you seen the state he's in? Are things really that bad?'

She said, 'I don't know, but what I do know is that it's only two novels. You wouldn't even have to see Guy Royal. I'll deal with him.'

'Even so, do you really think it would work?'

'We can at least try.'

Kingston was thoughtful for a long time; he kept glancing at Hart-Wilson, who now cut a pathetic huddled figure, sitting with his head in his hands. He really did look like he was carrying the weight of the world on his shoulders.

Eventually, Kingston turned to Hart-Wilson, shook his arm and waited for him to look up before saying, 'Okay. It's against my better judgement, but I'll try to rescue these next two books.'

Hart-Wilson said, 'Really?'

'I'll try. I'm not making any promises, but I'll give it a go. Janice can bring me the finished manuscripts to work on. I don't want any contact with that odious individual, that prick Royal. If that becomes likely, I'll walk away. I'll just work on the manuscripts that Janice brings me and see if I can do anything with them.'

'Thank you.'

'Don't thank me yet, Seymour. If the first book's bombed as bad as you're saying, you're going to have a hell of a job convincing people to buy anything else supposedly written by this clown.'

As she listened to him, Janice could barely contain her feelings. She knew Kingston had been planning to leave for New York in a week's time. By persuading him to work on Royal's books, she felt like she'd given herself a little more time with the man who filled her every waking thought.

47

11.30 a.m., 10 October 1990
Bouldstone Press, Eastcastle Street, London

Rachel Moore and Jane Pope had driven to London for their appointment to see the head of Bouldstone Press.

Rachel studied Seymour Hart-Wilson as he fidgeted in his chair. His eyes were constantly scanning the room, and Rachel formed the impression this was a man very much on the edge.

She thanked him for taking the time to see them at short notice and said, 'What can you tell me about your dealings with Guy Royal?'

'What's to tell?' Hart-Wilson gave a nervous shrug. 'All I know is that his death is the worst thing that could have happened for this publishing house.'

'I don't understand?'

'Royal had signed a three-book deal with Bouldstone Press and had been paid a huge non-returnable advance to do so.'

'How much is huge?'

'I'd rather that stayed private, Detective. Suffice to say, it was a hell of a lot of money.'

'Is that normal?'

'Not really, but I needed to do something to fend off rival publishers. There were quite a few interested parties after the success of his first two books.'

'Has Royal's death caused you financial problems?'

Hart-Wilson rolled his eyes. 'Of course it has. Only one of the three promised books was ever written. He was murdered one month after the first book was launched. I've had my lawyers going over the small print in the contract, to see if there's any way I can claw some of that money for the advance back.'

'And is there?'

There was a haunted look in his eyes as he shook his head. 'Not a chance.'

Jane Pope said, 'How are sales on the book that was written?'

'Sales are shit. The book's shit. Guy Royal's a piece of shit.'

A little shocked by the vitriol of Hart-Wilson's outburst, Rachel said, 'I understood the first two books by Guy Royal were bestsellers. Is that not the case now?'

'The only place those two books are selling well now is in charity shops for pennies. Sadly, the second book, *A Fallen Star*, confirmed to the public what the tabloid press had been telling them for years, that Guy Royal was an arrogant, misogynistic piece of crap. It's my own fault. I totally misread the public's reaction.' He paused before continuing, 'I even thought that him dying, in the way he did, may boost sales for a while. Sad to say, even that hasn't helped. Nobody gives a shit about Guy Royal anymore.'

'Did anybody else work with Royal?'

'You can't seriously believe that a man like Guy Royal was capable of writing those two books?' He answered his own rhetorical question, saying, 'Of course somebody helped him. I employed a wonderful ghost writer, Kingston Jones, to write *A Rising Star* and *A Fallen Star*.

'Can we talk to Kingston Jones?'

'Only if you've brought a Ouija board with you.'

'Excuse me.'

'Unfortunately, he took his own life just before Guy Royal was murdered.'

Jane and Rachel glanced at each other, trying not to show their surprise. 'Any idea why he'd do that?'

'Haven't a clue,' Hart-Wilson said in a flat, indifferent tone.

'Is there anybody else who had regular contact with Guy Royal when he was under contract with Bouldstone?'

'The only other person who had any regular dealings with Royal was Kingston Jones's personal assistant, Janice Millership. Jones was an American who didn't want to drive in the UK, so Janice would drive him to Royal's house in Nottingham whenever they had meetings.'

'Can we talk to Janice Millership?'

'I believe Ms Millership left the company yesterday. I'll see if our admin department have an address for her.' He picked up the telephone and said, 'Hello, Linda, I need the home address for Janice Millership.' There was a brief delay, and then Seymour scribbled down a few notes before saying, 'Okay, thanks.'

He ended the call, handed the note to Rachel and said, 'That's the only address we have for Ms Millership. Apparently, she told Linda she intended visiting her parents and wouldn't be returning to London until tomorrow evening.'

As the two detectives left the building, Rachel said, 'We'd better find somewhere to stay for the night. This is one strange state of affairs. There's no point driving all the way back to Nottingham, to then drive back here tomorrow. I'll clear it with the boss first, but I know what he'll say. Does an overnight stay cause you any problems?'

Jane Pope smiled. 'Only if you book us into some grotty dive for the night, Sarge.'

Rachel laughed. 'I'd better see what rooms there are at the Hilton, then.'

48

11.00 a.m., 11 October 1990
7 Berkely Court, Church Drive, Carrington, Nottingham

Rebecca Marney paid the taxi fare and wheeled her suitcase to the rear of the flats. She cursed under her breath when she saw the car she'd bought for Jamie to use was still sitting in the parking bay allocated to her flat.

She'd tried to call Jamie the night before, when she booked the train tickets from Norwich. As soon as everything had been put in place for the twenty-four-hour care her mother needed, Rebecca's first thought had been to get back to Nottingham. She needed Jamie to pick her up from Nottingham Midland Station and had phoned the flat as soon as she arrived. And now it looked like the phone call was unanswered because the lazy sod was still in bed.

She wearily climbed the concrete steps that led to her first-floor flat, cursing the weight of the suitcase every step.

She slipped the Yale key into the lock and stepped inside, shouting, 'Jamie!'

She was surprised when there was no answer to her repeated shouting. She had expected him either to be in the lounge with the television blaring out, or still asleep in his bedroom. She hadn't expected him to be out.

Hearing no sound from the lounge, she abandoned her suitcase and walked down the hallway to his bedroom. Starting to feel a little anxious, she tapped on the door and said, 'I'm home, Jamie. Are you decent?'

When there was no sound from within, she knocked again, a little louder this time. She waited a few seconds, then rapped loudly on the door before slowly opening it.

The bed hadn't been slept in, and the curtains were open.

Slightly puzzled, she walked from the bedroom to the lounge door.

The door was slightly open, and the first thing she saw was the upturned coffee table. With a feeling of unease rising inside her, she pushed the door wide open and said, 'Jamie, are you in here?'

As the door opened, she was confronted with a sickening sight. Jamie was lying flat on his back, his white shirt covered in dark crimson, almost black blood. His mouth gaped in a silent scream, and his eyes were wide open, staring sightlessly up at the ceiling.

Rebecca retreated out of the room, unable to comprehend what had happened, and staggered back into the hallway, struggling to fight the nausea building inside her.

She leaned against the wall and allowed herself to slide

down onto her haunches. Drawing in deep lungfuls of air, she tried to make sense of what she had just witnessed.

After several minutes in that position, she reached for the telephone in the hallway.

With shaking hands, she dialled three nines. She told the operator she required the police and waited to be put through. After a moment she heard a woman's voice, 'Police. What's your emergency?'

Rebecca said, 'You need to come to my flat. My flatmate's dead.'

'What's your name, and where do you live?'

'Rebecca Marney. I live at number seven Berkely Court, Carrington.'

'Okay, Rebecca. Officers are on their way, and I've despatched an ambulance to your location. Have you checked your flatmate for a pulse?'

'I haven't touched him. I know he's dead. I think he's been stabbed. There's blood everywhere.'

'What's your flatmate's name?'

'His name's Jamie Hart. Are the police going to be long? I'm scared.'

'Is there anyone else in the flat?'

'No.'

'The officers will be with you any minute, Rebecca. Just stay on the line talking to me until they arrive.'

A few minutes later, Rebecca heard a knock on the front door, and a voice said, 'Police.'

Rebecca put the telephone back on the cradle and called out in a shaking voice, 'I'm here.'

49

11.40 a.m., 11 October 1990
7 Berkely Court, Church Drive, Carrington, Nottingham

Danny Flint stood on the walkway directly outside Rebecca Marney's flat. As he struggled into the forensic suit, he looked at Tina Cartwright and said wearily, 'What have we got?'

'The flat's owned by Rebecca Marney; she's the woman who made the three-nines call. She travelled from Norwich this morning by train after being away for a few months caring for her elderly mother.'

'Okay. And who's the deceased?'

'Rebecca has identified him as being her flatmate, Jamie Hart.'

'What do we know about Hart?'

'There are several Jamie Harts on the PNC but none who

fit our deceased's age and profile. Rebecca doesn't know his date or place of birth. All she could tell us about him was that he had a strong northeast accent, and she thought he was from Newcastle.'

'How did he become her flatmate?'

'They met about a year ago, and he now works for her as some sort of minder.'

'Minder?'

'It seems Rebecca Marney earns her money as an escort. Hart looks after her.'

Danny's forehead creased in puzzlement. 'Seems a bit of a strange set-up. Is the pathologist here?'

'She's inside.'

'No Seamus today?'

'No. The pathologist is Dr Margaret Tanner. I've never met her before, but she's covering Nottingham city for a couple of months while Seamus is on a course in Canada.'

'Anything forensically?'

'Tim's inside with his team. They've just paused what they were doing to allow the pathologist in. It's tight for space in there.'

'Okay. Show me the way, and we'll make it a little more crowded.'

As he walked into the lounge, he could see a slim woman in her late fifties bending over the deceased. The hood on her blue forensic suit was covering her hair. She turned to look at Danny and barked, 'Gloves on, Detective!'

Her round spectacles and the pinched expression of her mouth gave her an owlish look.

Danny said, 'Good morning, Dr Tanner. I'm DCI Flint. Do you have a cause of death yet?'

'On first inspection, I can see several stab wounds have penetrated the chest cavity. A couple of them are very adjacent to the heart, so that looks like the probable cause of death.'

'Any idea on a time of death?'

'As you well know, DCI Flint, that's a very inexact science. My estimation going on the temperature of the body and the level of rigor mortis would be sometime last night. I'm sorry I can't be any more precise that that.'

'That's fine. As you say, it can only ever be an estimation.' Danny paused before asking, 'Have you seen any defence wounds?'

'None that are obvious. The only injuries I can see thus far are the stab wounds I've mentioned. There's no bruising around the head and face or on his hands. This doesn't look like a fight that escalated into a stabbing. From what I can see so far, it looks like he was surprised by the offender and stabbed before he could react. This is also borne out by the fact that although there's a lot of blood, it's very localised. I think he was stabbed, fell to the ground, then stabbed some more where he fell. I think he died right here.'

'As you say, there's a lot of blood. Would you expect our offender to be heavily bloodstained?'

'That's a distinct possibility.'

'Where will you be holding the postmortem?'

'I'm using the City Hospital as my base while I'm covering this area, so I'll arrange for the body to be taken there.' She continued, 'I've provisionally booked the postmortem for three o'clock this afternoon. Will you be attending?'

'I will. I'll get out of your way and leave you to your work and see you at the hospital later. Thanks.'

Danny stepped outside the lounge and whispered to Tina, 'Well, Margaret Tanner takes no prisoners. That'll teach me to make sure my gloves are fully on in the future. Where's Tim hiding?'

'He's in the kitchen, boss.'

Danny walked through to the kitchen, where the scenes of crime supervisor, Tim Donnelly, was chatting to three of his scenes of crime technicians. Danny said, 'What have you got for me, Tim?'

'All we've found inside the flat are glove marks. However, the good news is we've lifted a fingerprint from the doorbell at the front door.'

'You're kidding me?'

'I'm not. And it's a full print too.'

'Bloody hell. Nobody's that dumb, surely?'

'We both know it's happened before. The offender rings the bell before putting his gloves on. They do walk among us, boss.'

'So it would seem. Let's hope we've a match on our system. That could make this a very quick job. Anything else?'

'When we first arrived, we made a cursory search of the deceased's bedroom. It's early days, but there's something a bit weird going on here. The woman who called the police to the scene identified the deceased as Jamie Hart. When we searched the bedroom, we recovered a driving licence in the name Garry Poyser. The date of birth looks about right for the age of the deceased, and the address on the licence is a Gateshead one.'

Danny turned to Tina and said, 'Didn't Rebecca Marney say the deceased was from the northeast?'

Tina nodded. 'I'll do a name check on Garry Poyser.'

Danny said, 'Anything else, Tim?'

'In the same place we found the driving licence we also recovered a clear plastic bag containing thirty or so white tablets. Obviously, they'll need to be tested, but they look like MDMA to me.'

Danny took the exhibit bag containing the pills. 'You think these could be ecstasy?'

Tina acknowledged the result of the PNC check for Poyser on the radio, turned to Danny and said, 'Can I have a closer look at those tablets, boss?'

Danny passed her the exhibit bag, and she said, 'These tablets have the red dragon motif that's been mentioned in the spate of recent overdoses in the city centre nightclubs.' She then added, 'The PNC check for Garry Poyser, using the date of birth on the driving licence, shows he's known to the police.'

'Go on.'

'There's an interest marker on the PNC that was put on by Northumbria police. Poyser's wanted in connection with the death of a young woman who died from a suspected MDMA overdose at a nightclub in Newcastle.'

Danny was thoughtful. 'Where's Rebecca Marney?'

'She's at the police station in Sherwood.'

'Who's with her?'

'I've tasked Jag with obtaining her full statement.'

'I want you to go to Sherwood and let him know what's been found here. Rebecca Marney needs questioning properly. She could be Poyser's partner in crime, which would mean she's involved in peddling this shit around the city's nightclubs.'

'I'm on my way, boss.'

'Just a second, Tina. Who else is here?'

'There's only Simon, Helen, Nigel and Jeff. They're currently door knocking on the neighbouring flats.'

'Okay. Ask Jeff to go to Sherwood and interview Rebecca Marney with Jag. I'll need Nigel at the mortuary with me, for the postmortem exhibits. That will free you up to stay here and supervise the scene with Tim.'

'No problem. I know you should be off today, and you've come straight from home, so there's something else you need to know, not connected with this job.' Tina paused, gathering her thoughts. 'The control room left a message at the MCIU this morning, informing us that one of the women being treated at Queen's for a suspected overdose has died. Control wanted to know if the MCIU will be taking on the investigation?'

'Did they give the name of the woman?'

'No.'

'Bloody hell.' Danny looked horrified. 'I need to go to the QMC. It could be Glen Lorimar's daughter who's died. Get in touch with Rob and Andy and make sure they speak to the drugs squad about this new information. They may already have some information on this Garry Poyser, aka Jamie Hart. Contact the control room and let them know we'll be taking on the overdose investigation as well. I'll make sure I seize all the intubation equipment that was being used on the dead woman at Queen's Med, while I'm there.'

'Will do, boss.'

Danny got outside the flat and quickly ripped off the forensic suit before sprinting to his car. His mind was spinning with unanswered questions.

He knew the death of the woman would be treated as a murder enquiry and that it would be down to him and the MCIU to investigate it.

But what if it was Sandra Lorimar who had died?

What if Garry Poyser was the person who had supplied the ecstasy that had put her in harm's way?

Had Glen discovered who the dealer was and taken his own retribution?

50

12.30 p.m., 11 October 1990
Queen's Medical Centre, Nottingham

Danny felt breathless as he got out of the lift at the Queen's Medical Centre. He had jogged down the steps of the multistorey car park and through the hospital grounds, scanning the signs for the ICU.

In the distance, at the end of a long corridor, he could see Glen Lorimar and his wife sitting outside the main entrance to the Intensive Care Unit.

Glen had his arm around his wife and his back towards Danny. A chill ran through him as he approached the couple. He couldn't see their faces, so he couldn't gauge what was happening. He got to within ten yards of the couple before Glen turned to face him.

As soon as he saw Danny, Glen beamed a smile and said, 'It's good news, boss. The doctor's just been out to see us.

Sandra's awake and responding well to her treatment now. They're removing most of the tubes and lines, and he says we may be able to take her home tomorrow morning. They want to keep her in another twenty-four hours, for observations, just to be on the safe side.'

'That's brilliant news, Glen. Thank God.' Danny reached out and squeezed his friend's shoulder in affection and relief.

Glen patted Danny's hand, but his face took on a puzzled expression. 'Why are you here, boss?'

'A message was left at the MCIU informing us that one of the women being treated here for an overdose had died. They didn't identify the woman in the message.'

'And you thought it might be Sandra?'

'I didn't know what to think. I just knew I had to be here, either way.'

'The other woman passed away just before midnight. I was here when it happened; my wife had gone home to try to get some sleep. It was bedlam.'

'It's awful that she died.' Danny was thoughtful. 'But why bedlam?'

'The young woman is Stav Georgiou's daughter.'

'Stav from the Black Aces Casino?'

Glen nodded. 'He was here last night, crashing around the unit like a wounded bull. It got so bad I had to ask him to leave the unit and wait in the corridor. I don't think he recognised me; he was obviously wildly distraught over his daughter.'

'Was he here on his own?'

'No. There was a lot of people here with him. A woman I assumed was his wife, and a few big men who looked like security from the casino. They were becoming very intimidating towards the nurses; that's why I had to step in and say something.' Glen drew in a deep breath before continuing, 'Stav was bellowing at a couple of these big guys to get him an address. No, it wasn't an address, it was the address. He kept shouting, "Get me the address."'

'Anything else?'

'He shouted something about a heart, or her heart. Something like that. He wasn't making much sense; he was in such a state. I've got to be honest, if it were the other way round, I would probably have been similar.'

'Was Stav here all night?'

'No. He left his wife here with a couple of men, then shot off with another guy.'

'What time was this?'

'I'm not sure. Sometime after midnight, possibly around one o'clock. I know the nurses were relieved to see him go.'

The door to the ICU ward opened, and a nurse stepped outside. 'Mr and Mrs Lorimar, you can come in now. Sandra's awake and wants to see you both. She's still a little groggy, but she'll be fine.'

Danny shook Glen's hand and said, 'I'm so relieved for you, mate. And for you, Mrs Lorimar. Go now; your daughter needs you. Take as much time as you need.'

Glen returned the handshake. 'Thanks, boss.'

Danny spoke to the staff nurse in charge of the ICU, then walked to the security office, near the main entrance of the hospital. There was a telephone in that office that he knew the security staff would allow him to use.

He dialled the MCIU number and was relieved when it was answered on the second ring by Fran Jefferies.

'Fran,' he said, 'it's Danny. I need you to get in touch with DI Cartwright and ask her to attend the postmortem at the

City Hospital at three o'clock. I'm not going to get there. Is anybody else in the office?'

'There's only Phil and Sam here. Everyone else is at the crime scene in Carrington.'

'With my compliments, tell them both to attend the Queen's Medical Centre and take possession of the medical equipment used on the overdose patient who died last night. The surname of the deceased is Georgiou. I've already spoken to the staff on the ICU, and they know not to get rid of anything.'

'Will do, boss.'

'Lastly, contact Rob and Andy and ask them to meet me at the home of Stav Georgiou. We took a set of elimination prints from him at the casino, so we'll have his address in the system somewhere.'

'No problem, boss. I'll get it all sorted.'

51

2.00 p.m., 11 October 1990
Violet Road, Carlton, Nottingham

Danny had been updated on the car radio with the current address for Stav Georgiou. As he drove onto Violet Road at Carlton, he could see the CID car with Rob and Andy sitting inside.

He parked twenty yards behind them and walked to the passenger side. Rob wound down the window and said, 'That's Stav's address, the dormer bungalow with the blue front door. I've done a PNC check on the Sierra parked on the drive. It's registered to Stavros Georgiou.'

'Has Tina updated you about what's been recovered at the Carrington murder scene?'

Rob nodded. 'We got the message about the MDMA found there and that the victim has been tentatively identified as Garry Poyser, whom Northumbria police want to speak to about another fatal ecstasy overdose.'

'I've just come from the Queen's Medical Centre. I've spoken to Glen there, and he's given me information that could be significant. You'll be pleased to hear that his daughter is now expected to make a full recovery. However, as you know, a young woman died on the ICU last night as a direct result of taking ecstasy.'

'That's great news about Glen's daughter.' Rob nodded, genuinely relieved. 'But what information?'

'The reason I've asked you to meet me here is because the young woman who died last night was Stav Georgiou's daughter. Glen told me Stav was at the hospital last night, demanding that his men fetch an address. He also mentioned the word "heart".'

'So what's the connection between Poyser and Georgiou?'

'The woman who called the police to the murder scene at Carrington, Rebecca Marney, identified the victim as Jamie Hart, not Garry Poyser. I think it's possible that Georgiou knew who had supplied the ecstasy that killed his daughter.' Danny paused before continuing, 'There's something I need to check at the Black Aces before we detain Georgiou. I'm hoping it doesn't take too long.'

'What do we do if Georgiou looks like he's on the move?'

'You'll have to improvise,' Danny instructed his officers. 'We haven't enough to arrest him; just don't let him out of your sight until you hear from me. Keep your radio to hand. I won't be long.'

52

2.30 p.m., 11 October 1990
Black Aces Casino, Hockley, Nottingham

As Danny was shown into Toni Pappas's office, the casino owner was slipping on his overcoat. He said, 'I was just leaving, Detective. I have urgent family business to attend to; my godson's family needs me. Can't this wait, whatever it is?'

'I'm sorry to hear that. Is something wrong?'

'It's family business, nothing to concern the police.'

'I promise I won't keep you a minute longer than necessary. I understand family comes first.' Danny paused. 'But I urgently need a list of all the clients who are in debt to the casino.'

'I'm sorry, Stav's not here right now. He deals with all matters concerning debts.'

'This is urgent, or I wouldn't have called in person. I need that list.'

Danny said the last part of his sentence in a tone that left Pappas in no doubt he wasn't leaving without the list.

'Very well.' Pappas tutted under his breath. 'Just a minute.'

He walked to the door of the office and started barking orders. Within a minute the giant, Theo, arrived carrying a sheet of A4 paper, which he passed to Pappas.

Pappas in turn thrust the paper towards Danny and said, 'These are the names and addresses of everyone who's currently in debt to the casino. The amount owed is not on there. Do you need that too?'

'Names and addresses will be fine for now, Toni. I don't want to delay you seeing your family. Are you sure there's nothing I can help you with?'

The casino owner looked away and said in a sombre voice, 'It's a family bereavement. There's nothing you can do, Detective.'

Danny held up the paper and said, 'I'm sorry to hear that. Thanks for taking the time to get me this.'

'This way, Detective. I'll show you out.'

As Danny walked back to his car, he quickly scanned the list. He started the car engine and picked up the radio. 'DCI Flint to DI Buxton. Over.'

Rob Buxton had been waiting patiently for the radio message and answered immediately, 'Go ahead. Over.'

'Is Stav still at the house? Over.'

'He's still here. He came out to the car once, then went straight back inside. Over.'

'Excellent. I want you to get uniform to back you up at

your location, then arrest Stav Georgiou on suspicion of the murder of Garry Poyser. Over.'

'Have you got the evidence you wanted from the casino? Over.'

'Jamie Hart of 7 Berkely Court, Carrington, owes money to Black Aces. I think Stav has somehow found out that Jamie Hart, aka Garry Poyser, was dealing the ecstasy that put his daughter in hospital. Stav must have recalled that Jamie Hart was also on the casino's list of debtors. That was the address he was yelling for at the hospital. Over.'

'Received. Over.'

'One other thing, Rob. I think Toni Pappas is on his way to your location. No doubt he'll arrive with a bunch of heavies, so make sure you get sufficient backup there before you attempt to arrest Stav. Over.'

'Andy's already got the local uniform travelling to us. Over.'

'Good work. Get him detained; then take him to Mansfield. I'll see you there. Over.'

53

4.30 p.m., 11 October 1990
MCIU Offices, Mansfield, Nottinghamshire

Danny was in his office with the scenes of crime supervisor, Tim Donnelly, about to discuss any forensic opportunities from the Berkely Court murder scene.

There was a knock on the door, and Tina Cartwright walked in.

She said, 'Fran said you wanted to see me as soon as I got back from the postmortem.'

Danny said, 'How did it go at the mortuary?'

'No great surprises. The cause of death was stabbing. All the wounds are of a similar size. It looks like a very slim blade was used; the pathologist suggested either a flick knife or a stiletto blade.'

'Did the pathologist suggest any other theories?'

'Only that she felt it was quite a frenzied attack. There were twenty-seven stab wounds in all, four of which pierced Poyser's heart. She felt the attacker is probably right-handed, as most of the stab wounds are on the left side of the victim's chest.'

'Any defence wounds?'

'None at all. Which could mean that Poyser was probably taken by surprise when he was attacked.'

'When will we get the pathologist's full report?'

'She was hoping to get it to us tomorrow or at the latest the day after.'

'Good work, Tina. Sorry I couldn't make it back in time myself.'

Danny paused, then said to Tim Donnelly, 'Have you found any fingerprints at the scene, other than the one on the doorbell?'

'The only marks that have been found in the living room and the hallway are glove marks. We've lifted fingerprints from both the bedrooms, the bathroom and the kitchen. Now that I've obtained a full set of prints from the deceased, as well a set of elimination prints from Rebecca Marney, we'll soon know if we have any unidentified fingerprints. I can tell you that the fingerprint recovered from the doorbell doesn't come from Rebecca Marney or the deceased.'

'That's fast work, Tim. Well done. Talking of Rebecca Marney, any update on her statement?'

'Jag and Jeff are still with her,' Tina replied. 'When she was shown the bag of MDMA tablets, she couldn't stop talking. She maintains she had absolutely no idea that Jamie was dealing. She can prove that she's been in Norwich since the end of April. Interestingly, it was about a month later that the drugs squad noticed a rise in incidents of ecstasy overdoses. It could be Poyser has taken advantage of her absence to start dealing.'

'Could be. What does she say about the false name used by Poyser?'

'Again, she had no idea of his real name. He told her, when they first met, that his name was Jamie Hart. She claims she had no idea his true identity was Garry Poyser.'

'Do Jag or Jeff have any concerns over her account?'

'Not that they've mentioned to me. They're taking a witness statement from her, which suggests they're happy with the account she's given so far.'

'Okay. I want to see her witness statement as soon as possible. I also want all the paperwork from the fatal ecstasy overdose in Newcastle. The one Poyser was circulated for on the PNC. Try to contact the appropriate officer, and let's get some liaison going.'

'Will do, boss.'

'Tim, anything else from the scene?'

'Yes. There's one significant finding. In the living room, we recovered a cloth bag that contained three thousand pounds in various denomination banknotes.'

'Whereabouts in the living room?'

'On the floor beneath one of the two sofas.'

'And the killer just left it there?'

'He may not have intended to leave it. Maybe he couldn't find it.'

'Was it hard to find?'

'Not really. Obviously, we photographed it in situ, but to me it looked like it had been dropped and just fell under the sofa.'

'That seems slightly unusual,' Danny said. 'So when will the photo album be ready?'

'You'll have that tomorrow morning, sir.'

'Good. Any sign of the murder weapon at the scene?'

'No. And we've also searched the grounds of the flats.' Tim added, 'Plus, we've checked every drain for a one-hundred-yard radius.'

'Anything else?'

'Just to repeat what was said earlier, there was a hell of a lot of blood at the scene. I'd be amazed if the killer wasn't heavily bloodstained.'

Danny looked at Tina. 'With that thought in mind, have the door-to-door enquiries turned up any witnesses?'

'Nothing. Do you want me to extend the parameters for the house to house?'

'Yes, please. Extend the cordon to five hundred yards.'

Tina nodded. 'I'll grab a map and see how many streets that takes in. We may need the assistance of the Special Operations Unit on a house-to-house of that size.'

'I'll put a call into Special Ops and see what availability they have this week. Has there been any update from Rob on the arrest of Stav Georgiou?'

'There's been nothing on the radio.'

'We already have a set of elimination prints for Stav Georgiou,' Tim added. 'Do you want me to arrange a comparison against the lift found on the doorbell?'

'As soon as you can, please, Tim. Stav was seen leaving the hospital with a second man, whom we still need to identify.' He looked at them both, then said, 'Good work today. I know you didn't have a lot of staff to work that scene, but you've done a cracking job.'

Tina turned as she was leaving the office and asked, almost as an afterthought, 'Any update from Rachel and Jane in London?'

'Rachel did contact me to say the enquiries down there could take another couple of days. I've authorised their expenses to stay over. It's pointless them driving up and down the motorway, and I'd rather they just completed what they need to do down there.'

54

5.30 p.m., 11 October 1990
MCIU Offices, Mansfield, Nottinghamshire

Danny walked into the main briefing room, seeking out Tina Cartwright. 'I've just come off the phone to Chief Inspector Chambers at Special Ops,' he said. 'He's providing us with a full section of officers, for the next three days, to try to bottom out the house-to-house enquiries in Carrington. How big a job is the area I suggested?'

'It will be a big job,' Tina replied. 'There's a lot of flats in old three-storey buildings in that area. We'll be lucky to be anywhere near completion after just three days.'

'I want you to master the area this evening so you can brief Sergeant Turner tomorrow morning. His section will be on scene at Carrington, at eight o'clock, for a full briefing.

I've arranged for the mobile police station to be in the car park at the rear of Berkely Court tonight. Local officers will staff it overnight, and then Fran will take over at seven o'clock tomorrow morning. You never know, we could get a few walk-ins from members of the public with information. Sergeant Turner will also use it as his base for the house-to-house enquiries.'

'I'll take Fran with me now; she can help with the mastering this evening.'

Danny nodded and was about to go back to his office when Rob and Andy walked into the briefing room.

Rob said, 'Stav's locked up downstairs. I've got uniformed officers searching his house for any likely weapons or bloodstained clothing. I do feel for them; they're getting a ton of grief at the house.'

'Is it contained?'

'There's enough of them there to maintain control, but it's a tense situation.'

'Have you arranged for Georgiou's car to be brought in?'

'Vehicle examiners are in the process of carrying out a full lift of the vehicle,' Andy said, 'and I've already arranged for it to be taken to the forensic bay at HQ. Tim's aware that it will be arriving this evening.'

'Did Toni Pappas turn up at the house?'

Rob nodded. 'That's why it's so volatile,' he said. 'He turned up with Georgiou's wife just as we were putting Stav into our car. Then a car full of the casino's security staff also turned up.'

'What was Pappas's reaction?'

'He was raging that we'd got Stav in handcuffs. He was demanding we release him so he could be with his wife to comfort her over their daughter's death.' Rob looked a little awkward as he went on. 'When I told him that Stav was under arrest on suspicion of murder and wasn't going anywhere, Pappas went mad. I genuinely thought it was going to get very nasty at that point. That's why it's taken us a little longer to get back here and get Stav booked in. I had to try to quieten Pappas and his goons down before we left. He was going crazy, and his security staff were swaggering about, trying to intimidate the uniformed cops who were there.'

'What happened?' Danny asked, concerned at how knife-edge the whole scenario sounded.

'Eventually, everyone calmed down, and I felt it was okay to leave the cops to search the property.'

'Good job.' Danny nodded his approval, and relief. 'Did Georgiou say anything when you arrested him?'

'He said we were wrong, but mostly he was muttering about his daughter.'

'Understandable. Did he talk to you on the way back to the station?'

'Not a word. I've got to be honest, boss. Stav Georgiou looks awful. This business with his daughter has completely broken him. There was no anger when we arrested him, just a weary air of detachment. It's as though he's shutting himself off from what's happening around him. The only rage or resistance we encountered was from Toni Pappas and his heavies.'

'Does Georgiou want a solicitor?'

Rob nodded. 'Yes, and Toni Pappas gave him a card for a London firm to represent him during any interviews.'

'Will that delay any interviews?'

'The legal firm have been contacted. They said they can be here between eight and eight thirty, so not too long.'

'Okay. In the absence of Glen Lorimar, I'll be interviewing Georgiou with you,' Danny instructed. 'Now, let's use those hours to put an interview plan together.'

55

9.00 p.m., 3 September 1990
Clifford Towers, Ainger Road, Camden, London

Kingston Jones stared out the window of his first-floor flat. The street below looked dark and cold, and the streetlights were already on. The rain hammering against the sash window didn't help his general feeling of melancholy.

The very thought of working on another Guy Royal book filled him with despondency. Even though he'd agreed to do it in such a way that meant he would have no personal contact with the former television star, he still had an overwhelming sense of being trapped and forced into doing something he didn't want to.

His thoughts turned to New York, and he started wondering what he would be doing if he'd been in the Big Apple tonight instead of a gloomy, rain-soaked London.

He sat down on the sofa next to the telephone. He was about

to pick it up to call his only friend in the city, Janice Millership, when it started to ring.

He snatched up the handset and said, 'Kingston Jones.'

'Kingston,' a man with a strong New York accent said, 'you don't know me, but we have a mutual friend, Ralph Hooper.'

There was something about the tone of the mystery man's voice that filled him with an icy dread. Hardly daring to ask the question, Kingston said, 'Is Ralph okay?'

There was a long pause, and he could hear the man's breath down the phone.

'No, Kingston. Ralph's not okay. I'm sorry to have to tell you like this, but Ralph's dead.'

Kingston was stunned into silence.

The caller continued, 'Ralph passed away at the Cherry Tree Hospice, here in New York, yesterday evening. I've been trying to trace you ever since.'

Kingston finally found his voice and blurted out, 'Who the hell are you?'

'It doesn't matter who I am. I was a good friend of Ralph's, and I was with him at the end. Ralph truly loved you, Kingston. His dying wish was for me to contact you and apologise on his behalf for the way he treated you.'

Hearing this stranger speak so fondly, almost lovingly, about the one man he had ever truly loved turned Kingston's shock into a mixture of anger and frustration. Anger because he couldn't understand why Ralph had thrown him out if he truly loved him, and frustration because he hadn't been in New York by his side when he died.

With all that emotion in his voice, he growled through gritted teeth, 'If Ralph loved me so much, why the hell did he throw me out like yesterday's trash?'

'I understand this is all too much for you to take in right now.

But what you need to understand is that when Ralph acted the way he did, he was already sick. He knew he was ill and couldn't face telling you.'

'What do you mean sick? What was it, cancer? Is that why he was in the hospice?'

'It wasn't cancer.' There was another long pause before the stranger continued, 'Two months before he asked you to leave, Ralph was diagnosed as HIV positive.'

A cold chill ran the entire length of Kingston's body as he tried to process what he'd just been told. A lot of things started to make sense now. Why he'd been experiencing endless uncomfortable night sweats, weight loss and continuous sore throats. His hand shot to his neck, and he could feel how swollen his lymph nodes were. Tears formed in his eyes.

He blinked hard and felt those tears roll down his cheeks as he said, 'Are you telling me Ralph died from AIDS?'

The voice on the line remained silent for a long time before saying, 'I don't know how intimate you guys were before you split up, but I think for your own peace of mind, you should get tested as soon as you can, Kingston.'

Kingston allowed time for the stranger's last comment to sink in and then said quietly, 'How was his passing?'

'I've been with him over the weeks. Ralph fought so hard, for so long. He was in dreadful pain at the end, but the doctors couldn't provide him with any more morphine. It would have risked him dying from an overdose. In the end his heart couldn't take any more.' The man's voice, so steady until now, started to break. 'His heart, Kingston, it just gave out.'

But Kingston couldn't stand to hear another word. He terminated the call.

Any thoughts of Guy Royal, Stan Jennings or Seymour Hart-Wilson had now vanished.

He sat alone in the darkness of his flat.

He sat alone, fearful of the darkness of his own future.

The noise of the rain outside was now matched by the sound of his own desperate, anguished crying as Kingston mourned the loss of the only man he ever truly loved.

56

7.00 p.m., 5 September 1990
Clifford Towers, Ainger Road, Camden, London

Kingston Jones sat alone in his flat. *The curtains were closed, and the only light came from a standard lamp in the corner of the room.*

The only sound came from the overloud mechanism of the ornate wall clock positioned above the gas fire.

Just four hours ago, he had been given the devastating news at the nearby hospital.

Not only was he HIV positive but he'd already developed full-blown AIDS. The medical staff had been compassionate and expert; they had offered prescriptions for several drugs they hoped would slow the progress of the disease.

His mind numb, Kingston had accepted the drugs and all the leaflets offering advice on the best way to manage his condition. Everyone, including Kingston himself, knew there was nothing that could be done to stop the disease, and that the outcome was as inevitable as it was terminal. The only unknown was the precise time when death would come calling.

After sitting quietly in his flat for an hour, he had made the decision that he wasn't prepared to suffer in the same way his lover had suffered.

With that personal clarification, his mind became clearer, and he felt the need to explain his actions to someone. He sat down and wrote a letter to his only friend in this city, Janice Millership. He wished her every success with her writing. He expressed his hope that she would hear something positive from one of the many publishers he'd posted the manuscript of her first novel to. In the letter he offered the prospect of working with Guy Royal, and how trapped he felt by Seymour Hart-Wilson, as his reasons for ending things in the way he had chosen to.

Even in his moment of deepest despair, his troubled mind wouldn't allow him to declare, in writing, his true sexuality. Being a homosexual man was ultimately what would cost him his life, but even now at the end of that life, he felt this was nobody's business but his own.

Having finished the handwritten letter, he walked from his flat to the nearby High Street, where he purchased a single box of thirty-two paracetamol tablets from three different shops. He then dropped the letter for Janice in a red post box before buying a bottle of his favourite Californian Merlot from the local off-licence.

Alone now in his flat, he pulled the cork from the wine bottle and poured three large glasses of the red liquid. He lined the glasses up in a row on the coffee table in front of the sofa. The full glasses stood like crimson sentries, towering above row upon row of white paracetamol tablets.

He put his favourite CD into the player and sat down on the sofa as the music of the O'Jays played softly in the background.

He made himself comfortable and popped the first tablet into his mouth. Having placed the single pill on his tongue, he took a sip of the red wine and swallowed.

Tears filled his eyes as he robotically repeated the process.

A tablet, a sip of wine, swallow...

A tablet, a sip of wine, swallow...

A tablet, a sip of wine, swallow...

57

7.00 p.m., 11 October 1990
Flat 52, Jacqueline House, Fitzroy Road, Camden, London

The lift in the block of flats was out of order, and climbing the concrete steps had left Rachel and Jane slightly breathless. They scanned the numbers of the doors on the fifth floor until they found number fifty-two.

Rachel knocked loudly and waited.

After a moment the door was opened by a slim, middle-aged woman with short brown hair. She looked as though she'd been asleep, her hair was unbrushed, and the plain dress she wore was creased.

Rachel held out her identification and said, 'I'm Detective Sergeant Moore, and this is DC Pope. I'm looking for Janice Millership?'

Rubbing sleep from her eyes, the woman looked at the identification and then said, 'That's me. How can I help you?'

Rachel said, 'We'd like to ask you a few questions about the work you did on the books written by Guy Royal. May we come in, please?'

'Of course. I've just got back from visiting my parents, so you'll have to excuse the mess.'

As they walked through the small one-bedroom flat to the living room, Rachel was shocked at just how untidy the place was. It was far more than a couple of days' worth of neglect. Obviously, housework wasn't high on Janice Millership's list of priorities.

The two detectives sat down on the settee opposite Millership, who occupied the single armchair. There was no offer of a drink or any small talk from Millership, so Rachel simply said, 'I understand you recently worked at Bouldstone Press?'

'Until a couple of days ago, I did. I couldn't stand working there any longer; there's such a toxic atmosphere around the place.'

'Toxic?'

'It's just not the same since Kingston left.'

'I believe you worked with Kingston Jones on the Guy Royal books,' Jane said. 'Is that right?'

'I wouldn't put it quite like that. It was Kingston who did all the work. I was his PA, that's all.'

'And what did being his PA entail?'

'Kingston didn't drive, so I'd drive him to any meetings he had outside London. I would make shorthand notes of those meetings and then type up the completed manuscripts.'

'And what was Kingston Jones like to work for?'

Janice's eyes took on a dreamy look as she gazed across at the two police officers. 'Kingston was a wonderful man,' she said. 'Kind, considerate, charming and handsome. He was a beautiful human being. I still can't quite believe what happened to him.'

'We've been told he took his own life, which is always very sad.'

'Especially so,' Janice said, an edge to her voice now, 'if you've been driven to it by other people.'

'That's a strong accusation,' Rachel said. 'Exactly what do you mean, driven to it?'

'That wonderful man was being forced to work with Guy Royal on a new series of books. Kingston loathed the man. I believe that's what drove him to do what he did.' She paused before continuing, 'I've left Bouldstone Press now, so I'm not bothered about talking out of turn.'

'Why did Jones dislike Guy Royal so much?'

'I witnessed first-hand how Royal abused that lovely, generous man, making his life a misery and getting him fired from the job he adored.'

'That can't be right,' Rachel interrupted. 'I thought Kingston Jones was still working on Royal's books. Why do you say he was fired?'

'He was fired after Royal demanded that Seymour Hart-Wilson sack him. All because they'd had words over the content of the first novel in his proposed trilogy. Kingston tried so hard to make that book decent, but Royal refused his advice and rejected all the rewrites Kingston worked so diligently on.'

'If Kingston was sacked, how come Hart-Wilson never told us?'

'Probably because the sly old bastard didn't want to

mention how he'd tricked Kingston into working on the next two Royal projects, just to try to make them decent after the first one bombed.'

'And you say Kingston wasn't happy about that. How do you know that? Did he tell you himself?'

'Yes, he did.'

'When was the last time you spoke to Kingston?'

'The day before he did what he did. He explained everything to me.'

'You physically spoke to him the day before he took his own life?'

There was a long pause before Millership replied, 'Yes.'

'Did you have any idea what he intended to do?'

'I knew he was extremely depressed with his situation and that he felt trapped, but I had no idea he was contemplating suicide. If I'd known he was that depressed, I would have gone to him. I adored him and would have done anything for him.'

'Of course,' Jane murmured before she said, 'Have you ever been to Guy Royal's house?'

'Several times. I always had to drive Kingston to meet Royal there, as that odious little man refused to come to London.'

'And after Kingston took his own life, were you interviewed by the police?'

'Yes, but I was still working for Bouldstone then, so I didn't feel able to tell them about the work situation.'

'Can you remember the name of the officer who talked to you?'

'No, sorry. I did go to the inquest, but I wasn't called as a witness. When I heard the coroner say it was suicide, I cried for two days afterwards.'

'We are sorry, truly, for your loss,' Rachel said. 'You've been really helpful, Janice, thank you. Is there anything else you think we should know?'

She shook her head, then said, 'Only that Guy Royal and Seymour Hart-Wilson have Kingston's blood on their hands. They're directly responsible for pushing that beautiful man to his death.'

58

8.00 p.m., 11 October 1990
Royal National Hotel, Bedford Way, London

Rachel Moore found a payphone in the hotel lobby and dialled the number for the MCIU office. Fran Jefferies answered the call and put Rachel straight through to Danny's office.

Danny said, 'How are your enquiries going?'

'We talked to several other employees at Bouldstone today, who confirmed what Hart-Wilson told us yesterday. It was obviously in the interest of everyone employed at Bouldstone for Guy Royal to fulfil the contract he had signed. Reading between the lines, it appears the non-returnable advance paid to Royal for the three-book deal has put a massive financial strain on the company, especially as there's now no chance of achieving any sales against that advance.'

'So with Royal dead, it will be Stan Jennings who stands

to gain massively from his death – in this respect, too. Everything keeps pointing back towards Jennings. Do you know who negotiated this deal?'

'The contract was agreed between Seymour Hart-Wilson, the CEO at Bouldstone, and Stan Jennings.'

'Did Hart-Wilson say anything else about the contract?'

'Only that his lawyers had tried to find a way to claw back some of the money, and failed. He also said it was highly unusual to pay such an advance, but he was worried that another publishing house could snatch Royal from under their noses.'

'I bet he wishes they had now.' There was a pause, and then Danny asked, 'Who worked on the books with Royal?'

'Bouldstone employed an American ghost writer, Kingston Jones, to write the first two autobiographies. From what we've heard so far, it seems there was a lot of animosity between Guy Royal and this American.'

'Have we got to look at Kingston Jones as a viable suspect?'

'No, sir. Kingston Jones took his own life before Royal was murdered.'

'How awful,' Danny said, the shock clear in his voice. 'Have you managed to speak to anyone else who had dealings with Royal?'

'We saw Jones's PA today, Janice Millership. She gave us some insights into the inner workings of Bouldstone Press and how much animosity there was between Jones and Royal. She also gave us some interesting information on the reasons behind Jones's suicide. We've arranged to speak with the police officer who prepared the inquest file tomorrow morning. I want to see how the official line compares to what we were told by Millership. I thought we might as well be thorough while we're down here.'

'I agree. Do what you think needs to be done. If it means another night, so be it. I hope you've found a half-decent place to stay?'

'Well, Jane insisted on the Hilton, but we've settled on the Royal National Hotel. It's not five star by any means, but it's comfortable, and the cooked breakfast is great.'

'Don't get used to it.' Danny chuckled. 'Hopefully, I'll see you back here sometime tomorrow.'

59

9.00 p.m., 11 October 1990
Mansfield Police Station, Nottinghamshire

Rob introduced everyone present in the interview room and reminded Stav Georgiou that he was still under caution.

As soon as Rob had finished speaking, Georgiou's solicitor said, 'I have instructed my client not to answer any of your questions at this time, Detective.'

'No problem,' Rob said. 'I still intend to ask him my questions.'

He looked directly at Georgiou and said, 'You've been arrested on suspicion of the murder of Jamie Hart. Are you responsible for the death of Jamie Hart?'

Georgiou looked up briefly and made eye contact before looking back down at the desk and mumbling, 'No comment.'

'Are you aware Jamie Hart's home address was number seven Berkely Court in Carrington?'

Georgiou stared at the desktop, never once looking up as he answered, 'No comment.'

'Have you ever visited that address?'

'No comment.'

'Have you ever been inside that address?'

'No comment.'

'Have you ever seen Jamie Hart at the Black Aces Casino?'

'No comment.'

'What is your role at the casino?'

'No comment.'

'Are you responsible for managing clients who owe the casino money?'

'No comment.'

'Have you ever used force to recoup a debt?'

Georgiou's solicitor intervened. 'I don't see the relevance of this line of questioning.'

Rob said, 'We're aware Jamie Hart was in debt to the casino. We believe it's your client's job to recover debts from clients who owe money to the casino. That's the relevance.' Rob paused, then repeated his question. 'Have you ever used force to recover money owed to the casino?'

'No comment.'

'Have you ever instructed anybody else to use force to recover such a debt?'

'No comment.'

'Tell me about your daughter, Androulla?'

Georgiou didn't say a word, but he looked up slowly, and Rob could see the anger and hatred in his eyes.

He maintained eye contact with Georgiou and said again, 'Tell me about your daughter?'

Once again, the solicitor intervened. 'Really, Detective. This is not on. You're fully aware what's happened to my client's daughter. If you persist in trying to goad my client, I'll have no choice but to call a halt to this interview.'

Danny spoke directly to Georgiou. 'We have evidence that Jamie Hart owed money to the casino and that you knew his home address. We also suspect that Hart was responsible for dealing ecstasy at nightclubs and pubs in the city centre. When did you find out Hart was dealing ecstasy?'

With an element of surprise registering in Georgiou's eyes, he stared at Danny and muttered, 'No comment.'

Danny pressed, 'Do you blame Jamie Hart for Androulla's death?'

There was a long silence; then Georgiou twisted his chair around until his broad back faced Danny.

The solicitor said, 'I think my client's actions make it clear that he's not prepared to answer any more of your questions. I think we should end the interview. I would deem it oppressive if you carry on at this time, and will register a complaint accordingly.'

Danny nodded and said, 'I'm prepared to stop the interview for now, but we will be speaking to your client again.'

In the chair, Georgiou silently rocked back and forth.

60

1.00 a.m., 12 October 1990
Mansfield, Nottinghamshire

Danny was wide awake. He tossed and turned in bed until, finally giving in to the fact that sleep was never going to come, he sat up.

Sue flicked on her bedside lamp, sat up and said, 'What's wrong? You've been fidgeting about ever since we came to bed.'

'I don't really know,' Danny said. 'Something's bothering me from work today, that's all.'

'Why? What's happened?'

'Rob and I questioned a man about a murder. This man has just lost his teenage daughter to a bad reaction to MDMA.'

'The same drug that hospitalised Glen Lorimar's daughter?'

'We believe so, yes. Anyway, during the interview, I heard myself using that young woman's death to try to persuade her father to admit killing the man we suspect of supplying the ecstasy that caused his daughter's death. What I was doing felt totally wrong.'

Sue remained silent, knowing her husband wanted to say more.

After a long pause, Danny continued, 'I know I've got a job to do, but I felt ashamed after the interview. I was going to say something to Rob about it, but thought better of it.'

Sue was thoughtful, then said, 'Do you think you felt that way because you have a daughter yourself, and you were putting yourself in the suspect's shoes?'

'What do you mean?'

'Wondering, as a father, what you would be prepared to do if you knew the man responsible for killing your daughter. Asking yourself how you would have reacted?'

'It's possible.'

'Were you asking yourself if you'd be prepared to take the law into your own hands?'

'I can't answer that.' Danny shrugged. 'I'd like to think I wouldn't, and that I'd let the law seek justice for me. But, honestly, who knows?'

'Maybe you should take yourself out of the interview room if you feel that conflicted. It's obviously bothering you if you can't sleep for thinking about it.'

'I'm not going to lie; it does bother me. Part of the reason is the demeanour of the suspect. He appears to be completely broken by what's happened. Today, he turned his chair around so he didn't have to look at me as I questioned him. It was something I've never encountered in the interview room before.'

'Surely, you've got to be guided by the evidence. What's that telling you?'

'Any evidence we have is circumstantial at best. Yes, he has a strong motive, the death of his daughter, and he had the opportunity. But I'm still not convinced he did the killing.'

'It's tough, Danny.' Sue tilted her head to one side, her eyes full of sympathy. 'I don't know what else to suggest to you.'

'The whole situation is complicated by the fact that Guy Royal was also in debt to the same casino and has also met a violent death.'

'Do you think the two murders could be connected?'

'I don't know. Royal was shot, and the other man stabbed. Different methods but both extreme violence. I intend to question him about Royal's death today.'

Danny reached for his dressing gown before continuing, 'Hopefully, things will become a little clearer this morning. I'm going to get a coffee. Do you want one?'

Sue flicked off the bedside lamp. 'No, thanks. I need to get some sleep; I've got a busy day tomorrow. Don't be up all night, sweetheart. You look exhausted.'

'I won't.' Danny leaned over and kissed his wife. 'Thanks for listening.'

61

7.30 a.m., 12 October 1990
MCIU Offices, Mansfield, Nottinghamshire

As Danny draped his suit jacket over the back of his chair, there was an urgent knocking on his office door.

He shouted, 'Come in!'

The door opened, and Danny was surprised to see Tim Donnelly walk in. 'Good morning, Tim. What brings you in so early?'

With a grave expression on his face, the scenes of crime supervisor said, 'I've got bad news, boss.'

'Go on.'

'We worked late on the forensic samples we took from the Carrington scene. All the marks we found inside the property relate to either Garry Poyser or Rebecca Marney.'

'I half expected that would be the case.'

'That's not the bad news.'

Danny remained silent, waiting for the scenes of crime supervisor to carry on.

Tim said, 'You've got Stav Georgiou in a cell downstairs, and the mark we lifted from the doorbell isn't a match for him.'

'Are you certain?'

'Unfortunately, yes. I double-checked the result late last night against the elimination prints we had. The fingerprint isn't his.'

'And we already know it isn't a match for Poyser or Marney.'

Tim shook his head. 'That's right.'

'Are you doing a general check now?'

'Yes. But without a suspect, that could take forever.'

Before Danny could respond, the telephone on his desk began to ring. He snatched it up. 'DCI Flint.'

'Sergeant Carr at the front desk, sir. I've got a Toni Pappas here, wanting to speak to you. He said it's urgent and that he won't talk to anybody else.'

Danny was thoughtful for a few seconds; then he said, 'Put him in one of the interview rooms, get him a drink if he wants one, and I'll be down in the next five minutes. Thanks, Sarge.'

Danny turned to Tim. 'Well, this day is full of surprises, so far. Anything else you need to tell me about the Carrington scene?'

'We're still working on other samples. We lifted fibres and tapings from the deceased's clothes, but any results from them will take a bit longer, as we've had to submit them to the Forensic Science Service.'

'Have you started the examination of Georgiou's car yet?'

'That's being done later this morning.'

Danny grabbed his jacket off the chair and said, 'Thanks for coming in to let me know. I'll call you later to see if you've any further updates.'

'No problem, boss.'

Danny followed the scenes of crime supervisor and was pleased to see Rob Buxton already in the main briefing room. He said, 'Don't take your jacket off, Rob. Toni Pappas has come in wanting to speak urgently with me. I need you to come with me and hear what he's got to say.'

Rob took one last sip of his coffee and said, 'Ready when you are.'

62

8.00 a.m., 12 October 1990
Mansfield Police Station, Nottinghamshire

Toni Pappas stared across the desk at the two detectives; then he made eye contact with Danny and, in a voice barely more than a whisper, said, 'You've arrested the wrong man, Detective. My godson didn't kill that drug-dealing scumbag.'

Danny had been expecting this to be the reason Pappas wanted to see him so urgently. He said, 'You're bound to think that. If Georgiou's so innocent, why doesn't he answer our questions?'

Pappas tutted. 'Because the man is grieving the death of his only child. He shouldn't be in one of your cells.'

'I have a witness who heard Georgiou demanding an address and repeating the word "heart". I believe the address he was demanding was the home address of Jamie Hart.'

Pappas shook his head. 'You are wrong, Detective.'

Danny said, 'When did Georgiou realise it was Hart who had supplied the ecstasy that killed his daughter?'

'From the moment Androulla was rushed into the hospital, I've had my men out on the street, asking questions. I think we both understand that my men's style of questioning is different to your detectives'.'

Danny nodded. 'When did your men discover who was supplying the ecstasy?'

'A doorman at the Manhattan told one of my men about another bouncer he'd seen pushing pills at the nightclub.'

'At the Manhattan?'

'Yes. That was the nightclub Androulla had been dancing in before she became ill.'

'And did this bouncer give up the name of his colleague to your men?'

Pappas allowed himself a grim smile. 'What do you think, Detective? When Stav was told the name Jamie Hart at the hospital, he knew the same guy was on the debtors' list at the casino.'

'How?'

'Detective, you've seen first-hand how Stav's memory works. The only thing he didn't know was Hart's address. That's the address he was demanding at the hospital. I'm sure you'll have seen Jamie Hart's name and address on the list I gave you at the casino.'

'None of this proves Georgiou's innocence or suggests he played no part in the murder of Jamie Hart,' Danny said firmly. 'If anything, what you've just told me is damning evidence against him. Especially when I've a witness who saw Georgiou leave the hospital in a wild rage, accompanied by another man.'

Pappas let out a long sigh and said, 'I can give you the killer.'

'What did you say?'

'Release my godson, and I will give you the killer. Stav needs to be at home with his wife, not in a prison cell.'

Danny leaned forward, placing both elbows on the desk. 'No deals,' he said in a clipped tone. 'Tell me everything you know, or this conversation is over.'

Pappas sat in silence for a few moments before starting to talk once more. 'The man who left the hospital with Stav that night was his best friend, Andreas Ersoy. Both men grew up in the same village in Cyprus and have been friends since they were small boys. Stav got Andreas his job on the security team at the casino so he could provide a comfortable life for his wife and family back in Cyprus. Andreas believes he's in debt to Stav.'

'Are you telling me Andreas Ersoy killed Jamie Hart?'

'Patience, Detective. When the two men left the hospital, Stav broke down. He was crying uncontrollably, in a really bad way, so Andreas took him home. He helped to clean his friend up, then put him to bed, promising he would personally take care of Hart. He left Stav sleeping in his own bed.'

Rob now spoke for the first time. 'I can't believe Stav didn't go with Ersoy to deal with Hart. It was his only child in the hospital, not Ersoy's.'

Pappas stared at Danny and said, 'Have you spoken to Stav, Detective?'

Danny replied, 'Yes, we both have.'

'Do you think he looks right? I'm telling you this whole thing has affected him badly. He's a broken man.'

Danny was thoughtful, recalling the interview he'd had with Georgiou. He remembered the vacant look in the man's eyes. The misgivings he'd felt immediately afterwards. He also thought of his conversation with Sue the previous night, recalling his own instincts and feelings on whether Georgiou was capable of murder.

He said, 'How do you know all this, Toni? Have you spoken to Ersoy?'

'Andreas has confided in Theo at the casino what happened that night, and Theo has told me.'

'Where is Andreas Ersoy now?'

'He is with Theo at the casino. I didn't want him to disappear on the next flight to Paphos.'

'Will Theo make a statement about his conversation with Ersoy?'

'Theo will do whatever I ask him to do.'

'We'll talk to Ersoy and see what he has to say.'

'And Stav can come home with me?' Pappas pressed.

'Stav is going nowhere until I know exactly what happened that night at Hart's flat. There's the added complication of Guy Royal's death. Also in debt to your casino, also on that list, and also murdered. You can either wait here or go and be with Stav's wife.'

'Stav had nothing to do with Royal's death,' Pappas said with a surge of anger in his voice now. 'That murder has nothing to do with my casino. We're not gangsters. I need people to pay their debts. I don't need to kill or maim them so they can't. I'm a businessman.'

Danny nodded, but still he insisted, 'We'll talk to Ersoy before we decide any course of action.'

Pappas clearly wasn't happy, but he shrugged and said, 'I'll wait at my godson's house. I'll call the casino and tell Theo you're coming, and that he's to co-operate with you.'

'Is that wise?' Rob asked. 'Won't Theo simply give Ersoy a heads-up?'

Pappas held Rob's gaze. 'Like I said, Theo will do exactly what I ask him to do. Andreas will be waiting for you at the casino.'

63

10.00 a.m., 12 October 1990
Black Aces Casino, Hockley, Nottingham

The man mountain, Theo, was waiting at the main entrance of the casino. He opened the double doors when he saw the four detectives approaching.

Danny walked in first, followed by Rob Buxton, Andy Wills and Sam Blake.

'Good morning,' Rob said. 'Where's Andreas Ersoy?'

Theo said, 'This way, Detectives. I've got Andreas locked in Mr Pappas's office. Don't worry, he isn't going anywhere.'

Theo unlocked the door, and Danny stepped inside. Andreas Ersoy looked physically very similar to Stav Georgiou, a little taller with a bit more muscle, but the two men could have been brothers.

Danny said, 'Andreas, my name's Detective Chief

Inspector Flint. I am currently making enquiries into the murder of Jamie Hart.'

Andreas remained tight lipped, saying nothing.

'I want to take a set of your fingerprints for elimination purposes. Will you agree to that?'

Theo clapped a giant hand on Ersoy's shoulder and said, 'Of course he will. Mr Pappas has told all of us to co-operate fully with the police.'

Andreas spoke for the first time: 'Okay.'

Danny glanced at Sam Blake, who stepped forward with the ink strips and the fingerprint form, quickly obtaining a set of elimination prints from Ersoy. Once that was done, Danny said, 'I believe you have information that will help us understand how and why Jamie Hart was killed.'

Andreas Ersoy allowed a fleeting smile to pass his lips and looked at Theo, who simply shrugged his massive shoulders. Then he turned to Danny and said, 'It's okay, Detective. I understand what's happening now. No problem, let's go.'

'Andreas Ersoy,' Danny said, 'I'm arresting you on suspicion of the murder of Garry Poyser, also known as Jamie Hart.'

'Like I said, Detective. No problem.'

64

12.30 p.m., 12 October 1990
MCIU Offices, Mansfield, Nottinghamshire

Danny, Rob and Tina were sitting in Danny's office, discussing the arrest of Andreas Ersoy. They were all waiting patiently for the telephone call from HQ. DC Blake and DS Wills had taken Ersoy's elimination prints directly to headquarters so Tim Donnelly could compare them against the fingerprint lifted from the Carrington flat where Jamie Hart had been murdered.

'I've just been on the phone to the custody sergeant,' Tina said. 'Ersoy has declined a solicitor and wants to talk.'

Danny said, 'I'll give it five more minutes; then we'll go and interview him. But it would be nice to know if it was his fingerprint on the doorbell first.'

Suddenly, the phone on his desk started ringing, and Danny snatched it off the cradle. 'DCI Flint.'

His voice jumpy with excitement, Tim Donnelly said, 'It's a match. The fingerprint lifted from the doorbell is identical to Ersoy's right index finger. He was at the murder scene, boss.'

'Brilliant. Thanks, Tim.'

Rob said, 'I take it that was positive?'

'Ersoy rang the doorbell,' Danny said. 'Let's see what he has to say about the murder.'

65

1.00 p.m. 12 October 1990
Mansfield Police Station, Nottinghamshire

As soon as Danny had finished introducing the people present in the interview room, he reminded Andreas Ersoy that he was still under caution.

Andreas said, 'Can you speak a little slower, Detective? I do understand English, and I can speak it okay, but I sometimes need longer to understand.'

'If it makes things easier for you,' Danny said, 'I can arrange for an interpreter to be present.'

Ersoy shook his head. 'That won't be necessary, Detective. Just take your time, please.'

The Greek Cypriot paused and then said, 'Before you ask me your questions, I need you to understand how things are between me and Stav.'

Danny said, 'Okay. Let's start there, then. Tell me about you and Stav?'

'We are brothers in the true sense of the word. Not blood, but equally as close. I've known him all my life. He always looked out for me and me him. It's just what we do, what we've always done. I was upset when he left Cyprus to come to the UK to work. I felt I had lost my closest friend, but I didn't blame him, because times were hard on the island, and money was scarce for all of us.'

'Is that why you also came here to the UK?'

'I came because Stav arranged everything. He knew how I was struggling to feed my wife and kids, so he got me this job and sent money so I could travel. Even now, when I'm working, earning decent money myself, Stav still sends extra money over to my family.'

'How many children do you have?'

'Three. I have two boys and a daughter who's the same age as Androulla, Stav's daughter.'

'I can understand why you feel so close to Stav,' Danny said. 'So my first question is, are you doing all of this out of a sense of loyalty towards him?'

'Doing what? You already know I killed that drug dealer. Why don't you want me to tell you about that?'

'Okay, tell me what happened when you left the hospital with Stav.'

'When we first left the hospital, I didn't know what was going to happen. Stav was so angry he could barely speak. As I drove out of the multistorey car park, he started sobbing. He kept muttering his daughter's name over and over. Gradually, the sobbing became louder until he was crying like a child. I stopped the car and asked if he was okay.'

'Did he answer you?'

'No. He said nothing. He had his head in his hands, and his whole body was shaking. I was worried, so I said I would take him home. Still, he said nothing.'

'What happened?'

'I drove to his house and took him inside. I virtually had to carry him into the house. He couldn't stand. I've never seen Stav like that. He's normally the strong one, the boss man. This was frightening for me to see him like this.'

'What did you do?'

'I tried to calm him down. I took him upstairs and put him on his bed. He just curled up in a ball.'

'Did he say anything about Jamie Hart?'

'Not while we were in the car. At the hospital he said he wanted to go to the man's flat and confront him over what he'd done to his daughter.'

'Was that all he said about Hart?'

'Yes. I didn't know what he intended to do once we got to Hart's flat, but we never got there.'

'Neither of you went to Hart's flat?'

'That's not right, sorry. Stav never went to Hart's flat, but I did.'

'Why did you go there?'

'I went because I knew that's what Stav wanted to do. He told me at the hospital we were going to see Hart, so when he wasn't in a state to go, I decided to go for my friend, my brother.'

'Had Stav asked you to deal with Hart in any particular way?'

'Stav didn't ask me to do anything.' The man looked at Danny. 'I told you, Detective. He was incapable of saying anything when I left his house.'

'Tell me,' Danny said. 'When you drove to Carrington, whose car were you in?'

'My car.'

'Where is your car now?'

'Parked behind the casino.'

'So when you went to Carrington, had you got something in mind? Did you know what you were going to say and do to Jamie Hart?'

'I didn't really have any plan. I just wanted to confront him over what he'd done.'

'Tell me what happened at the flat?'

'I parked the car round the back of the flats. I rang the doorbell and put gloves on while I waited. I shoved my hands in my pockets and could feel my flick knife.'

'Why had you taken a knife?'

'It's always in my coat pocket. I've carried a knife since I was thirteen.'

'What happened when Hart came to the door?'

'I told him Stav had sent me, and I was there to collect what he owed the casino.'

'Did you know what he owed?'

'No. I just said that so I could get inside.'

'And did he let you in?'

'Yeah. I think he recognised me from the casino.' Ersoy paused, as if remembering. 'He took me into the lounge and told me he had all the money he owed. I waited there while he got the cash.'

'How much did he give you?'

Ersoy shrugged. 'He came back carrying a cloth bag. He said there was three grand in the bag, enough to pay off his entire debt. He opened it so I could see the cash inside.'

'Did you take the money?'

'No. I asked him how he'd managed to raise all that cash in such a short time.'

'What did he say?'

'He just laughed and said the kids in this city couldn't get enough of his happy pills. He was gloating and saying things like he couldn't sell them fast enough to the stupid idiots who had more money than sense. Then he said he wished he had more pills left, as he could make a small fortune.'

Andreas paused and looked down at the desk.

Danny pushed. 'Then what happened?'

'I could feel the knife in my pocket. And I could see this disgusting pig's face laughing and bragging. Something inside me snapped.'

'What did you do?'

'I pulled the knife and hit the flick mechanism all in one go. He saw the knife coming but was too slow to block it. The blade hit him in the chest, just below his armpit.'

'Did he try to defend himself?'

'He never had a chance. After that first blow, I just kept stabbing him again and again. Something inside me was raging at the thought of young people like Androulla dying just so this piece-of-shit bastard could make money. I kept stabbing him until he went down.'

'Did you know he was dead?'

'I knew.' Andreas nodded. 'I walked out of the flat and got back in my car.'

'What have you done with the bag of money he owed the casino?'

'I left it there. I wasn't interested in his blood money.'

'And after you left Hart, where did you go?'

'I drove back to my place, had a shower and got changed.'

'Why did you change?'

'My clothes were covered in blood.'

'Where are they now?'

'I put them in a plastic bag and chucked the bag down the rubbish chute at the flats.'

'Where's the knife you used?'

'I dropped the flick knife down one of the drains near my place. I can show you which one.'

'Did Stav or anybody else order you to do this, Andreas?'

'No. I didn't even know I was going to do this.' Ersoy looked Danny in the eye. 'If that pig hadn't bragged about it, the knife would have stayed in my pocket. He shouldn't have laughed. It felt like he was laughing at Androulla, laughing at Stav, laughing at me.' His voice softened, and he repeated, 'He shouldn't have laughed.' Then he paused for a long moment before continuing, 'Androulla didn't deserve to die.'

'Is there anything else you want to tell me?'

'Only that I'm glad I killed him. This bastard, this man Hart, he was the scum of the earth.'

66

5.00 p.m. 12 October 1990
Mansfield Police Station, Nottinghamshire

Danny was waiting for Stav Georgiou in the foyer of the police station. After Andreas Ersoy had been charged with the murder of Garry Poyser, Georgiou's solicitor had immediately pushed for his client's release.

Georgiou had been released on bail, but with heavy conditions. Until a trial date had been set for Ersoy, Danny didn't want to risk Georgiou leaving the country. He had contacted Toni Pappas to tell him his godson was about to be released and had stressed upon him the need for Georgiou to comply with the bail conditions or risk being arrested again.

Pappas had been delighted at the news and assured Danny he would make sure his godson complied.

Danny was standing next to the casino owner when Georgiou and his solicitor came through the door that led to the cell block.

He was immediately embraced by Pappas, and Danny waited for the two men to finish their greeting before saying, 'Georgiou, it's imperative that you comply with every single one of your bail conditions. If you don't, you will end up back here. Is that understood?'

His eyes flat and expressionless, Georgiou still looked a beaten man. He shrugged and said, 'I understand, Detective. My solicitor has explained everything to me. Can I go home now?'

Danny nodded. 'We'll need a full witness statement from you about what happened after you left the hospital with Andreas, but we can do that another time.'

'I don't remember much about that night, Detective. I hope my recollection comes back, and I'll give you your statement, but not today. Today, I just want to go home to my wife. That's where I should be right now.'

As the group walked out of the police station, Toni Pappas turned and mouthed the words 'thank you' to Danny.

Danny walked slowly back up the stairs to his office, where he found Rob Buxton waiting for him.

Rob said, 'How was Georgiou?'

'Glad to be going home. But he still doesn't look right.'

'I'm not surprised. Can you ever hope to get over something like that happening to your child?'

'I don't think I could, Rob.'

'Does Georgiou know what's happened to his friend Andreas?'

Danny nodded. 'His solicitor told him when he was

getting his bail organised.'

'What was his reaction?'

'He never said a word; he just sat there and sobbed.'

'Ersoy has a wife and three kids in Cyprus.'

'I'm sure Pappas will look after Ersoy's family,' Danny said. 'Especially after the sacrifice Ersoy has made for his godson. Without his full cooperation, I doubt we would ever have got to the truth. Who knows, we may even have charged Georgiou with the murder. He may not have been convicted at Crown Court, but there was certainly enough evidence to charge him.'

'I think it would have been a stretch to charge Georgiou based on the evidence we had,' Rob said with a shake of his head. 'If you consider the fact that it wasn't his fingerprint on the doorbell, any half-decent defence barrister would have got any charge thrown out at court.'

'You're probably right.' Danny sighed deeply. 'How did you get on with the searches?'

'The flick knife's been recovered from the drain indicated by Ersoy, and a bin bag full of heavily bloodstained clothing has been recovered from the communal rubbish bins at his flat. I'm just about to complete all the paperwork to submit everything to the Forensic Science Service for a full analysis; we need to ensure it's Garry Poyser's blood on the knife and the clothes.'

'What about his car at the casino?'

'That's been recovered and will be fully examined at HQ. The vehicle examiners have been in touch and said there's what looks like blood on and around the driver's seat.'

'Good work, Rob.' Danny reached out and shook his colleague's hand. 'I'll leave you to it. I've a couple of phone calls to make.'

67

5.30 p.m. 12 October 1990
MCIU Offices, Mansfield, Nottinghamshire

Danny was about to call headquarters and give Chief Superintendent Slater an update on the Garry Poyser murder enquiry, when the telephone started to ring.

He picked it up and said, 'DCI Flint.'

Rachel Moore said, 'Evening, boss. Is now a good time? I just wanted to give you a quick update on progress down here.'

'Now's fine,' Danny said, pleased to hear from her. 'What have you got?'

'We've spent the day with the officer who prepared the coroner's file for the inquest on the Kingston Jones suicide. There are a few discrepancies between what Janice Millership said to us, and what she told the investigating officer.'

'Go on.'

'She told the officer she'd been unable to contact Kingston Jones for over a week prior to his death. Whereas she told us she'd spoken to him the night before he died. That's the first.' She paused before continuing, 'The post-mortem of Jones revealed a very interesting fact. Janice Millership told us that Jones had committed suicide because he was depressed over work and that he blamed Guy Royal for those feelings of depression. It turns out that Jones, a homosexual, had full-blown AIDS when he died.'

'This is all very interesting,' Danny commented, 'but is it taking us any closer to Royal's murder?'

'Bear with me, boss. The cop who did the file for the inquest has done a cracking job. He established that Jones had been informed about his AIDS diagnosis on the day he took his own life. He traced the route Jones would have taken from the clinic, where he was given those test results, to his flat. He managed to track down three separate shops that all sold Jones boxes of paracetamol tablets that day. He has the CCTV from those shops and statements from the shopkeepers.'

'He has been thorough.'

'It was the same with the local off-licence where Jones purchased a bottle of red wine. He's obtained their CCTV as well.'

'So you think Janice Millership was wrong about the reason Jones took his own life.'

'She must have heard about his AIDS diagnosis at the inquest, so she was either wrong, or she deliberately lied to us.'

'Why would she lie?'

'I don't know. There's something about Janice Millership

that just doesn't feel right,' Rachel said. 'She's a forty-something woman who's quite a plain Jane, who kept talking about this younger, handsome, gay man like he was the love of her life. It wasn't just me who noticed it; Jane commented on it too. We're both sure that Janice Millership was holding a torch for Mr Jones. It's possible she was still trying to deny the fact that Jones was homosexual. If you were a woman with strong feelings for a man, would you want to admit to yourself that man was a homosexual who couldn't possibly hold similar feelings for you?'

'I suppose not, but does it take us anywhere?'

'I don't know, boss,' Rachel admitted. 'I want to go back and re-interview Millership at her flat this evening, just to iron out these discrepancies. If that doesn't take us any further forward, we'll drive back tomorrow morning.'

'I suppose it's only one more night. Do what you think's right, and be careful. I'll talk to you tomorrow.'

68

6.30 p.m., 12 October 1990
Flat 52, Jacqueline House, Fitzroy Road, Camden, London

The lift in the flats was still out of order, so the detectives made the same weary climb up the concrete stairs until they were standing outside Janice Millership's flat.

Rachel knocked hard on the door and waited.

When there was no reply, she repeated the process, and this time lifted the letterbox to scan the hallway. The flat looked the same, but there were no coats hanging up, and no shoes on the floor.

Rachel turned to Jane and said, 'Jane, can you fetch the caretaker up here with his duplicate keys? I think we need to get inside, and I don't want to force entry if I can help it.'

Jane sighed, not relishing the walk down to the ground floor where the caretaker had his flat, and even less the climb back up the concrete stairs. She grimaced and said, 'I'll be as quick as I can.'

Rachel didn't hear her sarcastic comment, as she was already knocking on the door again.

Five minutes later Jane reappeared with the caretaker, who said, 'This lass tells me you think somebody may have harmed themselves inside, is that right?'

Rachel glanced at Jane before taking out her identification and saying, 'We're from the police, and we need to get inside. I think what my colleague told you could be right, and we don't want to cause damage to the door if we don't have to.'

The old caretaker grumbled as he sorted through the bunch of keys. 'We're not supposed to do this unless you have a warrant.'

Rachel snapped back, 'And if I'd brought a warrant, that door would have been off its hinges by now. Somebody could be dying inside that flat right now, so please, can you get the door open?'

Finally locating the right key, the old man said, 'All right, all right. I've found it.'

He opened the door and went to take a step inside. Rachel gently took hold of his arm and said, 'I think it's best if you wait outside until we know what we're dealing with.'

Rachel and Jane began moving methodically through the flat, quickly searching each room. It didn't take them long to establish the flat was empty, and there was no sign of Janice Millership. All the furniture was still in its place, but there was no trace of anybody living there. There were no clothes in the wardrobes and drawers, and no food in the fridge or the kitchen cupboards.

The detectives stepped back outside, and Rachel said to

the caretaker, 'Are these flats rented with all furniture included?'

'That's right, love. Everything's included. Is the tenant okay?'

'Looks like she's gone,' Rachel said. 'None of her belongings are in there.'

'Another bloody moonlight flit. I'll never understand why these people don't just say if they're leaving. It would save all this messing around.'

Rachel thanked the man for his help and said, 'There's no need for you to stay. We'll need to have a look around the flat before we leave, and we could be a while. We can secure the door on the Yale lock when we go.'

'Thanks, love. My missus was just about to dish my dinner up. It's shepherd's pie tonight, my favourite.'

'Lovely, enjoy,' Jane Pope said kindly. 'I'll knock on your door when we're leaving, okay?'

The old man was already making his way towards the stairwell as he said, 'Okay, love.'

'That must be one good shepherd's pie.' Jane chuckled. 'He couldn't get away from here fast enough.'

Rachel said, 'Did you find anything in the rooms you searched?'

'Nothing. All her clothes and personal belongings have been removed.'

The two detectives walked back inside the flat. Rachel went into the galley-style kitchen and said, 'Did you check the rubbish bin?'

'No.'

Rachel lifted the plastic swing bin and tipped the contents into the aluminium sink. As the two detectives started to sift through the rubbish, Jane lifted a food-stained envelope and said, 'This is addressed to Janice.'

She carefully removed the contents of the envelope, placing the handwritten note onto a dry work surface.

The two detectives read the note. At the end was the signature of Kingston Jones.

Jane said, 'It's pretty obvious that Jones told her he blamed Guy Royal and Seymour Hart-Wilson for what he was going to do.'

Rachel picked up the envelope and said, 'I don't get this. If Janice saw him the night before he killed himself, why would Jones feel the need to send her a letter explaining his actions. The postmark is dated the day after he died, which means it was posted on the day he took his life.' She paused, looking about the deserted flat, before continuing, 'Something isn't right. We need to go back to Bouldstone Press. Somebody there may know where Janice Millership has gone.'

69

9.00 a.m., 13 October 1990
Bouldstone Press, Eastcastle Street, London

Rachel and Jane were waiting outside Seymour Hart-Wilson's office when he arrived.

Seeing the detectives, he said, 'Back so soon, Detectives? Have you thought of a way I can get my money back from that thieving bastard Jennings?'

Ignoring the barbed comment, Rachel said, 'I need all the paperwork you have here relating to your employment of Janice Millership.'

'You know Janice Millership no longer works here, so I don't know what you expect us to have.'

'Any references you provided for her, her original application forms. That sort of thing.'

'Ms Millership didn't want a reference when she left.'

Jane said, 'What about the references she used to get the job here?'

'All destroyed when she left the company, as we're obliged to do, Detective.'

Rachel said, 'We know she used to drive Kingston Jones to all his appointments. Do you have a record somewhere of her vehicle?'

'This is London. Like every other office block in the capital, parking here is extremely limited. Janice Millership was never allocated a parking space, so we would have no reason to record the details of her vehicle. I believe she either walked or used public transport on the days she was working from the office.'

'So you've no record of where she came from, or where she is now?'

'No, I don't. Is that a problem?' He paused briefly, and when no answer came, he said, 'In that case, I really need to get on with some work. You could try talking to some of her colleagues in the typing pool; they may have some idea where she intended going. Good day, Detectives.'

70

4.30 p.m., 13 October 1990
MCIU Offices, Mansfield, Nottinghamshire

It had been a long, tiring drive from London to Nottingham, and Rachel wanted to brief Danny about Janice Millership as soon as possible.

She was now sitting alongside Jane Pope, opposite Danny in his office, and outlining her concerns.

Danny interrupted, 'I hear everything you're both saying, but why do you think this woman could be involved in the death of Royal?'

Jane replied, 'It was just the way she spoke and the language she used whenever she referred to Guy Royal. There was always real venom and a genuine hatred in her voice. I think she blamed him totally for what happened to Kingston Jones.'

Danny turned to Rachel and said, 'Is that what you think as well?'

Rachel nodded. 'One hundred percent. We both picked up on it.' She continued, 'This woman obviously held extremely deep feelings for Kingston Jones. I don't think it's too much of a stretch to say she was probably in love with the man.'

Danny looked puzzled. 'But didn't the inquest say he was homosexual?'

'No. I said he had been diagnosed as suffering with full-blown AIDS on the day he committed suicide. While we were making enquiries at Bouldstone Press this morning, I put a call in to their New York office, where Jones used to work.'

'And?'

'It seems that the people who worked with Jones there thought he may have been gay. They based this opinion on the fact that Kingston shared an apartment with an artist called Ralph Hooper. Interestingly, nobody there would say for definite that Jones was gay. It seemed he kept his private life just that, private.'

'Have you been able to speak to Ralph Hooper?'

'No. He also died recently.' Rachel sighed heavily before she went on, 'I did put a call into the medical examiner's office and discovered that the cause of death listed for Ralph Hooper was acquired immune deficiency syndrome.'

Danny was silent, deep in thought. Finally, he said, 'What more can we do to try to trace Janice Millership?'

Jane said, 'The only thing we got from Bouldstone Press that could help us is a grainy image taken from one of their security cameras. The quality is awful, though.'

'Could we get that image enhanced? Didn't Bouldstone have any paperwork for her at all?'

'Everything they did have was destroyed when she left,' Rachel said. 'We spoke to several of her colleagues, and although none of them knew where she intended going, a couple of them told us she originated from somewhere around the Newcastle area.'

'So we've got sod all, basically. I suppose if we manage to get the image enhanced enough, we could try a press appeal.'

Jane said, 'What about putting it on *Crimewatch UK*?'

'The television programme?'

'Yeah. When I was on the CID at Canning Circus, we put an unsolved armed robbery on there. It was dead easy to do, and it generated a stack of leads.'

Jane waited to hear Danny's response, and when none came, she continued, 'If it's something relating to the murder of Guy Royal, I'm sure they would want to feature it on the programme.'

'It would be a first for this office,' Danny said. 'We've never put any of our enquiries on *Crimewatch*.'

'It's simple to arrange, boss. Do you want me to talk to the press liaison officer? She helped arrange everything for us at Canning CID.'

'See if you can get the image enhanced first. It's pointless if we've got nothing to show them. If the image looks half decent, we'll do it, but at this time I think it would be prudent if we only refer to Janice Millership as a person of interest in the Guy Royal murder enquiry. It's a bit too soon to be calling her a suspect.'

71

10.15 a.m., 23 October 1990
Crimewatch UK Studios, London

As the train pulled into St Pancras, Danny reached for his overnight bag on the luggage rack above his head. He could see Rachel Moore and Jane Pope doing the same. The fourth member of the party that had travelled to London for the *Crimewatch* programme was DC Simon Paine. He stood up, stretched his back after the cramped two-hour journey, and said, 'Where are we staying?'

Jane replied, 'We're booked into the Royal National Hotel, near Russell Square. It's only five minutes in a cab.'

As they waited to get off the train, Danny glanced at his watch. 'The briefing at the studio is eleven o'clock; we need to get a move on. I want to dump the bags at the hotel first and then get a taxi to the studios.'

'The studios aren't far away,' Jane said. 'We've got plenty of time.'

Half an hour later, and with their bags dropped at the hotel, the four detectives arrived at the studios. Waiting for them was Sebastien, a runner employed on the show. He took details of their identities and, as he walked them through the studios, said, 'There are two other crimes featuring on tonight's broadcast. The briefing you're going to receive now covers not only your own case, but the other two as well.'

Danny said, 'How come?'

'We find it's easier if all the detectives who come to the studio are available to answer the telephones once the programme finishes. The lines don't open until then, but it can sometimes get busy – the lines are hot, with people queuing.'

'Do you know what the other cases are?'

'One is the rape of a woman at Blackpool Pleasure Beach three months ago. And the other is an armed robbery that happened in June. That involved a security van delivering wages to a factory in Sevenoaks. Like I say, you'll get a full briefing shortly on all the cases featured. At the same time, you'll also be given a typed handout that contains all the details of each case. I know one's been sent into the programme from your press liaison officer, highlighting all the details of the murder case you need help with. I imagine the other forces will have provided similar details for their cases.'

'Okay. What happens after the briefing?'

'Once that's over, I'll need to take DCI Flint on to the set, so he can prerecord a piece to camera, ready for tonight's broadcast.'

Danny said, 'Okay.'

Sebastien made eye contact with Danny and said, 'Are you comfortable doing that? Have you got everything you need?'

'I'll be okay with that,' Danny said with a nod. 'What I'm asking for isn't that complicated. We're just trying to trace a woman who may be able to assist us with our enquiries.'

'That's great. Has your press liaison officer sent us all the images you want to put out?'

Jane said, 'Yes. That's all been done, and receipt acknowledged.'

'Fabulous.'

He stood by a closed door and told them, 'Right, the briefing's in here. As soon as that's finished, I'll be back to show you all around the call centre. I'll explain how the phones work and how any calls received should be logged. We utilise a strict number system that must be adhered to. It's dead simple, so it won't cause anyone any issues. Any questions?'

Danny shook his head.

Sebastien opened the door and pointed out a group of similarly suited and booted detectives sitting at the far side of the room. 'If you'd like to join your colleagues, we'll get the briefing started,' he said.

72

9.50 p.m., 23 October 1990
Crimewatch UK Studios, London

Danny sat alongside Rachel in the call centre. From his position, he could see a monitor that was relaying the live feed of the programme as it was broadcast live to the nation.

He was a little shocked to see his head and shoulders appear on the small screen as the director cut to the piece he had prerecorded earlier. He could hear himself saying that the woman they sought had used the name Janice Millership to gain recent employment as a secretary at Bouldstone Press in London. She was known to have links with the northeast of the country, as well as London, and spoke with a distinct Newcastle accent.

The screen suddenly showed the only image they had of Millership. It had been enhanced but still wasn't great. The piece finished with Danny saying that they believed this woman held vital information that could help solve the murder of the TV personality Guy Royal and that they needed to speak to her as a matter of urgency.

The image of Janice Millership was then shown on the screen again before the director cut to the programme's presenter to close the broadcast.

Danny couldn't help thinking that, compared to the other forces' presentations, theirs had been a little sparse on content. He had voiced those same concerns to the director after he'd recorded his interview. She had tried to reassure him, saying sometimes less was more and that she expected there would be a good response to the request for information on Millership.

He was about to find out. He could now see the credits rolling on the monitor and could hear the programme's theme tune being played. Immediately in front of him sat row upon row of detectives all facing telephones. The telephones had lights on the receivers, instead of bells, to determine which of them was ringing.

Suddenly, the lights on several phones started flashing. The calls were starting to come in for all the featured cases.

Danny wondered how many, if any, would be about Janice Millership.

The light on the telephone in front of him started to flash. He picked it up and answered as he had been instructed, '*Crimewatch UK*. Can I help you?'

A woman with a Lancashire accent said, 'I'm calling about the rape in Blackpool. I think the same man tried to attack me a month ago...'

Danny grabbed the pro forma notepad and took down the woman's personal details, as well as her contact details, before promising that a detective would contact her tomorrow. As the woman tried to go into detail about what had happened to her, Danny was forced to explain, as politely as he could, that he could only take the bare minimum information tonight so that the line could be freed up for other people to call in. He again promised the woman that a detective involved in the case would speak to her properly in the coming days; then he terminated the call.

Instantly, the light on the telephone flashed again.

73

11.10 p.m., 23 October 1990
Crimewatch UK Studios, London

The Crimewatch telephone lines had closed ten minutes ago, and Sebastien had collected all the pro forma contact documents completed by the various detectives over the last hour.

He was now dividing the calls into three piles, one for each of the cases featured.

The case that had generated the most calls was the rape in Blackpool; the lead detective on that case was feeling confident because three separate callers had put forward the same suspect's name. Next most popular was the armed robbery at Sevenoaks in Kent. That case had also generated a lot of calls naming potential suspects.

As Danny had half expected, the request for information

about Janice Millership hadn't generated anywhere near the same level of public response.

He stood in the green room, sipping a strong coffee, feeling quite deflated. He could hear the animated voices of detectives working on the other cases as they discussed the potential leads that their presentations had generated.

Rachel approached Danny and, feeling his mood, said, 'Don't be too downhearted, boss. We've generated several leads, and at least one of them looks promising.'

'Do you know something, Rachel. I sat there for an hour and never took one call about our case. What promising lead?'

'It's one of the calls I took. It was from a prison officer who works at a jail located in County Durham. He told me the photograph we showed of Janice Millership bore an uncanny resemblance to a woman who had served time in prison for a fraud offence.'

'When?'

'He said it was about three years ago,' Rachel told him, 'and he thought that woman's name was Jan Miller.'

'Jan Miller not Janice Millership. What do they say good fraudsters do?' He paused before answering his own rhetorical question. 'They only change part of their name if they can get away with it.'

'That's exactly what I thought, boss. It's got to be worth a trip to Durham to have a conversation with this prison officer.'

Danny nodded, and with his mood lifted a little, he gestured for Jane Pope and Simon Paine to join him and Rachel.

He said to Jane, 'Have you got all the calls made about Millership?'

Jane held up about twenty contact sheets and said, 'This is it, boss. But Sebastien said sometimes the BBC receives calls after the show has aired. Any that do come in for our case will be automatically diverted to the incident room.'

Danny glanced at his watch and said, 'Let's get back to the hotel. It's been a long day, and we've got an early train to catch tomorrow. We can debrief all the contact sheets properly when we get back to the office. Let's hope there's something in those papers that will lead us to Janice Millership – whoever she might be.'

As he waited for their taxi to arrive at the studio, Danny couldn't help but feel a tinge of excitement as he thought about the call from the prison officer. Maybe *Crimewatch* hadn't been such a waste of time after all.

74

11.00 a.m., 25 October 1990
HMP Low Newton, Brasside, County Durham

Rachel parked the CID car in the allocated visitor's bay, directly opposite the huge blue door that formed the main gate of HMP Low Newton.

Danny said, 'What's this guy's name again?'

'Prison Officer Jack Dodds. He knows we're coming this morning. Everything was arranged with his supervisor yesterday.'

'Let's get inside, then.'

Fifteen minutes later, Danny and Rachel were sitting in the staff canteen, drinking mugs of strong tea that felt very welcome after the long drive north from Nottingham.

The door opened, and a uniformed officer walked in. Jack Dodds was in his early fifties and, judging by his appearance, had a wealth of experience in the prison service. His steel grey hair was cut very short, and his uniform looked impeccable. The silver chain that carried his keys was lengthy, indicating many years of service. He was carrying a slim manilla folder.

He gave a warm smile as he approached the table and said, 'I hope I haven't dragged you people all the way up here for nothing.'

Danny waited for the prison officer to sit down, and then said, 'We're very interested in the call you made to *Crimewatch* about Jan Miller. What can you tell us about her?'

'When the supervisor told me you were coming today, I spent an hour in the admin block, going through old records. I managed to find the file for Jan Miller. The prison keeps a skeleton record of all inmates for five years after their release. It was only three years ago that Jan Miller was released, so we still had her file.'

As he opened the folder, he said, 'There's not that much in it, like.' The first document was an A4-size photograph of Jan Miller. Rachel took out the photograph they had for Janice Millership. There was indeed a striking resemblance between the two women in the images.

Danny said, 'What can you tell us about Jan Miller?'

'Funnily enough, she's one I remembered quite well. She wasn't one ounce of bother all the time she was in here. I remember her because I reckon she fancied herself as the next Catherine Cookson.'

Rachel said, 'In what way?'

'She was always scribbling down stories and reading them to the other women. Some of them weren't half bad, as it goes. When she wasn't writing, she was talking about writing. And she would read whatever she could get her hands on.'

Danny said, 'Did you ever talk to her about her home life?'

'I do recall her being extremely worried about her mam and dad. They were both elderly, and I think she acted as their unofficial carer.' He paused and then said, 'I think that was one of the reasons she was released so early. She only served about a third of the two-year sentence she got. Nobody begrudged her; like I said, she was good as gold in here.'

Rachel asked, 'Do you know anything about the offence she was imprisoned for?'

'Only what it says in that file, pet. It was some sort of fraud offence.'

Rachel flicked through the file. It was basic information without any details. The offence was listed as obtaining goods by deception, which could mean anything. There was no arresting or charging officer listed. The only police reference in the entire file was Dunstanburgh Police.

Danny said, 'Before we go, I want you to have another long look at the image we have for this woman. Are you sure that the woman in this photo is the same woman you knew as Jan Miller?'

Jack Dodds looked thoughtful as he studied the grainy image. Finally, he said, 'She's quite a bit slimmer than I remember her, but yes, I'm sure it's her. That's Jan Miller.'

'Thanks, Jack. Are you okay for time? I'd like to get a quick witness statement from you before we leave.'

'No problem.'

75

5.00 p.m., 25 October 1990
Middle Engine Lane Police Station, Wallsend, Tyne and Wear

The long drive from the prison in Durham to Middle Engine Lane Police Station had been well worth it. The local intelligence officer at the station was a font of knowledge.

He passed Jan Miller's file to Danny and said, 'Jan Miller was arrested for quite a complex deception. It involved relatively small sums of money, but from a large number of victims. People had been paying cash into a Christmas Club Miller had set up, on a weekly basis. It was so they could save for the Christmas holidays. Unfortunately, when the time came to get paid out, none of the cash was available. Miller had been spending the money as fast as she collected it. It was her only offence and a dumb one. She's no criminal mastermind.'

Rachel said, 'And she got two years' imprisonment on her first offence?'

The LIO said, 'I think it was the number of victims and the amount of cash involved; that's why it was sent to Crown Court after she entered a guilty plea.'

'And nothing since she was released?'

'Not a thing. God knows why she did it in the first place.'

Danny said, 'What addresses do you have for her?'

'The only address we've got is her parents' house at Dunstanburgh. Are you wanting to go there this evening?'

'We might as well. Once we've checked it, we can get back to Nottingham.'

'I'll get the control room to radio the local officers. They can drive over and meet you here. You might as well follow them. Unless you know this area, it's easy to get lost out there when it's dark. They won't be long.'

'Thanks,' Danny said; then he picked up the file on Jan Miller and began reading.

Forty minutes later Rachel drove the CID car into Dunstanburgh. She had been pleased to follow the local police car, as all the lanes looked identical, and the road signs were few and far between.

The car in front indicated, and brake lights came on.

Danny said, 'Looks like we're here.'

Rachel parked the CID car behind the police vehicle and said, 'Doesn't look that promising; it's all boarded up.'

'We still need to check it.'

The two detectives got out of the car and, together with the two uniformed officers, made a check of the property.

The large, detached house was in total darkness, and the metal shutters on the doors and windows were all secure.

Nobody was inside the house.

As they walked back to the cars, Danny said, 'What happened to Miller's parents?'

PC Sanderson, the older of the two uniformed officers, said, 'The old lady got Alzheimer's, I believe, and went into a home. She was quickly followed by the old man, Harry.'

'Did you know her father?'

'Everyone round here knew Harry Miller. He was a bit of a local war hero. I'm sure I read somewhere that he was one of the most decorated soldiers of the Second World War.'

'Can you remember when the house was first boarded up?'

The younger officer, PC Mitchell, said, 'It was around Christmastime last year. I was asked to check it regularly when it was first boarded up to make sure squatters or tramps didn't get in.'

'And are the parents still alive?'

PC Sanderson said, 'Nah. They both died within a week of each other, earlier this year. It was in the local paper because of Harry's wartime exploits. The funeral was quite a big deal.'

'You might as well take us back to Wallsend, then, gents.'

The older officer said, 'Harry did have a caravan out near Dunstanburgh Castle, not too far from here. I don't know if he still owned it when he died. I remember going out there after it was broken into, a couple of summers ago. Do you want to check that before we go back?'

'We might as well while we're out here. It's got to be worth a look.'

As Danny drove, Rachel said, 'That's odd. I'm sure when we spoke to Janice Millership, she said she'd been away visiting her parents. Do you think she meant visiting their graves, or was she lying?'

'Good point.' Danny shrugged. 'But why would she lie?'

76

6.30 p.m., 25 October 1990
Proctors Stead, Caravan Park, Dunstanburgh, Northumberland

There was no lighting of any kind to illuminate the dark caravan park on the blustery hillside overlooking the North Sea. Only three caravans were parked on the site, all some distance from each other. Two of the caravans were in total darkness; the third parked closest to the hill that led down to the sand dunes showed a single dim light inside.

The only car on site was parked next to the caravan showing the light.

Danny said to PC Sanderson, 'Can you get close enough to see the car registration plate? It looks like an old Ford Cortina to me.'

The uniformed officer said, 'No problem, boss. If memory serves me correctly, old man Miller had a Cortina.'

He crept forward; then, returning moments later, he turned to his younger colleague and said, 'Stevie, nip back to the car and do a PNC check on Foxtrot, Juliet, Hotel, nine, five, eight, Charlie. It should be a red Ford Cortina.'

PC Mitchell said, 'Right you are, Frank,' before eagerly jogging back to the lane, outside the caravan park, where they had left the two vehicles.

Danny said, 'When you were in closer, could you hear any noise coming from inside the caravan?'

PC Sanderson said, 'Oh, aye. But I don't know how long they're going to be here, like. I watched a woman putting stuff into the car boot before hurrying back inside the caravan.'

A breathless PC Mitchell returned. 'The car's registered to Harry Miller.'

Danny said, 'I think it's fair to assume that Jan Miller's in the caravan, and it sounds like we need to act fast. Frank, you know the woman, so you come with me, and we'll knock on the door. Rachel, Stevie, follow us, but keep your distance. I don't want her to panic, which she might do if she sees too many people all at once.'

As Danny and PC Sanderson approached the caravan, a curtain twitched.

PC Sanderson said, 'Did you see that, sir?'

'She knows we're here. Come on, Frank.'

Danny ran the last few steps and knocked loudly on the metal door of the caravan. The door was opened immediately, and Danny recognised the woman he now knew was Jan Miller. Having opened the door, she immediately stepped back inside, followed by Danny and PC Sanderson.

The caravan was tiny inside. The single light that they had seen from outside was hanging above a small Formica-topped table. Wooden bench seats ran along each side of the table.

Jan Miller sat on the far bench, her eyes staring straight ahead, her face expressionless. She stared at the two police officers but remained silent. Her hands were hidden below the table.

PC Sanderson took a step forward and said, 'Hello, Jan. This man's a detective from Nottingham. He needs to ask you a few questions.'

Jan Miller never said a word. Her eyes remained fixed on some imaginary point in the distance, not even acknowledging the presence of the two police officers inside the caravan.

Danny squeezed himself down onto the bench seat until he sat opposite the pale-faced Jan Miller. In a quiet, calm voice he said, 'I need to talk to you about Kingston Jones.'

Suddenly, Jan Miller hissed angrily, 'Don't you dare speak that man's name.'

After the initial silence from the woman, it came as a shock to hear her speak with such venom and anger in her voice. Danny was also concerned at the level of hatred apparent in the woman's wild, staring eyes.

'Come on, Jan. Don't be like that, pet,' PC Sanderson said. 'All we want to do is talk.'

Miller hissed through gritted teeth, 'I don't want you here. I want you both to leave. Get out.'

The barrel-chested cop took another step forward and said, 'We can't do that, Jan. If you don't talk to my colleague here, we'll have no choice but to take you to the police station.'

Miller began to fidget, and Danny said quickly, 'Take it easy. Nobody's going to hurt you. All I want is to understand what happened to Kingston.'

'I've asked you once not to speak his name. He was too beautiful to be sullied by any of this mess.'

'What mess, Jan?'

'I don't want to talk about it. Just leave, now.'

PC Sanderson had edged forward until he was standing next to Danny's right shoulder.

Danny began to say, 'We can't just leave, Jan...'

But before he could finish his sentence, the burly PC Sanderson lunged forward and made a grab for Jan Miller.

She dodged him and for the first time raised her hands from beneath the table. Danny saw immediately that she was holding a black handgun in her left hand. She spun in her seat and aimed the gun towards the uniformed officer, pulling the trigger as she turned.

Danny saw PC Sanderson fall backwards as the bullet found its mark.

The sound of the gunshot, in such a limited space, was deafening, and Danny flinched before reaching forward to try to grab the gun. He too missed his chance, and this time Miller turned the gun on him.

Suddenly, Danny was staring at the black muzzle of the handgun, which was now less than a foot away from his face. Everything seemed to slow down. Danny could see the wisps of gun smoke curling from the barrel. He could also see the caked-in rust on the barrel and the trigger guard. He could see Miller's finger beyond the trigger guard and saw her knuckle turn white as she began to exert pressure on the trigger for a second time.

He locked onto Miller's wild eyes, expecting to hear a

second explosion. All he heard was a loud click, then another as Miller repeatedly tried to fire the ancient handgun.

After what seemed an eternity, he reacted and lunged for the handgun a second time. This time he grabbed it by the barrel and snatched the still warm weapon from the deranged woman's grasp.

At the same time, he heard the caravan door swing open and PC Mitchell shout, 'Frank, are you okay!'

Still holding the handgun in his right hand, Danny reached over with his left hand and grabbed the front of Jan Miller's jacket. He used his grip on her jacket to lever himself out of the tight space between the bench seat and the table. Once standing, he forced Miller face down onto the table and held her there. As Miller tried to struggle from his grasp, Danny became aware of Rachel's presence by his side. She was holding handcuffs, which she deftly applied to Miller's wrists.

Seeing that the immediate source of danger was now secured, Danny turned to look at Frank Sanderson. The uniformed cop was sitting on the floor of the caravan, clutching his left shoulder. Danny could see the look of shock on his colleague's face, and the blood trickling between the man's fingers as his hand covered the bullet entry wound.

Danny yelled to PC Mitchell, 'Get on the radio! And get an ambulance here as quick as you can!'

The young officer sprinted off into the darkness, and Danny looked again at PC Sanderson. He unbuttoned the man's tunic and ripped open his shirt, exposing the gunshot wound, before grabbing a tea towel from the aluminium sink. He placed the towel on the area of the wound.

He firmly applied direct pressure to stem the bleeding and said, 'Don't worry, Frank. The bullet passed clean through, and it doesn't look as though it's hit anything vital. You're not losing too much blood; looks like you'll be okay.'

The tough cop smiled and managed to say, 'Looks like we've both been lucky, then, sir.'

'You saw what she tried to do?'

'I saw it. God knows why the gun didn't go off, but if it had, you'd be a dead man.'

Danny glanced down at the gun still in his hand. He could see it was an ancient German Luger. He knew nothing much about guns, but he could see the top slide on the automatic handgun wasn't sitting right.

He held the weapon up for Frank Sanderson to see. The cop looked at it for a few seconds before saying, 'Looks like it's jammed to me, sir. That's at least one of your nine lives gone.'

Danny turned to Rachel and said, 'Get her in the back of the uniform car while we wait for the ambulance.'

Fifteen minutes later, Danny could hear sirens approaching; then an anxious PC Mitchell burst through the caravan door. 'The ambulance will be here in a couple of minutes,' he announced. 'How's Frank?'

Before Danny could reply, the older cop answered for himself, 'I'm fine, Stevie. It hurts like a bastard, but I'll be okay. I want you to make sure you tell my missus that I'm all right. I don't want her panicking over nowt.'

'Will do, mate. I'll get back to the lane and make sure the ambulance crew knows where you are.'

'Aye, you do that, bonny lad.'

'I'm so sorry about this, Frank,' Danny said. 'I should never have approached the caravan without armed backup.'

'Come off it, boss. How were you to know she'd be armed and dangerous?'

'Because I suspected her of killing Guy Royal, and he was shot. I should have allowed for all possibilities.'

'Aye. In a perfect world, Detective. None of us ever do though, do we? We all knock on doors and walk in, never really knowing what's waiting for us on the other side. It goes with the job, sir.'

Danny half smiled at the cop's stoic outlook. 'I suppose so, Frank.'

PC Sanderson winked and said, 'Besides, it was your head that nearly got blown off as well as mine, sir.'

After the ambulance crew had patched up the wounded PC Sanderson and driven him away in the ambulance, Danny approached PC Mitchell. The man was standing next to the police vehicle, talking to colleagues, who had arrived after the first radio call for assistance.

Rachel sat inside the police vehicle next to the troubled Jan Miller. The woman hadn't said a word since the shooting.

Danny said to PC Mitchell, 'Where will you be taking Miller?'

'Back to Middle Engine Lane nick, sir. It's the nearest one with a cell block.'

'Okay, Rachel will stay with Miller in the back of the car, and I'll follow you, so drive slowly, please. I don't want to get lost in these country lanes.'

PC Mitchell said his goodbyes to his colleagues and jumped in the driver's seat of the vehicle.

Danny walked slowly back to the CID vehicle. He took the handgun from his pocket and placed it in an evidence bag before putting it on the passenger seat. He turned the ignition on and drove slowly behind the marked vehicle, the one that carried the woman who had almost ended his life.

He wound down the window and gulped huge lungfuls of cold air; he needed them to ward off the feelings of panic and nausea he was experiencing. His mind couldn't quite come to terms with what had almost happened.

Glancing down at the black handgun on the passenger seat, he unconsciously gripped the steering wheel harder, desperately trying to stop his hands from shaking.

77

8.00 a.m., 26 October 1990
Middle Engine Lane Police Station, Wallsend, Tyne and Wear

The cell block sergeant greeted Danny and Rachel, then said, 'Did you manage to get any sleep after what happened last night, sir?'

'I did, thanks. No nightmares. How's Frank doing at the hospital?'

'I called the hospital just before you got here. He's doing okay. He had a comfortable night, and knowing Frank, he's probably revelling in all the attention those young nurses will be giving him.'

'He's a good man.'

'Aye, he is that, sir.'

Rachel said, 'And what about the prisoner, Miller? How's she been?'

'She was quiet all night. No histrionics. Very polite, says please and thank you. No bother at all, really. When you look at her this morning, it's hard to imagine what she did last night.' The sergeant paused, then said, 'While I remember. There's a message here for you, Chief Inspector.'

He handed Danny a handwritten note. Danny scanned it and said to Rachel, 'The fingerprint bureau's matched the smudged print found in Royal's blood at Hunters Croft to Jan Miller's fingerprints. The match is good enough for identification purposes only and wouldn't be admissible as evidence at Crown Court.'

Rachel said, 'I bet the handgun's a ballistic match, and that will be admissible at court. There can't be many German Lugers out there.'

'One was nearly one too many last night.'

Rachel said, 'I wonder how she came to be in possession of it.'

'All the lads who work here reckon it was probably a memento her dad brought home from the war,' the cell sergeant said.

Danny said, 'More than likely, Sarge. Can you sign Miller out to my custody, please? We're taking her back to Nottingham, to question her about the murder of Guy Royal.'

'No problem, boss. As I understand it, your force will be dealing with her for the weapon offences that happened last night, as well. Is that correct?'

Danny nodded. 'It's what was agreed with your assistant chief constable last night. It makes sense to deal with everything at the same time.'

'I'll go and fetch her from the cell. She's got no property with her.'

The sergeant returned moments later, followed by the slight, ineffectual-looking Jan Miller.

Danny said, 'You were arrested last night for the attempted murder of PC Sanderson and other firearm offences. I'm arresting you now on suspicion of the murder of Harvey Jarvis, also known as Guy Royal.' He cautioned Miller and said, 'Do you understand?'

Miller nodded and said, 'I understand. How is PC Sanderson?'

'He's going to be fine. We're going to take you to Nottingham, where we'll question you about all these offences. We won't talk to you about any of these matters during the journey, so if you ask either of us anything about them, we'll ignore you. That's not us being rude; that's how it must be until we reach the police station in Nottingham. Do you understand?'

Jan Miller nodded. It was obvious she didn't intend saying another word.

Danny thanked the cell sergeant, and as he walked out of the cell block, he said, 'I'd like to be kept informed of Frank Sanderson's progress, please, Sergeant.'

'Thank you, sir. Will do.'

78

4.00 p.m., 26 October 1990
MCIU Offices, Mansfield, Nottinghamshire

As Danny walked into the main briefing room with Rachel, the gathered detectives broke into a spontaneous round of applause. Danny turned to Rob Buxton and said, 'What's all that about?'

'Word has already got down from Northumbria about your lucky escape last night.'

Danny felt a mixture of embarrassment and annoyance. He quietened everyone down and said, 'What happened last night is no cause for celebration. I was lucky I didn't get myself killed, and more importantly, I'm extremely fortunate that I didn't get a uniformed colleague killed. As it is, that officer is still in hospital recovering from a serious gunshot wound. I'm sure you've all got work to do, so get cracking.'

Danny then turned to Rob and said, 'I want all supervisors in my office in five minutes.'

Danny walked into his office and closed the door. He picked up the telephone and called home.

Sue picked up on the third ring, and Danny said, 'Hi, sweetheart, just wanted to let you know I'm back from Durham.'

'Good, did it go okay?'

'It went all right, a bit eventful, but I'll explain everything when I get home. I just wanted to hear your voice.'

Sue was quiet for a few moments and then said, 'Are you okay?'

He could feel tears stinging his eyes, and he knew his supervisors would be coming in shortly, so he said brusquely, 'I'm fine, Sue. I'll be a couple more hours; then I'll be home. See you soon.'

He quickly put the phone down and used the heels of his hands to rub his eyes.

There was a single knock on the door, and Rob walked in, followed by Tina, Rachel and Andy.

Danny said, 'I didn't appreciate what just happened out there. It was uncalled for and unnecessary, and I don't ever want to see a repeat performance. I want – no, I demand – a high level of professionalism, and that wasn't it. Understood?'

The four supervisors all nodded, and Rob said, 'It was spontaneous, but we'll make sure it doesn't happen again.'

Danny mellowed a little and said, 'I think I understand why it happened, and I feel the same sense of relief as everyone does that things didn't turn out worse, but we need to move on.' He paused and added, 'When we booked Miller in, the custody sergeant stated she can't be interviewed tonight, as she needs a rest period. The interview will be tomorrow morning at nine thirty. I'll lead the interview, and Rachel will accompany me, as she spent a lot of time with Miller yesterday when she was detained and has spoken to her before in London. I want us to use this time to plan the interview and gather all the available evidence. Tina, I'd like you to fast-track the forensic testing of the handgun we seized in Northumberland. The sooner we know that was the weapon used to kill Guy Royal, the better. I've no idea how Jan Miller will respond when questioned. She has indicated she wants a solicitor, and I've asked the custody sergeant to arrange for her to be examined by the police surgeon. She seems a lot more rational today than she did the previous night, but I don't want her legal team to cause problems later by claiming we didn't have the correct safeguards in place prior to her questioning.' He paused briefly and said, 'Any questions?'

When the room remained silent, he went on with his instructions. 'Rachel, you and I will work on the interview strategy. Tim, Rob, I want you to gather the rest of the evidence we have. It shouldn't take long, as we don't have that much. That's why the handgun is vital, Tina. I'm relying on you to get a result on it as fast as you can.'

79

7.00 p.m., 26 October 1990
Mansfield, Nottinghamshire

Danny slid the key into the lock and opened the door. He had been rehearsing what he was going to say to his wife about the events of the previous evening.

He heard Sue's voice from the lounge. 'Is that you, sweetheart? Do you want a drink?'

Danny walked into the lounge, and Sue's smiling face instantly changed as she saw the expression on his ashen face.

She walked towards him and said, 'Whatever's the matter? You look awful.'

Totally forgetting his rehearsed speech, he spluttered, 'Something terrible happened last night.'

'What?'

'I was almost shot.'

He hadn't meant to blurt it out in such a hard fashion, he just didn't know how to tell his wife that he'd almost been killed.

A look of horror descended on Sue's face, and she said in confusion, 'What do you mean, shot?'

'We went to a caravan to arrest Jan Miller, and she had a gun. She shot the officer I was with, then pointed the gun at me and pulled the trigger.' He then quickly added, 'But it jammed and didn't fire.'

The horror on her face changed to anger, and she started to pound Danny's chest with her balled-up fists. 'What the hell were you thinking? You knew Guy Royal had been shot. Why did you try to arrest that woman without armed backup?'

'It all happened too fast. I thought she might get away, so I did what I always do, I went in.'

'How dare you say that?' Sue demanded. 'Don't you ever consider me or that little girl sleeping upstairs before you act? I just don't understand why you didn't allow armed cops to arrest her. Was it because she was just a woman? Is that it, you idiot? How could you be so bloody selfish?'

Her reaction surprised him. He'd expected the level of anger she had shown to be aimed towards the woman responsible.

He hadn't expected that anger to be turned into recriminations against him.

He attempted to explain the chain of events in more detail, but she wasn't listening now. She shouted over him, asking about the condition of the officer who had been shot. She raged at him. 'Your stupid arrogance got that poor man shot. What the hell were you thinking?'

Danny had no more words. He stepped forward and wrapped his arms tightly around her, pulling her in close. At first, Sue resisted, still furiously telling him that he was a naïve, selfish idiot.

Eventually, the heat and rage of her raw emotion drained from her, and he felt her body slowly relax in his arms. With tears stinging his eyes, he stood still and allowed that feeling of unadulterated relief to wash over them both.

Danny had never felt as tired as he did in that moment.

They stood like that for several minutes before she glanced up at him and whispered, 'It's not just you anymore, Danny. You have to think about all of us.'

80

9.30 a.m., 27 October 1990
Mansfield Police Station, Nottinghamshire

There had been no miracle fast track for the handgun seized in Northumberland, so that evidence was still unavailable when Danny had given disclosure to Jan Miller's solicitor.

A duty solicitor had been provided for Miller, and Danny knew her well. He had worked many an interview room with Jackie Harris representing the accused.

He had always regarded her as a solicitor who, while striving to represent her clients to the best of her ability, was never one to play games or try to abuse the system. After he'd given her full disclosure, she had said, 'Without the evidence of the handgun, there isn't an awful lot to connect my client to the murder.'

Danny had responded by saying, 'We can place your

client at the house where the murder happened. We know that Guy Royal knew her and would happily allow her access into the house, and we both know the handgun evidence will be available soon. It would be foolhardy for your client to come up with some fanciful defence that will subsequently be proved wrong.'

'I appreciate what you're saying, Chief Inspector, but I'll be advising my client not to answer your questions. I don't know if she'll heed that advice. When I spoke to her this morning, she seemed hell-bent on telling you the whys and wherefores of everything.'

'Time will tell. How long will you need with your client?'

'Thirty minutes should do it.'

Forty-five minutes had passed since that conversation, and now Danny and Rachel sat opposite Jan Miller and Jackie Harris in one of the interview rooms.

Danny introduced everyone present, reminded Miller she was still under caution, and said, 'You've been arrested on suspicion of the murder of Harvey Jarvis, also known as Guy Royal. Do you have any knowledge of that offence?'

Jan Miller made eye contact with Danny. There was none of the wild, staring energy in her eyes that he had witnessed at the caravan, just a calmness that made her appear almost detached from her current situation. When she spoke, it was in hushed tones that displayed none of the anger and frustration she had shown at the caravan. 'You need to understand what sort of creature that man was.'

'What man are you talking about?'

'Guy Royal, Harvey Jarvis, whatever his name is. He was a monster who treated people appallingly all his worthless life.'

Jackie Harris touched her client's arm to get her attention

and said, 'Jan, you understood the advice I've given you. There's no need for you to answer any of the detective's questions.'

Jan Miller nodded and said, 'Thank you for your advice, but I need them to understand why I did what I did, and that I'm not an evil person.'

With an air of resignation, Jackie Harris picked up her pen and prepared to make notes on the A4 pad in front of her.

'Take your time,' Danny said. 'Can you tell me what happened at Hunters Croft?'

There was a long pause before Miller said, 'It was almost eleven o'clock at night when I arrived at Royal's house. I could see his manager's car on the driveway, and I nearly turned round and drove off again. I sat staring at the house for some time before I walked up to the door.'

'Why did you delay?'

'Because I wasn't sure what I was going to say or do. I was just so angry about things. I was trying to rationalise what I wanted to do.'

'And what was that?'

'I wanted Royal to suffer the same fate that Kingston had. I wanted him dead.'

Danny paused before saying, 'What happened when you eventually knocked on the door?'

'It was a long time before it was opened. I could hear the key turning in the lock. I fully expected Stan Jennings to open the door, so I was surprised when I saw Royal standing there in his flashy silk dressing gown.'

'Did Royal ask you inside?'

'Not at first. He said that Jennings wasn't there and that I should come back tomorrow. I told him I'd come to talk to him not Jennings, and he let me in.'

'How was Royal at that time?' Danny asked.

'On something or drunk or both. He was staggering around all over the place, he reeked of whisky, and he was swearing at me, calling me Kingston's bitch.'

'Where did you go when you went inside the house?'

'I followed him into the lounge. The one with the big fireplace. I told him what had happened to Kingston. How that wonderful man had taken his own life and that it was all down to the way he'd abused him when they had worked on his books.'

'How did Royal respond to that?'

'He laughed in my face and said he already knew why Jones had topped himself, and that it had nothing to do with him.' Jan Miller paused before she went on, her voice steady. 'We argued, going back and forth at each other. I could feel myself getting angrier by the second. Then he said something unforgivable.'

'What was that?'

'He said the real reason Jones had killed himself was because he was gay, that he had AIDS, and was going to die a horrible death anyway.'

'How did that make you feel?'

'I was hurt and raging inside. It was such an awful thing to say.'

'Why did that single comment hurt you so much, Jan?'

She remained silent for a long time before saying quietly, 'Because it wasn't true. Kingston wasn't gay. We loved each other. That nonsense about him being gay was a pack of lies, invented to cover up what had really happened.'

'What do you think really happened, Jan?'

'That beautiful man had been hounded to his death by Royal and Hart-Wilson. The AIDS story was something they'd made up to cover their backs.'

'So Guy Royal repeated that to your face, goading you. How did you react?'

'I could feel the weight of the gun in my coat pocket, so I took it out, pointed it at him and told him to shut up.'

'What did he do?' Danny asked her.

'He laughed at me. Called me Kingston's bitch again and turned his back on me, saying I'd never have the guts to shoot him.'

'What did you do?'

'I told him to turn round, and when he did, I looked him in the eye and pulled the trigger. I shot him full in the face.' There was a brief pause, and then she continued, 'After he went down, I walked over and touched his neck, to see if he was dead. I couldn't feel a pulse, and when I took my hand away, it was covered in blood. I walked out of the house, wiped my hand on the damp grass to get rid of the blood, then drove away.'

'Did you lock the door as you left?' Danny asked her.

'No. I think I closed the door, but I didn't have a key to lock it.'

'You obviously knew Royal was seriously injured; did you think about calling an ambulance or rendering any sort of first aid?'

For the first time in the interview, Miller allowed a smile to pass over her lips. 'Why would I do that?' she said in a cold tone. 'I wanted that bastard dead more than I wanted anything else in the world. He'd effectively ended the life of the only man I've ever loved, so it was right I should end his.'

Danny glanced at Rachel, then said, 'Where did you get the gun?'

'It belonged to my father. He took it from a dead German officer, a man he killed on D-Day.'

'Had you taken the gun with you to London when you left home?'

'No.'

'Then how did you have it with you when you went to Royal's house?'

'I drove to Dunstanburgh first to get it.'

'You drove all the way from London to Dunstanburgh and then back to Nottinghamshire?'

'Yes.'

'Why did you think you would need the gun,' Danny said, 'if you hadn't already decided what to do about Royal?'

'I didn't know for certain,' she explained calmly. 'I did know that I wanted him dead and that I couldn't do it physically. That's why I went to get my dad's gun.'

'Did you know it was loaded?'

'Yes. Dad showed me how to load and unload it. He kept it unloaded because of the spring inside, something like that.'

'So when you collected it from your parents' house, it was unloaded?'

'Yes, but the box of bullets was hidden in the same place as the gun, in the loft.'

'When we visited your parents' house, it was all boarded up,' Danny told her. 'How did you get in?'

'I knew it would be boarded up. I had arranged for it to be made secure, as everyone knew the house was empty after my parents died, and I didn't want vandals or squatters getting in before I could arrange to sell it. Anyway, I knew it was like that, so I took my electric drill. I unscrewed the metal grille that covered the back door, smashed the glass and climbed in. I got the gun and ammunition from the loft, then screwed the grille back on, covering the back door. Once I'd replaced it, you couldn't see the glass in the back door had been smashed.'

'You went to an awful lot of trouble to get your hands on that gun,' Danny observed. 'I think you always intended to shoot Guy Royal, and the only reason you delayed briefly was because you thought Stan Jennings might be in the house.'

Miller curled her top lip into a sneer and said, 'And what if I did? That pig deserved to die. I'm glad I shot him.'

'And what about PC Sanderson? Are you glad you shot him too?'

'Of course not. When he tried to grab me, I just panicked. I didn't intend the gun to go off.'

'After shooting PC Sanderson, you pointed the gun at my face and pulled the trigger several times. Fortunately, the gun malfunctioned, or you would have shot and killed me as well. Why were you trying to shoot me?'

Miller shrugged and said, 'I don't know. I just saw red. You were in my way, and I wanted to leave.'

'I see,' Danny said. 'After you shot Royal, where did you keep the gun?'

'At the caravan.'

'Why not put it back in the house?'

'I still needed it.'

'What for?'

'There was someone else who needed to answer for what happened to Kingston.'

'Who?'

'Seymour Hart-Wilson used Kingston in the most abominable way. He forced him into working with that ignoramus Royal and threatened him if he didn't do what he asked.' She took a deep breath, as if struggling with her emotions. 'He threatened to prevent Kingston from ever working in the publishing industry again.'

'How did you intend to make him pay?'

'I always intended to deal with him the same way I had dealt with Royal. When your detectives questioned me at my flat, I knew time was running out, so I drove back to the caravan to retrieve the gun and ammunition. I was about to leave when you arrived.'

'Why had you waited so long to get even with Hart-Wilson?'

'I needed to leave Bouldstone first. I had already found out his address in Surrey. I was going to drive there the night you arrested me. That man should be dead now.'

'Your intention was to drive to his home address and kill him?'

'Yes. I just needed the gun first.'

Danny looked at Rachel. 'Is there anything you want to ask?'

Rachel said, 'Why did you think Royal was lying about Kingston Jones? You attended every day of the inquest, and you heard the coroner describe his death as suicide. The coroner also said that his suicide was as a direct result of acute depression brought on by his recent diagnosis of AIDS. Was the coroner lying as well?'

'Probably. That lot all stick together, don't they?'

'Why did you think Kingston Jones was in love with you?'

'I just knew.'

'Did he ever tell you he was?'

'No.'

'Did he ever do anything physically that would give you that impression?'

'No, he didn't.'

'Have you ever kissed him or had any intimate sexual relations with him?'

Miller's thoughts turned to a sun-filled morning in the spring when she had walked arm in arm with Kingston Jones along the banks of the Thames in London. When they had stopped, and she had stood on tiptoe before planting a soft kiss on his cheek.

That thought evaporated, and she said gruffly, 'None of your business.'

Rachel pressed. 'Did you?'

'No.'

'So I'll ask you again. Why did you think Kingston was in love with you?'

'He was. I just knew he was.'

Rachel said, 'I've nothing else to ask.'

Danny glanced at Jackie Harris. 'Do you want another chat with your client?'

The solicitor placed her pen on the pad and said, 'Yes, please.'

81

4.00 p.m., 27 October 1990
Mansfield Police Station, Nottinghamshire

Danny leaned against the cell block wall as he watched Rachel reading out the long list of charges against Jan Miller. He inwardly winced as he listened to her read out one charge in particular.

Rachel said, 'You are also charged that on the eighth of October 1990 at Dunstanburgh in the county of Northumberland, you attempted to murder Daniel Flint...'

As Rachel read, Danny zoned out of the words and concentrated on Miller's face. Her expression did not change. There was no remorse, no protest, no anger. There was nothing, just an empty, almost vacant look, which somehow made her actions on that night even more chilling. To Danny, it seemed Jan Miller just wasn't bothered, one way or the other.

He swallowed hard at that thought. He was still struggling to come to terms with the chain of events on that dark, blustery night that had almost cost him his life.

The conversation he'd had with Sue the previous night had been a difficult and emotional one.

As Rachel read out the murder charge, he observed Jan Miller closely. She hadn't batted an eyelid at any of the other charges, but now she allowed a cruel smile to form on her lips. There was no sign of remorse, just an inward celebration that she had achieved what she set out to do. Which was to kill Guy Royal.

Rachel finished reading the charge relating to the murder of Harvey Jarvis, the real name of Guy Royal, then reminded Miller of the caution and asked, 'Is there anything you want to say in response to these charges?'

Miller stared straight ahead and muttered, 'Even Royal's name was phoney. Good riddance to bad rubbish.'

82

10.00 a.m., 28 October 1990
Nottinghamshire Police Headquarters

A lot had happened in the few weeks since Danny had first met Detective Chief Superintendent Mark Slater. During the drive to headquarters, Danny had felt quietly positive. The first meeting had gone better than he ever expected, and now he had good news on the current caseload of the Major Crime Investigation Unit.

He walked briskly up the stairs and into the command corridor. He knocked once on Slater's office door and waited.

There was no reply, and Danny was just about to knock again when he heard Slater's voice behind him. 'Good morning, Danny. You're early.'

Danny spun round and saw Mark Slater walking towards him, holding a mug of fresh coffee in each hand.

Slater said, 'I thought I'd get us both a brew, ready for our meeting. Can you get the door, please?'

Danny opened the door and followed Mark Slater inside. Slater put the coffees on the desk and gestured for Danny to sit down.

As the two men sat, Slater said, 'I haven't put sugar in either. Hope that's okay.'

Danny nodded. 'That's fine, sir. Thanks.'

Slater sat back in his chair and said, 'Your unit's been busy over the last couple of weeks. Where do you want to start?'

Danny said, 'The murder of Garry Poyser at Carrington was one of those jobs where everything dropped into place very quickly.'

'I saw you charged a Cypriot national with the murder. Are you confident of a conviction?'

'When interviewed, Andreas Ersoy made full admissions, and there's a wealth of forensic evidence to support that incriminating interview.'

'Can you give me a brief recap on the circumstances?'

Danny took a sip of the hot coffee and said, 'Poyser was actively engaged in the supply of ecstasy to clubbers in the city centre. That ecstasy was responsible for hospitalising several late-night revellers, and subsequently caused the death of a young woman, Androulla Georgiou. Ersoy is a close associate of that young woman's father, so when he discovered who was responsible for supplying the drugs, he took it upon himself to deal with the matter.'

'By dealing with it, you mean he stabbed Poyser to death.'

'Yes, sir.'

'Some would say a somewhat Mediterranean response to the problem.'

Danny didn't agree with his line manager's comment but remained silent.

Slater scribbled down a few notes before saying, 'Tell me about Jan Miller?'

'Jan Miller has been charged with a number of offences, including the murder of Harvey Jarvis.'

'Jarvis, also known as Guy Royal?'

'Yes. She blamed Royal for the death of a man she considered to be the love of her life.'

'Considered to be?'

'It appears those feelings were not reciprocated.'

'But she chose to shoot Royal anyway.'

'That's her story.'

Slater sat forward in his chair. 'That's great work by you and your team, Danny. But now we need to talk about the not-so-great aspect of the Miller job.'

'I take it you're referring to the arrest of Miller at Dunstanburgh?'

Slater leaned further forward to emphasise the seriousness of his next words. 'The assistant chief constable of the Northumbria force is pushing for you to face a disciplinary hearing for your reckless actions on the night Miller was detained.'

'What?' Danny said in shock.

'Don't forget, those actions resulted in one of her officers being shot at close range...'

'And me almost being killed,' Danny protested. 'Let's not forget that part.'

'Quite so.' Slater paused before he went on, 'Talk me through the arrest, from your perspective.'

Danny was thoughtful before saying, 'When we located Jan Miller at the caravan, it looked as though she was about to leave. She has said as much during her interview. I had very little time to react to a rapidly changing situation, and I didn't want to risk Miller getting away, so I took the decision to approach the caravan and effect a quick arrest. When PC Sanderson and I entered the caravan, Miller was quietly sitting at a table, not presenting any threat. We both spoke to her, and at the time she seemed quite rational, if not overly co-operative. It was only when PC Sanderson made a grab for her that she produced the handgun and fired it at him.'

Danny paused, a cold sweat enveloping him as he relived the ordeal.

After a few moments, he spoke once more. 'As Frank Sanderson fell backwards, I reached across the table that separated me and Miller, and tried to grab the weapon. She evaded my grasp and turned the gun on me, pulling the trigger several times while pointing it directly at my face.' Danny wiped the sweat that was beading on his brow. 'When I realised it hadn't gone off, I grabbed the gun, and she was detained. I then gave first aid to PC Sanderson.'

'I know hindsight's always twenty-twenty vision,' Slater said, 'but what do you think you could have done differently?'

Danny was feeling drained and becoming irritated. 'Oh, I don't know, sir. I could have waited for a full armed response team to attend and make the arrest of a forty-something, five-foot-two female with one previous conviction for fraud. Having said that, I doubt that Jan Miller would have waited for the armed team to arrive, and at some stage we would have been forced to make the arrest anyway whether she had a gun or not.'

A little taken aback by the outburst, Slater sat back and said, 'I appreciate your frustration, but there's no need for your facetious comments. You need to take this seriously. ACC Patricia Ealing certainly is, and she's got the backing of her force federation rep.'

'Has anybody taken into account what PC Sanderson has to say?'

'Sanderson would have followed your orders, Danny. Any flak coming is all yours, I'm afraid.'

'I know that, sir. What I meant was, has anybody asked him what he thought of any perceived threat?'

'I don't know the answer to that,' Slater admitted, 'but I'll be pushing to find out.'

'Where do I stand now? Are you suspending me?'

'Good God, no. The chief constable has travelled to Northumbria Police headquarters today for a meeting with their chief and with Pat Ealing to try to resolve this matter. In the meantime, you need to carry on doing what you're doing.' Perhaps to try to lighten the mood in the room, Slater then said, 'Are you sure you wouldn't prefer that desk job now?'

'I'm sure, sir. Do you want to hear about the ancillaries from the Guy Royal murder enquiry?'

'Sounds interesting.'

'Stan Jennings, Royal's manager, faces charges of supplying Class A drugs. He has a pending court date and is currently on bail. Tyrone Armstrong also faces charges of supplying Class A drugs. Because of his previous record and flight risk, Armstrong is charged and on remand at HMP Lincoln.'

'Do murder enquiries always throw up additional suspects and charges like this?'

'It depends how many suspects there are and where those enquiries take my detectives. Every lead is followed to its natural conclusion. Even when a suspect is cleared from the murder enquiry, that conclusion can sometimes lead to other serious charges for the suspect.'

'You see, this is the work I want to hear about,' Slater told him. 'I've never been one for the "shoulda, woulda, coulda" squad. Hopefully, the chief will be able to smooth things over and disciplinary charges won't become an issue. All in all, it's been a good couple of weeks for the MCIU.'

'Thank you, sir. Hopefully, discipline charges won't spoil that.'

Slater nodded. 'I heard about the problems facing DC Lorimar. Have you any update on his daughter's condition?'

'Glen's daughter is back home and being cared for by her family. I've granted Glen additional leave to be with his family.' Danny went on to say, 'I'm thinking of booking a long holiday myself. After what happened up there in that caravan, I think I need to get away and spend some time with my own family.'

'I think that would be very wise, Danny,' Slater agreed. 'Something like that is going to take some getting over. Submit your annual leave pass today, and I'll make sure it gets signed through. Neither of your detective inspectors have got any leave booked, have they?'

'No, sir.'

'Good. Get yourself away somewhere hot for a few weeks, and try not to worry about ACC Ealing. Jack Renshaw can be a very persuasive man when he wants to be.'

EPILOGUE

10.00 a.m., 26 November 1990
HMP New Hall, Flockton, West Yorkshire

Jan Miller sat opposite her legal team in one of the visitor's private interview rooms. She looked relaxed and well. Prison life suited her. There was nothing to worry about, nobody to care for; everything she needed was provided for her.

Facing the prospect of a long custodial sentence meant she had been given her own cell, and there was no need for her to share with another inmate. Some of the other women on the wing terrified her, but she only had to see them at mealtimes and association.

Since arriving at New Hall, she had kept herself to herself, trying hard not to bother or upset anybody. But she was no pushover, and whenever the occasion called for it, she gamely stuck up for herself.

All things considered, life behind bars wasn't too much of a trauma for Jan Miller. She had no family or friends to consider. If she left prison tomorrow, she would be on her own. At least being inside meant there were always other people to see and talk to.

It was with all that in mind, she had decided to enter guilty pleas on all the charges she faced at the earliest opportunity.

Her solicitor, Jackie Harris, looked a little shocked at the decision and said, 'Are you sure that's what you want to do?'

Miller said, 'Let's face it, we both know the evidence the police have will convict me even if I have a full trial. It's all a waste of time, and I just don't see the point.'

The solicitor said, 'On the plus side, the judge will have to give you credit for an early plea. That could reduce the time you have to serve on your life sentence considerably.'

'How can you reduce a life sentence?'

Jackie Harris explained patiently, 'Murder carries a statutory term of life imprisonment. That doesn't mean you're going to spend the rest of your life in prison. The judge, when he sentences you, will stipulate what that life term means.'

'I don't understand.'

'When it comes to the actual sentencing, the judge will say something like life imprisonment to serve a minimum of sixteen years or a minimum of thirteen years. Whatever he decides is suitable for this case.'

'What do you think I'll get?'

The solicitor shrugged. 'If it was just the murder of Guy Royal, I'd say maybe twelve to sixteen years. Your biggest problem is the two charges of attempted murder on the police officers. The courts take a dim view of any attack against the police, especially when a firearm has been used. With those offences factored in, you could get anything between sixteen and twenty-four years.' The solicitor let those numbers sink in before saying, 'Are you still sure you want to enter a guilty plea?'

Miller was thoughtful before she said, 'Whatever the charges, it doesn't alter the fact they have the evidence to send me down, so I might as well plead guilty and hopefully get some time knocked off. I'd prefer not to become an old woman in here, but I don't think I have much choice anymore.'

The solicitor sat back and said, 'If you're sure that's what you want, I'll speak to our barrister, start preparing the paperwork and arrange an earlier court date.'

'Good. I want to get this over and done with.'

As Jan Miller stood up to leave, Jackie said, 'Sorry, Jan. I almost forgot. I've got a letter for you.'

She sat back down and said, 'How come?'

'It was forwarded to our office from your previous employers, Bouldstone Press. The letter had been addressed to you but delivered there. The admin department at Bouldstone contacted the police, who suggested they forward the letter to us.'

She reached into her briefcase and handed the cream-coloured envelope to Miller.

As she opened the letter, Miller said, 'This is a bit weird. I never had any mail delivered to Bouldstone when I worked there. I've no idea who this could be from.'

As she read the typed letter, tears started to well in her eyes. The solicitor, seeing her client getting upset, said, 'Are you okay? Who's it from, Jan?'

She brushed away the tears and began to smile. 'It's from a publishing house.'

'I know. Bouldstone sent it to us.'

'Not Bouldstone,' Jan corrected her. 'It's from Regency Publishing Limited. They want to offer me a contract to publish my book.'

'I didn't know you'd written a book.'

'I've always loved writing. This was the book I worked on with Kingston. I'd completely forgotten he sent the manuscript out to publishers before he died.'

'What will you do?'

'What can I do? I can't do anything while I'm stuck in here, can I?'

The solicitor said, 'I don't see why not. In my experience, I've encountered several prisoners who have written books while they serve their time. I don't know all the rules and regulations involved, but I'm pretty sure that providing you're not profiting from any crime you've committed, they can't stop you.' She looked directly at Jan. 'What's your book about?'

Feeling a little giddy, she gushed, 'It's titled *The Earl's Mistress*. It's a romantic fiction novel. Can you find out about the rules for me?'

The solicitor smiled, took the letter back and said, 'Of course I can. One last check, Jan. Do you want to enter a guilty plea on all charges?'

She stood up and said, 'Yes. Guilty on all charges, and let me know about the book as soon as you can.'

Any thoughts on the impending court case, or on spending most of her life in prison, had now vanished. All she could think about was how she was finally going to become a published author, and that it was all thanks to Kingston Jones.

How could that spiteful detective suggest he hadn't loved her?

Of course he loved her.

He had just proved it.

WE HOPE YOU ENJOYED THIS BOOK

If you could spend a moment to write an honest review on Amazon, no matter how short, we would be extremely grateful. They really do help readers discover new authors.

ALSO BY TREVOR NEGUS

EVIL IN MIND
(Book 1 in the DCI Flint series)
DEAD AND GONE
(Book 2 in the DCI Flint series)
A COLD GRAVE
(Book 3 in the DCI Flint series)
TAKEN TO DIE
(Book 4 in the DCI Flint series)
KILL FOR YOU
(Book 5 in the DCI Flint series)
ONE DEADLY LIE
(Book 6 in the DCI Flint series)
A SWEET REVENGE
(Book 7 in the DCI Flint series)
THE DEVIL'S BREATH
(Book 8 in the DCI Flint series)
I AM NUMBER FOUR
(Book 9 in the DCI Flint series)
TIED IN DEATH
(Book 10 in the DCI Flint series)
A FATAL OBSESSION
(Book 11 in the DCI Flint series)

Printed in Great Britain
by Amazon